SF Book

THE AI SERIES:
AI Destroyer
The AI Gene
AI Assault
AI Battle Station
AI Battle Fleet
AI Void Ship
AI Rescue
AI Armada

THE TRAVELER SERIES:
Galactic Marine
Sleeper Ship
The Zero Stone
The Institute
Neanderthal Planet
The Science of Mu
The Atlantis Equation
The Pyramid of Mars

Visit VaughnHeppner.com for more
information

The Atlantis Equation

(The Traveler #7)

Vaughn Heppner

ISBN: 9798311670050
Imprint: Independently published

You never know.

What don't you know?

That's the thing— you don't know until it happens. In my case, I didn't know that I'd never see my wife alive again except for a few precious seconds. I'd never see the unborn child in her womb because he would die soon after.

I know. I'm getting ahead of myself—a questionable tactic in storytelling and perhaps in poor taste, given the tragedy.

The name's Jake Bayard, by the way. I had lately become the king of Sky Island on the planet Mu. That wasn't bad for a former U.S. Marine, turned Traveler. I traveled through space via ancient obelisks and pyramids scattered throughout the former Harmony of Planets, doing so through interstellar teleportation.

That was quite the trick. And believe you me, I'd learned a hell of a lot during my travels. The problem was that I believed I understood most of the mysteries that had launched me into this crazy quilt of missions to the stars.

Does that confuse you? Or are you wondering what I'm talking about?

Hey, I thought I knew what the cave murals in subterranean Antarctica meant, the ones showing flying saucers, disintegrator rays, and mammoth riders with lances. I thought I had it down concerning shape-shifting Krekelens on Earth playing the part of reptilian skin-wearers, often posing as various government officials in Russia, China, America and so forth. Psi-Master Omilcar had told me I had the heritage of certain genetically modified humans that early man had worshiped as the Greek, Babylonian and Hindu gods. Omilcar also told me that human Mind Worshipers on Mu genetically created the Krekelens thousands of years ago.

I could list countless prehistoric and historical truths that I thought I had down pat. What a joke that turned out to be.

I will admit I knew a few things about all this. For instance, I'd learned that Ophidian lizard people ate Neanderthal carved steaks on the planet Saddoth. I knew that little *Homo habilis* geniuses calling themselves the First Folk ran something called the Institute somewhere in the stars. I'd found women for the horny Neanderthals on the prehistoric planet of Garm.

But how this all worked, who started what and precise timelines—you can say that I hardly knew my left hand from my right.

You see, Psi-Master Omilcar—the telepathic and telekinetic Mind Worshiper who had been instrumental during my previous mission—had been playing a double game all along. That meant he'd been spewing a ton of lies, particularly into my ear, even as he set up the situation for mayhem.

I didn't learn all that until…

You know what. Let's do this the old-fashioned way—the best way. By that, I mean a linear telling of events so this all makes sense in its proper sequence. It will be more satisfying that way for both you and me.

Are you ready then?

Good, because here goes.

My boots rang against the tiles of a long corridor in the Dark Citadel, illuminated by flickering fluorescent lights. The lights had just come on as we entered this section.

The massive Forkbeard and several of his pterodactyl riders followed me. Forkbeard was a veritable giant of a warrior, something over seven feet tall. He made me look small, and I'm no lightweight. Here, he was the largest man around.

Forkbeard had the brutal jaw of a ruthless leader of men and a long double-braided beard, a forked beard. He wore leather garments, thick boots, and a horned helmet like a Viking chief. He gripped a battleaxe and had a long sword strapped at his side. He reeked of power and strode as a lord of all he surveyed.

The riders with him weren't as tall, but they were equally tough looking, some with beards, and some with scars. All could have ridden with the Hell's Angels in their glory days.

They were my liegemen, as I was the king of Mu. Omilcar had given me the title. In reality, I ran Sky Island and toyed with grandiose plans.

I was also recently married to Livi, a beauty from Vega and a fellow Traveler. I'd impregnated her two months ago. That was as it should have been, as much of my time on Sky Island had been spent chasing my wife around the palace. Lately, though, I'd gotten more curious about the Dark Citadel below.

You see, Sky Island happened to be a literal piece of land several miles wide floating among the clouds. On the island were various block buildings and basements, much of them filled with technologically advanced equipment. The island also boasted what Omilcar had said was the key obelisk with its pyramidion—that was the capstone of the obelisk. Through the Sky Island Obelisk, Omilcar said I could control all the other ones scattered throughout the former Harmony of Planets, although I hadn't gotten to that yet. As I said, I'd been busy with other things.

Not so long ago, Sky Island had torn itself free from the Dark Citadel, leaving a gaping hole in the ground below. Shape-changing Krekelens and dragon-headed, giant, snake-bodied winged beings called Ispazars had been running experiments in the citadel. We'd slain all the Ispazars and some Ophidian soldiers they'd brought onto the floating island. That happened about three months ago. We'd also discovered that a monstrous snake had eaten whoever had been in sealed tubes down in the farthest subterranean parts of the citadel. Whatever Krekelens there had been must have fled just before we'd arrived.

As a quick aside, I'd once slain Krekelens that had reached Earth through similar sealed tubes. The Krekelen slaying had happened after my first Traveling voyage, taking place in the subterranean depths of Antarctica.

Today, I searched an archive section of the Dark Citadel, this also in a subterranean region. I didn't have any of my supposed Greek god-like weaponry that I'd used against the Ispazars with me. Instead, I had a sword strapped at my side and wore pterodactyl-rider garments.

Despite our primitive weaponry, this was a highly

technologically advanced adventure. For one thing, Sky Island used anti-gravity devices to float as it did. The archives I searched were kept in ancient computer systems down here.

I could have used Omilcar's help today, but the old man had told me he had a fever and would likely be bedridden for several days.

Livi had promised to look in on him and check his temperature while I was down here.

For the past month, Omilcar had been teaching me a few things about these ancient computers and how the Krekelens had been using them in their experiments.

As a quick refresher, Omilcar had helped me back on Earth, in Antarctica, about four months ago. With his aid, I'd slain several interrogating Krekelens and used the subterranean Antarctica obelisk to teleport to Mu. We'd been chasing the Krekelens who had taken Livi from the secret Antarctica base to Mu. They had appeared on Sky Island. Omilcar and I had appeared near the walled city of Tsargol.

Omilcar was a psi-master, and used a staff with a crystal to help amplify his mind powers. He was supposed to be 263 years old and was the Great Sark or Psi-Master of Mu.

I now stopped before a sealed door and typed in the code on a number pad beside the door. There was a beep, but that was it.

Annoyed, I typed in the numbers again.

The same beep sounded.

I frowned, trying to decide if I'd memorized the wrong code numbers. I didn't think so.

For the third time, I tried the control pad.

There was a third beep and that was it.

I wasn't crazy. So I wasn't going to try it again and expect a different result.

"Do you wish me to bash the door down, lord?" Forkbeard asked in his deep voice.

I turned to the giant. "Won't that break your axe?"

"There's only one way to find out, lord."

I sighed. I didn't care for this lord business. Once, Forkbeard and I had been enemies and then become friends. These past months, he'd become a loyal subject. Forkbeard and

5

I had both supped upon Omilcar's stories about the past, particularly how Livi and I had special genes from ancient humans with genetically modified abilities.

I stepped away from the sealed door, a steel one that was supposed to slide open. "Do what you can, my friend."

Forkbeard growled an order to the others. They stepped away from him. Forkbeard then set the double bladed axe-head on the floor, with the oak handle resting against one of his legs. He spat in his big rough hands, rubbed his palms together and grasped the axe haft. He raised the weapon, swung it back and then drove it forward, the steel edge smashing and ringing against the steel door.

I put my hands against my ears as the giant of a warrior hammered the door several times in succession. Soon, pieces of steel chipped and flew from his axe head. Forkbeard didn't let up, striking the door with even more force. More of his axe chipped, the pieces springing back against the wall, raining down and clattering across the tiles.

At that point, Forkbeard dropped the shattered axe, bellowed and hurled his mighty frame against the door. He bounced off. After collecting himself, he stepped back and charged again.

The warrior was going to badly bruise himself if he kept this up.

I opened my mouth to tell him to stop.

Forkbeard hurled himself against the door once more, crashing against it like a rhino.

Abruptly, the entire dented steel door blew off its hinges and clanged against the tiles of the archive chamber, with Forkbeard stumbling in after it.

The fluorescent lights in the chamber flickered, turning on, illuminating—

This was crazy.

I walked in behind Forkbeard, frowning at what I didn't see.

The giant warrior was hunched over, panting, rubbing his no doubt bruised shoulder. Then he straightened, looked about the chamber and then at me, obviously puzzled.

The chamber was empty, devoid of any computer systems,

devoid of anything, in fact.

"Is this the correct chamber, lord?" Forkbeard asked. Sudden astonishment filled his rough face. He bowed his head. "Forgive me, lord, for asking such an impertinent question."

My scowl grew. "None of that," I said. "I can make a mistake as easily as the next man. But..." I rubbed my chin, mentally going over our route down here. I took my time, thinking it through carefully. Omilcar had taken this exact route with me several days ago. He had put in the same code on the control pad outside, which had caused the door to slide open.

I stared at the giant. "This is the right chamber."

Forkbeard hesitated.

"Spit it out," I said.

"The code didn't work," he said, as if that was a point against my assertion.

"I'm well aware of that," I said.

"I mean no disrespect by saying that—"

"Forkbeard," I said, interrupting him. "Omilcar showed me this chamber last week. I distinctly remember everything about the visit, including the code he entered. He brought up certain records on the computers and suggested I study others. I'd have you go get Omilcar and bring him down here if he wasn't so sick."

"Lord?" Forkbeard asked, seemingly bewildered by the statement.

"What is it now?" I asked.

"You said Omilcar is sick?"

"That's right. He's sick in bed with a fever."

"I do not mean to contradict you, lord, but Omilcar was laughing just before we departed. He was whistling a merry tune, carrying equipment to his science chamber."

I blinked several times. "Did he do this yesterday maybe, when he was still feeling well?"

Forkbeard shook his head. "He did it several minutes after you'd mounted your pterodactyl and lofted into the air. I was late joining you, if you'll recall, and passed him as I hurried."

That was right. Forkbeard had been late, rushing to catch up with the rest of us. "You mean this happened less than an hour ago?"

"Yes, lord."

"Did Omilcar have a fever when you saw him? Was he coughing and stooped?"

"No. He was spry and hale. He seemed eager, delighted, filled with joy. I've never heard him whistle before this, but he was whistling an hour ago."

That didn't make sense. "Omilcar sent me word earlier today that he was sick with fever and would likely be bedridden for several days."

Forkbeard shook his head. "Omilcar has never looked healthier, lord."

"Why would Omilcar send me word like that then?"

Once again, Forkbeard shook his head.

I glanced around the empty chamber. A week ago, computers had crammed this place from wall to wall. A week ago, the key pad had worked and opened the door. Omilcar had given me the code in fact.

Forkbeard took several steps and crouched low, touching tiles. He looked back at me. "These are discolored as if used for years." He moved his hand, indicating the rest. "The other tiles are clean, looking new, as if someone has recently moved things from them."

I stepped beside Forkbeard, staring. He was right. Those tiles were discolored compared to the fresher-looking ones elsewhere. The discolored ones would be the row that we'd walked on between the now moved computers.

Omilcar knew I was coming down here today. Did he know the control pad no longer worked or that someone had moved the computers?

I straightened and grasped the hilt of my short sword. I found that I listened intently. Was I starting to think Krekelens or Ophidians might ambush us down here? We'd been tramping through these subterranean corridors for weeks without any incidents, without any hint of others.

I glanced at Forkbeard. The big man looked uneasy.

I thought about some of the inconsistencies with the Great Sark of Mu, with Psi-Master Omilcar. I'd never paid them much attention before this. Sometimes, especially in the

8

beginning, he had done or said some queer things. Could I have misjudged Omilcar's motives or sincerity?

"Forkbeard," I said. "Why did Omilcar go to the Dark Citadel the first time?"

"You mean when the old leader of the pterodactyl riders took him?"

"Yes."

Forkbeard scowled. "I don't remember the reason, although I told my friend not to go."

"You haven't always trusted Omilcar, have you?" I asked.

"No."

"Why was that?"

Forkbeard inhaled deeply, his eyebrows pulling together. "I don't wish to speak against anyone you hold in trust, lord."

"That's not the question."

"No," Forkbeard admitted.

"Let's cut the crap. Why didn't you trust him in the past?"

"Well... Omilcar used to visit the Draconians and Ophidians more than seemed right. He would often be gone for months at a time when no one knew his whereabouts. Then he would appear out of the Old Forsaken Lands."

Draconians were small lizard people who rode raptor mounts, acting the part of raiding nomads. Ophidians were bigger and more sedentary, but also armed with swords, spears and such. They had haunted the Old Forsaken Lands, once privy to possible nuclear detonations in the distant past. The Dark Citadel was in the center of those lands, surrounded by the various reptilian tribes.

"What else didn't you like about him?" I asked.

"Omilcar's desire to go the Dark Citadel always seemed suspect to me," Forkbeard said. "But events proved him correct and me wrong, did they not, lord?"

Was that the case? Omilcar had certainly helped me, especially in escaping from the Krekelens in Antarctica. His timing had been nothing short of miraculous.

As I thought about that, I wondered about miracles and coincidences. Had Omilcar's timing in Antarctica been too good? Would Krekelens have sacrificed some of their own for a greater goal? I knew too little about them to know the answer to that. However, according to Forkbeard, Omilcar hadn't been sick with fever today, but spry. If true, the psi-master had lied to me about that and had gotten up the instant I'd left. The door code here hadn't worked, almost as if to keep anyone from discovering that someone had moved the computers.

A bad feeling twisted my stomach. Suddenly—

"Come on," I said, hurrying out of the chamber. We need to get back to Sky Island—now."

-3-

We ran up the corridors, heading for the surface and our mounts there. Those mounts were among the most incredible sights I'd encountered on the various alien planets I'd visited during my time as a Traveler. Their kind had been on Earth once, but they couldn't have possibly been what I'd found on Mu.

I meant the pterodactyls the riders rode through the skies of Mu. The Hell's Angels-looking riders had been a scourge to civilized society here, acting similarly to historical Vikings on Earth.

The fact that such massive creatures could fly was undoubtedly due to several unique factors. Mu had thicker air density and lighter gravity than Earth. Combined with the pterodactyls' great musculature, this enabled them to fly despite their size and carry men on their backs.

We burst out of the underground cellars and ran to the

waiting creatures on the paved surface.

The grounded pterodactyls were colossal and awe-inspiring. Their bodies were covered in scales, a mix of dark greens, browns and grays. Like bigger eagles on Earth, pterodactyls were primarily scavengers, although they hunted on occasion.

The special Draco Pterodactyls had a massive wingspan, stretching over fifty feet from tip to tip. Their heads were elongated, with a bony crest on top. The beaks were long and pointed, lined with sharp teeth.

A pterodactyl's eyes were positioned on either side of its skull, providing a wide field of vision. They had superior vision like an eagle, well adapted for tracking prey from on high or detecting threats from a distance.

Each creature's legs were muscular and equipped with powerful talons. Those talons could inflict serious damage to any foe unlucky enough to come within reach. A long, flexible tail provided balance and helped stability during flight.

Our pterodactyls had specially designed saddles and reins. These saddles were fashioned from lightweight material and had a rope ladder on the side to help a rider climb into it. The reins were connected to various points on the pterodactyl's head and throat. These reins reached back, attaching to the front of the saddle in a circular fashion. Like a clock, pulling the one-strap or the two-strap made the beast respond as trained. The reins and pterodactyl goad that emitted severe shocks allowed for precise control over the beast's movements in the air and on the ground.

Several riders had remained on guard with the beasts and now turned toward us.

Forkbeard shouted to them as we ran.

The guards began to prepare our pterodactyls for flight, pulling off the hobbles.

I raced to mine so it twisted its neck to peer at me. I raised my hands and shouted its name. Then I hauled myself up the rope ladder, scrabbling into the saddle. I secured a saddle rope around my waist so I didn't accidentally fall out during flight. Only then did I haul back on the one strap.

My beast gathered its considerable bulk and leaped up as it

spread its wings and flapped with a bullwhip snap. I jerked back and forth as my pterodactyl climbed into the air.

Behind me, Forkbeard and the other riders urged their mounts as the rest of the pterodactyls followed mine.

I craned my neck and looked up at Sky Island. It was several miles in circumference, deeper in the center than on the edges, a wedge of land torn free and floating in the air thanks to its anti-gravity mechanisms.

As I gained height, my pterodactyl screeched its hunting cry—a terrifying sound. My beast screeched again, with consternation this time. I'd ridden enough to hear the difference.

I wondered about that, and then Forkbeard was racing beside me.

"Do you see, lord?" he pointed at Sky Island.

I studied the bottom of the island and then realized he must mean above it. There, swarming like crows were zigzagging pterodactyls. The beasts circled as if they were angry or confused. Yes, I could hear their drifting screeches.

My beast now started to buckle and resist. I glanced at Forkbeard. His pterodactyl did likewise.

"It's faint," Forkbeard shouted.

"What is?"

"Those are hypersonic blasts. The noise is unsettling our beasts and those above."

I twisted back. The other pterodactyls were having difficulty keeping a flying rhythm with their wings.

If hypersonic blasts emanated from the island, wouldn't that mean someone caused them? And if someone caused that, could the person have done so to keep us from returning on our pterodactyls?

With that in mind, I pulled on the three-strap, steering my pterodactyl away from Sky Island.

Fear twisted my stomach. In the past, Psi-Master Omilcar had positively helped all the pterodactyls fly higher than ordinary by affecting their brains. Someone who could do that could also cause something like this.

"The island is rising," Forkbeard shouted, who had continued to follow me.

I studied the island and saw the truth of the statement. I had seen the mechanisms in the island's guts before. If someone understood them, he could move the island as one moved an airship.

Then I understood with sick clarity. Omilcar was a traitor. I would suspect attacking Krekelens had done all this except that Omilcar had lied about being sick with fever this morning. How and why and for what reasons he had become a traitor, I had no idea. But all the little hints I'd worried about during the past few months coalesced into certainty. What was the purpose of this?

Livi, I thought to myself. Livi was on the island with Omilcar. Livi had conceived—
I had a terrible premonition. Could Omilcar have been waiting until I had certainly impregnated Livi? We were two different bloodlines. I still believed that mine was an ancient bloodline connected to those whom the simple people of Earth back then had mistaken for the gods of old, because of the various powers the so-called gods possessed.

I pulled on the one strap and the three strap. That caused my pterodactyl to move away from Sky Isle, even as the beast lofted higher and higher.

The rider-less pterodactyls that had swirled above Sky Island now peeled away as they screeched, soaring elsewhere.

My pterodactyl flapped smoothly once more. That meant the hypersonic, disrupting noises were only effective near the island. I had suspected as much, the reason I'd moved away.

A glance back showed me that Forkbeard and the others were still following me.

Through the saddle, I could feel my pterodactyl's heart beating and its muscles moving. We flew parallel with the island and then began to climb higher.

There was a guardrail around the entire island. In the center on the flat surface were dour block buildings, many several stories high. They had dark grim windows and looked like where many evil experiments had taken place, laboratories that Nazis would have loved. Pavement spread across much of the island. On one end was the obelisk with its red crystal pyramidion. On the other end was a large step pyramid, often

14

called a ziggurat.

I saw bodies sprawled on the paving—likely pterodactyl riders who had remained behind this morning.

I swallowed hard, thinking about experiments.

Was that what Omilcar was doing? Did he experiment on Livi, on the fetus?

Rage and renewed fear churned within me.

I flew my pterodactyl higher still until the island was far below us. Then I turned my great beast of prey as Forkbeard and the others followed my lead. Willing my pterodactyl to obey me, I sent it straight at the island.

The great beast glided, and screeched with rage and desperation, hating something on the island.

Omilcar was a psi-master, meaning he manipulated the minds of men, beasts, and aliens. Certainly, he would have the craft to have caused this. I'd seen it months ago.

I continued to force my pterodactyl down, using the goad against it, the shock device that caused sparks to fly from it against my mount.

My beast screeched at the ill treatment. I now pitted my will against the psi-master, with the pterodactyl the unwilling locus of our contest. The psi-master used hypersonic sounds, no doubt. I used the reins, the beast's training and a primitive instrument of punishment.

For the moment, I was winning. Like a Stuka dive-bomber (a WWII German plane), we dove at Sky Island, gaining velocity.

Suddenly, however, my beast could no longer hold its wings steady. At that point, we began to plummet. It seemed then that I was going to dash myself on the pavement of Sky Isle. That would give Omilcar—if indeed this was his doing— the   victory.

With a sick feeling, I realized that I was about to die.

-4-

As Forkbeard, his men, and I plummeted on our pterodactyls toward the surface of Sky Isle, I heard the floating words of Forkbeard: "The Edge, lord! Aim for the Edge!"

I believed I divined his plan, and by dint of the reins and my goad, I caused my beast to veer toward one edge. Then, it seemed as if the negative power affecting the pterodactyl's mind lessened incrementally, at least enough for the creature to hold its wings out.

Many dead or unconscious pterodactyl riders lay on the pavement down there. Had they tried to protect Livi? That was my fear, and it seemed the likeliest possibility unless others had used the ziggurat to land here.

Surely we would have heard great booms, if interstellar Travelers had used the ziggurat. That always happened when someone teleported onto a ziggurat.

I had no more time to worry about that. As the ground of Sky Island zoomed up, I sensed my pterodactyl was about to veer away for good. The beast gave a great cry of desperation.

I'd already ripped off the band tying me to the saddle. I now climbed onto the saddle so I crouched upon it. Then, from fifty feet above the pavement, I leapt, passed a wing and talons before continuing to plummet. If I hit the ground, I would break bones and possibly kill myself. I forced myself into a spread-eagle position and used skydiving techniques to aim for a pool of water.

At the last moment, I made fists, held my arms straight over my head and struck the water hard, slamming my head, neck and shoulders against it. I curled so that I didn't sink straight to the bottom of the pool. Even so, I ached all over and slowly floated to the surface.

Forkbeard and the others had not followed me in such a risky move. Instead, on their pterodactyls, they veered away from the island.

I swam to the edge of the pool, climbed out, dripping water, and looked up as a sense of urgency struck once again. Rising, I stumbled and then raced for my quarters, pumping my arms and legs. If this were Omilcar's doing, or even if it were someone else's, I needed a weapon—an offensive weapon more powerful than my sword. That meant the Staff of Zeus, as I now thought of it, the fiery staff that I'd used against the Ispazars and especially the queen and her crown three months ago.

Soon, I burst into our apartment, shouting Livi's name. It was empty, with strewn blankets and pillows all around. I threw myself flat onto the floor and peered under the bed. In the middle lay my fiery staff, what looked like a long metallic tube about five feet long.

I reached as far as I could, slid under the bed and curled my fingers around it. As I said, it was a long hollow tube and did not have a switch anywhere.

As I climbed to my feet, my genetic connection switched on the tube. I knew, as I felt a tingling sensation. Then a blue nimbus spread around me, outlining my body and head. That was a defensive shield.

Inside the hollow of the tube was microelectronics. When I willed it, fire would spew as if from a WWII flamethrower. The advanced electronics took something out of the very air to do this.

Gripping the metal staff with both hands, I sprinted out of our room, dashed down stairs and raced out of the block building onto the pavement. I looked around.

Where would Omilcar have taken Livi?

Lights flickered in one of the dark block building windows. Omilcar must be there. Should I blast the window with flames? No, it was too far away. Besides, that would alert him I was coming.

Instead, I sprinted across the pavement, passing dead or unconscious pterodactyl riders. Interestingly, their heads were all pointed in that direction.

Soon, I reached doors, finding them locked. I stepped back, aimed the tube, and summoned flames. The hollow tube or lance shivered in my hands and then fire ejected from the front and poured against the door.

I did that long enough, in my estimation.

I willed the flames to stop, lowered my shoulder and charged, slamming against the door.

The metal had weakened enough that the locks no longer held. The door burst open.

I wanted to shout with rage. I wanted to announce my coming, but I knew that was the wrong thing. If I could, I needed to take whoever was experimenting by surprise.

Then I heard a scream. It came from Livi, my dear and precious wife.

I ran down the hall and dashed up stairs, taking them three at a time. My heart was pumping, and I saw red, maybe because the air was so thin on Sky Island and I had exerted myself so mightily.

I reached the correct floor and headed for a door, one to Omilcar's laboratory.

I wanted to launch myself at the door. Instead, I slowed, heaving great gulps of air. In seconds, I tested the door. It was unlocked. I swung it open, and saw a scene like something out of a nightmare.

I burst into the chamber, and there, upon a table, lay Livi, my wife. Tubes were attached to her, and a mask covered her face. But the most hideous thing was her abdomen. Someone had cut it open, perhaps to extract the fetus, leaving a gaping, bloody wound.

As I rushed forward, Livi's eyes opened. I grasped her nearest hand.

Livi looked at me, and I heard whispers from the mask. As gently as I could, with my heart pounding and my hands shaking, I removed the mask from her sweat-streaked face. Pain twisted her features.

"Jake," she whispered.

My hand tightened on hers.

"He took our son," she said, shuddering and heaving a gasp.

I cried out in agony, feeling as if my soul had been ripped

apart. Here was my love, my sweet wife. We had produced an heir for our kingdom, a prince. I loved her so very much.

Livi shuddered again, and all the air and life seemed to drain from her as she deflated. Then, she was lifeless upon the table.

I stepped back as horror etched across me. I'd left her perfectly healthy this morning. Now…

I looked at her bloody abdomen again. Someone had torn my son from her. Someone had slain Livi to do this evil deed. She had been only two months along…

On trembling legs, I staggered toward the next door. It opened, and I heard down a corridor sizzling and hissing machines.

I increased my pace until I burst into another horrifying chamber. How could anyone conceive of such a hideous act? I saw the fetus of my son. His tiny body floated in amniotic fluid. He wriggled. Attached to his container by various nodes were wires. They threaded to a great machine with many blinking lights and making hissing sounds, the ones I'd heard.

Omilcar stood at the machine's controls, his long hoary beard flowing. Instead of the robes of a Sark of Mu, he wore the long white lab coat of an Earth scientist. He was the mastermind behind this hideousness, working levers and pressing buttons.

A sixth sense or his psi-mastery must have warned him. He whirled around. Our eyes locked, and I saw him as I had never seen him, a demon in human guise.

"What are you doing?" I bellowed. The shock of horror had dulled my reactions.

A hideous smile creased his leathery face. "Now you know," he said.

Before I could think, I aimed the tube at him and willed fire to consume him, but nothing happened except for a whiff of smoke curling from the front opening.

I spied his staff with the crystal on the end. The staff lay propped up against the machine. The jagged crystal on the end glinted with power.

Was that power blocking my weapon?

20

I kept aiming the tube at him as I approached.

"That's not going to work, you fool," Omilcar sneered.

I couldn't talk but only glowered as I neared him.

"Did you think you could defeat me, the great Omilcar, the Great Sark of Mu? Did you think that I was going to be your puppet all these years? Did you believe what I told you, you moron, you fool?"

I howled and charged, ready to hurl the tube like a javelin, even if only to use it as a blunt instrument. Then my limbs locked up, and I tripped and toppled, hitting the floor with my face, while awareness and pain coursed through me.

The psi-master must be doing this to me.

I felt Omilcar above, and he turned me over so my eyes stared up at the ceiling. The Mind Worshiper crouched and placed a small cold disc upon my forehead. I could no longer feel my limbs or the pain in my face.

There were questions perhaps in my eyes, and he no doubt saw that.

"You are not the progeny of the old gods," Omilcar said. "How could you be, because they never were? Did you really believe such a tale? Yes, you ate it up because you wanted to believe. And the coincidences of our union—"

He snorted, rose and moved away. Soon, I heard him moving levers. The machine hissed with power. Suddenly, there was a boom followed by sizzles and a bubbling liquid sound.

Omilcar let out a cry of dismay.

After that, the machinery wound down until the room was filled with an eerie silence.

A weary Omilcar holding his staff topped by the jagged red crystal looked down on me. I lay powerless on the floor. I did not see gloating in his eyes but bitter defeat.

"I can't believe it," Omilcar said. "I miscalculated in some manner. My carefully laid plans are now useless effort. I thought the fetus from you two would have the needed genetic—ah, it doesn't matter. It's over. They were right. I was certain this would work. Well, at least the Ispazars are no longer here, and the faction of the Krekelens that blocked us, they should have known better than to toy with me. I am

Omilcar. I am the Great Sark of Mu. Yes, I see now that I will have to use a different approach."

He studied me, then prodded my stiff, motionless body with the end of his long staff.

"I wonder if you can still be of any use to me. I don't know. You are a killer. You do know that, do you not? That is your one great ability. I can see the desire in your eyes to kill me, and yet you must know sorrow. How can I use you, hmm?"

After a moment, Omilcar shook his head.

"Your mind is too thick, and certain aspects make long-term domination nearly impossible. You're a dead end for me, but, hmm, perhaps I need to return to Earth first and check on a certain matter before I eliminate you."

How, I thought, *can you return to Earth? Certainly, you can't use the pyramidion, can you?*

"Oh, yes," he said, "after a fashion, I can use it."

Are you reading my mind?

"Of course, I'm the great Psi-Master. But I cannot leave you as a loose end. It seems foolish to leave you alive. Hmm. Let me see. What is the best thing to do?"

Omilcar pulled up a chair, sat down with his great staff across his knees, and stared at me, no doubt contemplating my fate as I despaired over what had happened.

6

In time, Omilcar rose. I heard his footsteps receding from me.

I wasn't sure what his plan was, but I strove with every ounce of my will. There was a metal disc on my forehead. Was it an inhibitor? Could I do anything to defeat it?

How could I do that when the Great Psi-Master of Mu had likely constructed it? He understood human neurons and the mind to an intense degree. He was a Mind Worshipper.

I still believed that part of his story had been true.

Once, he had put the champion Jarvo's thoughts and abilities into me, allowing me to become a master swordsman. I retained those skills but no longer had Jarvo's memories.

I thought back to that time and sought on some subconscious level how Omilcar had accomplished the transference. As I strove, grinding my teeth in rage, I pondered what had happened to Livi. Then I considered how Omilcar could use the pyramidion in the obelisk to escape.

Where would he go? Was Omilcar part of the Krekelens of Earth? It seemed he belonged to a faction trying to use my genetics, wanting something from my seed, from my son, through my union with Livi. That would imply Omilcar had manipulated Livi and me in order that we had the child.

Why had Omilcar used the fetus in the jar rather than Livi or me? I didn't understand it, and thinking about it was driving me mad with grief.

I strove against the inhibitor, grinding my teeth in rage. Whether it was an involuntary jerk or a spasm of my body, I felt something fall from my forehead, skittering across the tiles. Then I felt all my limbs begin to tingle with feeling as they slowly returned.

Awkwardly, like the pterodactyls earlier, I began to move. The sensation grew stronger until I stood, staring down at the inhibitor on the floor.

I crushed it under my boot heel, and looked around. Staggering, I picked up the hollow tube and then saw a mental band that a psi-master of Mu would use to amplify his psionic powers.

I shoved the band over my head and felt disoriented, almost as if I could see into the other room.

I cried out in despair at the horrors before me. How could such monstrosities and deviltry take place? This was hideous.

I staggered down the corridor with the tube in hand, wearing the psi-master's band. I reentered the room where Livi lay, her desecrated body—I dare not describe what I saw. A cry of rage, agony, and despair filled me.

I turned and staggered down the halls, following a dripping path of spotted blood. Omilcar held a gory, severed head in his hand. How I loathed the monster of a psi-master. I had left this morning, kissing good-bye my precious, pregnant wife, and now I was in a hellscape that I could hardly believe.

I wanted to drink myself into oblivion. I wanted to destroy worlds and kill every psi-master, starting with Omilcar, and then kill the Krekelens. I didn't understand how the shape-shifting reptilian beings were involved with this, but I was certain they were.

I raced down stairs and staggered out of the gray edifice of a building. I never would enter this place again except to retrieve Livi's body, to bury it and give it a benediction.

I'll avenge you, my sweet wife. I'll avenge you, my son.

Dark, vengeful visions filled me as tears streamed down my face. I saw damned Omilcar racing to the obelisk with the pyramidion. The monster clutched a severed head by her hair like a Celtic warrior, one of the headhunters of that ancient era.

I aimed my tube at him, sending a gout of fire, but the flames fell far short. I alerted him instead by my action.

He turned, raised his staff, and I saw the red crystal glitter, meaning he used his psi-powers.

I stood firm, blocking, hunching my shoulders like a wild man, feeling pain and agony sear into me. But not enough that I fell or quit or lost my sight or whatever Omilcar tried to do. Instead, I bellowed, charging after him.

Did he give a yelp? I sensed it, sensed we were side-by-side, sharing secrets. Our bodies were not close like this. Instead, our thoughts were. I studied his. It turned out that he was part of a faction of Krekelens and Psi-Masters. There were rifts among them. I sensed one word, which Omilcar tried to shield from me. That word was *Atlantis*.

It made no sense. Thus, I concentrated on sprinting after the 263-year-old monster.

He skidded to a halt and stood before the pyramidion, holding up Livi's severed head. With his mind powers, Omilcar used the engrams of Livi's freshly dead brain.

I understood in that moment. This was a one shot use of her genetics. Livi was recently dead, but perhaps the pyramidion sensed her brainwaves or brain pattern, that of a Traveler who could unlock the ancient mechanisms for star journeys.

The pyramidion crystal speared Omilcar with a beam of red energy that engulfed him.

I screamed until my throat was raw. I sprinted harder, willing this to stop.

It did no good. Omilcar stretched, thinned out and disappeared. He was teleporting to another planet or to a different part of Mu.

I sprinted until I skidded to a stop before the obelisk and

the pyramidion capstone. I used my mental power against it.

The pyramidion of the obelisk had turned dark and blank, not hearing my appeal to follow Omilcar.

Somehow, the wizard of a Mind Worshipper, the evil son of a bitch, had thwarted me and escaped completely.

I panted, beside myself with grief.

Dully, I realized Omilcar had inadvertently given me a clue. Then I fell to my hands and knees, overcome by emotion. Tears fell from my eyes at the terrible tragedy that had struck with swiftness, leaving me paralyzed and bereft.

Sobbing, feeling the anguish—

How could this have happened after all I'd been through?

I realized that Earth's enemies were far darker and more evil than I had ever suspected. Omilcar was high in their counsels. The Krekelens were nothing like us. Omilcar was an example of their ruthlessness, evil and disrespect of life.

Someone needed to stop them.

Then I, a former Marine, collapsed, unable to think of vengeance. I would mourn my loss. I didn't know what else I could do until I'd buried my sweet, sweet wife and my poor son.

I didn't want to think of the cooked remains of the fetus in the jar of fluids. How awful. How wretched.

I opened my eyes and slowly stood. The pyramidion was still dark. I turned. I would plan my next step carefully. I did not have plans of vengeance yet. First, I needed to take care of my dearly departed loved ones.

7

Omilcar escaped, taking a gruesome prize with him.

I did not go to the obelisk for several days. I was too distraught, too infected with paralysis and grief. I shut down various engines and devices, and soon Forkbeard and the others landed.

The towering warrior looked at my face and frowned deeply.

"What has happened?"

Haltingly, I told him what had happened. I did not sob, but I think Forkbeard understood men to an inordinate degree. I don't say I agreed with how he treated women, as he was a Viking chieftain indeed in that respect, as were most of his men. I had seen that in Tsargol many months earlier.

Forkbeard knew the depth to which I loved Livi, sweet Livi. She had been an agent from Vega, a different planetary system, but fully human nonetheless.

Vega had once been part of the Harmony of Planets. Interestingly, my father had come from Vega.

Now Livi was forever gone. I would never again touch her sweet skin, kiss her, or tell her I loved her. She was gone, forever gone. Oh, my sweet, dear Livi!

I drank. Forkbeard saw to that. We had a roaring fire on Sky Island, and his riders mourned my wife with me.

What hardy and good fellows they were. They did not berate me. They saw my grief, and they drank me into oblivion. They did it three nights in a row, until at last I said enough.

We buried her. I spoke over her grave from the Word of God, the Bible—"Dust to dust, ashes to ashes."

I buried my son in a plot beside Livi, even though he was only a small fetus. He had been drawn from my wife's womb. I know there are a slew of thoughts regarding the humanity of one so young. I'm not trying to take a side in the debate, but I buried him. He was my son, and Omilcar had slaughtered him by ripping him out of the womb too soon and using him in an experiment.

Enough! I couldn't dwell on that any longer or I would lose my sanity. Instead, it was time to decide what to do next.

Omilcar had once told me that I had the heritage of the Greek gods, or the ancient beings who had posed as them in prehistory. Now he'd told me that was fake and false.

How could I trust anything he'd said? I could only believe what I had seen and heard. I knew there had once been a Harmony of Planets. I had seen the obelisks and ziggurats on planet after planet. I had gone to many of them, and I had seen different factions and learned about ancient destruction. Thus, I knew that much was true because I'd participated in it.

I no longer knew if the Krekelens were vat creatures created on Mu. I no longer cared about their origin, just that I was on a mission concerning them.

Did I speak of vengeance? There beat in me the desire to kill, to eradicate and to extinguish the forces that had slain Livi and stolen what would have become our son.

This would be different from my other fights. Then, it had almost seemed like sport. Now, it beat like a holy mission.

Was I bitter? Was I enraged?

28

Oh, hell, yes I was.

Can you imagine trusting, loving, and then seeing it taken so callously…? I can no longer describe it.

I made my decision. Omilcar would die, preferably by my hand. I did not take an oath regarding that. Rather, it was my breath, my food and drink.

I knew that intense bitterness, and rage, and vengeance, were not productive to a good life. But that wasn't the purpose now. Omilcar would have to pay. If others benefited from that, so be it. I didn't care. Perhaps I'd free humanity from the Krekelens. I would engage in destroying the shape-changers until I died. It was as simple as that. This meant I'd be returning to Earth.

First, I needed to plan. I needed to think and get ready.

Forkbeard and the riders returned, but I told them I would not drink tonight. I needed my wits, intelligence, and hunter's instinct.

Forkbeard regarded me intently. "Whatever you do, I will follow."

I wasn't going to argue with him now. No, not yet. First, I needed to plan.

-8-

I slept, consumed by grief, and dreamed of Livi. When I awoke the next morning, the agony came crashing down again.

Fortunately, there was something to the pterodactyl riders' method of assuaging grief. They had let it flow for several nights.

Soon, my wits returned to me.

I slept in a different building, on a Spartan cot. Beside it lay the fiery lance of Zeus, my weapon of choice. I would use it in storming the Krekelen base in Antarctica on Earth. I had to go to Earth, as I was certain Omilcar had. He would search for sunken Atlantis.

Plato had written about it in some of his dialogues. Apparently, Solon of Athens had learned about it in Egypt. Legend held Atlantis had sunk in the past, although most moderns laughed at the idea.

My travels had taught me that many myths had a basis in

fact. It was as if the book and movie *The Chariots of the Gods* had posed many reasonable questions. Mu had turned out to be real, although it hadn't been an ancient continent in the Pacific Ocean. I'd seen flying saucers, saber-toothed cats, mammoths, Neanderthals, and even hairy *Homo habilis*.

That got me pondering. Could Atlantis be a planet like Mu? When I left, I would ask the pyramidion to send me there. Then I would learn the truth. Until I did, I was going to work on the running theory that Atlantis was on Earth. That meant I'd be returning to Earth.

The landing ziggurat on Earth was hidden beneath the ice of Antarctica, where the Krekelens had built a secret base. They had captured Livi and me there last time. After an interstellar teleportation, I would cause lightning to flash and thunder to boom as I was reconstituted in the ziggurat, alerting the Krekelens to my arrival.

That meant I needed to take the tube. I'd also need Livi's Phrygian cap. She'd been able to render herself invisible briefly with it. I'd have to learn to activate the cap and use it as well. With such a combo, I might be able to wreak havoc and eradicate the infestation of the Krekelens in Antarctica.

Humans known as the Terrans should have created the hidden base there, not the reptilian shape-changers.

Unfortunately, Colonel McPherson was dead. There had been a nuclear explosion in the Persian Gulf, originating from a Russian Poseidon torpedo. Well, that had been what the Krekelens had told me as they interrogated me in Antarctica. Was that true?

I did not know.

I had to find the other Terrans like McPherson, those who had battled against the Krekelens on Earth in secret.

I sighed.

That was too far in the future for me.

There was a loud knock on the door. "Enter," I said.

The door opened, and Forkbeard walked in, sitting down. "Lord—"

"Listen," I said, interrupting. "I'm not one of the old gods. That was Omilcar's lie, and we saw how false it was. I'm a

31

man. You see that I bleed. You see that I grieve. I'm not a god but a man just like you."

Forkbeard nodded sharply. "Whatever you are, know this: wherever you go, I will follow you."

"I'm going to go to Earth to find and kill Omilcar and Krekelens."

Forkbeard thumped his huge chest. "Then, I will do likewise."

I thought about that. Should I enter the Antarctica Krekelen base with 30 or 40 pterodactyl riders in tow? They could wreak havoc with their swords and axes if they got in close. If the Krekelens did not pull out phasors or other ranged weapons—

"This is a different kind of assault," I said. "That you're willing to join me on another planet—" I thumped my chest. "I'm touched. I would rather beg you—"

"No!" Forkbeard said. "Don't beg me. It is unseemly."

His response took me by surprise. After a moment, I nodded. "Then I ask you, my friend, that you do me a favor."

"Name it."

"Permanently station your pterodactyl riders on Sky Island."

Forkbeard considered that. "What if you never return?"

"Then you must do as you wish," I said. "No. I take that back. You must be the king of Mu, using Sky Island as your base."

Forkbeard squirmed before he said, "I either will serve you, the king of Mu, or I will be what I have always been, a raider doing as I will."

I took my time, thinking about this. "I hope you're going to be more than that. You're not just a raider any more. You must help humanity. Maybe you could bring the humans together on Mu. Once you do that, you must hunt down the Draconians and Ophidians who prey on humanity."

"Are you advocating war?" Forkbeard asked.

I sat back. Was that what I was doing? The Draconians and their saurian raptors were a plague to humanity on Mu. And the Ophidians, given half a chance, would eat human burgers.

"Yes," I said. "It must be war as you conquer the cities and peoples on Mu. Then, once you've consolidated, war against

32

the aliens unless they surrender, and are willing to go to a different planet."

"That sounds harsh," Forkbeard said.

"Maybe it is," I said. "From what I've seen so far, one species or another will dominate on a planet. Better that we humans dominate on Mu, as it is our kind. Therefore, you must unite humanity."

"In your name, Lord Bayard, I will do it."

I realized I couldn't disabuse him anymore if I wanted him to do this. I hoped I wasn't unleashing hellish genocidal wars onto Mu. I did think the human cities needed to be freed from snake and lizard people assaults.

It was possible I'd never return to Mu. I could easily die on my quest. Maybe this was a crazy plan, to have these ultimate barbarians as the bearers of civilization. Yet maybe that was a worthy quest. It might change them into protectors instead of mere predators. I was hoping to turn wolves into sheepdogs.

Forkbeard seemed to sense my troubled thoughts. "It has been an honor to know you, Jake Bayard."

I stood, he stood, and we embraced. Forkbeard, with his bone-crushing power, embraced me tightly.

I heard him grunt as I hugged him.

Right, this was a lighter planet than Earth, and therefore my muscles were pound for pound more powerful than his were. I was exceedingly strong on this planet, as I had been on many others.

We parted ways, as Forkbeard had duties to perform, and I still had much to think about.

-9-

The day of departure soon arrived, and I dressed in heavy garments for Antarctica. I wished I knew whether it was winter or summer in Antarctica. Either way, it would be intensely cold, but during winter, it would be prohibitively cold to walk on the surface. Breathing the frigid air could quickly lead to death then.

I'd have to find a way to leave Antarctica and reach America or Europe. If worst came to worst, perhaps I would find the obelisk in subterranean Antarctica and travel to the planet Garm to see how my Neanderthal allies were faring with their wives.

I hoped they were doing better than I had with my wife.

During mid-morning on Mu, I brought my equipment to the obelisk. The pyramidion was no longer dark, although I hadn't attempted telepathic communication with it. I brought the headband with me, the one that amplified mental powers. I think it could also help block psionic power used against me.

I shook hands all around with the warriors, wished them luck, and listened to their praise.

Then I said, "It is time, gentlemen. It has been an honor and a delight to ride the pterodactyls and count myself among your ranks."

"Jake Bayard," Forkbeard said, stepping forward, "know that we will call this the year Jake Bayard lived with us."

I grinned. The pterodactyl riders named their years. I was deeply touched that these excellent warriors, these fine friends, would remember me in this manner.

After that, I turned my back on the barbarians and approached the obelisk.

The obelisk resembled those in Washington, D.C., or at the Egyptian pyramids—a tall spire of stone, and upon it was the capstone or pyramidion. This one now began to glow red as the others on other planets had before. I felt a question in my mind. *Where do you want to go?*

"Do you remember the one named Omilcar?" I asked.

"Not that I know of," the pyramidion said.

I didn't really know if the pyramidion was machine intelligence or an alien thing trapped in the crystal. I was surprised I'd never tried to figure that out. I thought it odd it didn't know Omilcar. Then I realized the psi-master must have hidden behind Livi's Traveler brain pattern.

"I want to go to Atlantis," I said.

The pyramidion did not respond.

"Do you know where Atlantis is?"

No.

"Is it a planet?"

Not that I know of, the pyramidion said.

That was interesting and helpful.

"I want to go to Earth."

I am not to allow anyone to go to Earth.

"Who set this stricture?"

The one before you. He said it was important I obey him for the sake of the obelisks and the Harmony of Planets.

That didn't make sense, as the pyramidion had claimed not to know Omilcar. What was going on here? Usually, these pyramidions were extremely helpful with me.

"There is no Harmony of Planets," I said. "That passed away ages ago, according to what I know."

That is true, the pyramidion said.

Did this pyramidion have a glitch? I shook my head. It was time to get on with this.

"Send me to Earth," I said. "I am Jake Bayard, the Traveler. You can test my genes and my thought patterns. You know that I am a true Traveler."

Yes, you are. The one before you... There were oddities about him, and I feel soiled having sent her... him? I do not know. It was a strange mixture that I do not understand or comprehend.

"He played a trick on you, but now I have no more time to speak. Send me and all my belongings."

Abruptly, a beam flashed from the pyramidion. I felt myself thinning and elongating. It had not been that long ago since I had come to Mu, and now I was leaving it.

I looked back and saw Sky Island receding, and the ground behind it receding. I looked up and saw that I was shooting toward the stars. I did not see Earth, but I knew that I was being projected at great speed, faster than the speed of light.

How did all this work? I had no idea, as that was technology far beyond my understanding.

There was a time of passage where I did not have any thoughts, and in those moments, I felt wonderful peace. I did not think of anything, but I existed. There was no pain, no harshness and sadness.

Then I felt myself reforming. There were thunderous booms, strange gurgling sounds, and slowly, I was reforming on a block of stone.

I became aware again that I was Jake Bayard, the Traveler. I had lost my wife in a most tragic—not an accident, not an accident at all—but in vile spite in a search for power and dominance.

I was here. I could feel it. I was back on Earth in Antarctica. I made sure to keep lying back, because in the last red light of my reforming, I saw that I was inside a small stone chamber.

I slid off and gathered my belongings. Then I emerged out of the stone chamber into a shadowy place. I was atop a ziggurat, and I heard strange groaning sounds that I'd never heard before.

For a wild second, I feared I hadn't reached subterranean Antarctica. Then I calmed myself as the groaning ceased.

Whatever had caused the actual sounds, I was certain Krekelens were coming to imprison me, to kill or dissect me. I was going to turn that around and make this the beginning of my vengeance against those who had stolen everything I held dear.

-10-

Then the groaning sounds came again, and they seemed to come from all around me. It created a strange and eerie feeling in me until I remembered where I'd heard such sounds before: a nature show about whales and the groaning calls the giant mammals made to each other.

The groaning calls came again.

I looked up and all around, straining to see anything at all. I debated using my fiery staff to create enough flame so I could see what happened around me.

A sudden sixth sense warned me against that. Maybe my subconscious feared that I'd give myself away.

Instead, I made sure my garments were on tight and my backpack secure. I gripped my hollow lance with both hands—

At that instant, I heard a great pop, and light appeared all around me. It was murky, wavy, and in a second, I grasped why. Sunlight, perhaps, shone through water. According to what I saw, the surface couldn't be far away, a matter of fifty or more feet, surely no more than seventy.

Yet, that didn't make sense. If sunlight shone through water—

My eyes widened as understanding struck. I stood upon a ziggurat, the top. Broad steps led down all around me. However, the lower steps were submerged in water. Beyond, submerged underwater, were ruins resembling bombed-out structures, once-great buildings. Perhaps there was a circular design for roads and the placement of the ruins.

I saw all this through the prism of rushing waters, walls of them closing in around me. I felt as if the pop had been the sound of the air bubble—or something of that sort—breaking from the surrounding water pressure. The ziggurat must have formed the air bubble as I arrived.

The harsh, terrifying thunder of rushing waters reached me seconds before the mass swept me from the top of the ziggurat. Tons of rushing water slammed me from all sides, casting me one way and then another, and yet canceling each other out so I wasn't propelled in one direction for long or for far.

Luckily, I had taken a gulp of air seconds before the water struck. I struggled to maintain that air from the constant battering—Rather than spewing out the air in my lungs as the tidal waves hit me from all sides.

Too much water shot up my nostrils as the wave flung me about. I realize by the sting that this was salt water. Despite all this, I kept my mouth shut as I swirled end over end.

My self-possession in this might have come from a childhood memory at a beach in Santa Cruz, California. I'd ridden on an inflatable all day because my dad had taken me to the beach. I'd stayed out even as the waves got bigger and rougher. Then a big wave had crashed over my inflatable and me. That had smashed me down so I tumbled end over end. I'd hit the sandy bottom, bounced up, clawed my way to the surface, sputtering for air.

This was like that, only more so. I couldn't comprehend what had happened. Nor did I fathom how the water could be this temperature. It wasn't warm or freezing.

Perhaps I hadn't reached Antarctica but been transported—

teleported—somewhere else.

Could this be Atlantis, the planet?

That would mean the pyramidion on Sky Isle had lied to me on several fronts.

That didn't matter this second. I tumbled end over end as these myriad thoughts competed for my attention. Then I brought my left arm back around. Water had torn my left hand from the hollow tube. I now grasped it with both hands once more.

I was underwater—obviously—and I hadn't been or hadn't known seconds earlier. That surely meant my air bubble theory was correct. The ziggurat must have formed it upon my landing.

That meant I was presently soaked, weighed down by the heavy clothes I'd worn to help me withstand the intense cold of Antarctica. I had to shed most of those or I would never be able to swim to the surface and breathe again.

All thoughts of Omilcar and vengeance dwindled. I wanted to breathe again more than anything.

The first thing I did was to think critically, to force myself to do this. I recalled the wave from Santa Cruz. I'd learned from that. One went with the flow of surging water instead of trying to fight it. The human frame lacked the strength to fight such immense pressure and movement. One had to wait for the right opportunity.

I waited now as I tumbled around and around, keeping myself from panicking.

I knew this was important, as I'd once watched a trapper drown a captured gopher. The trapper had tossed the wire cage and gopher into a bucket of water. The gopher had drowned fast, almost in seconds, in fact. The creature could have lasted a lot longer if it had held its breathe. I'd said as much at the time.

The trapper had told me the gopher had panicked, as it was just a dumb beast and lacked logical sense. The lesson was that panic killed far more quickly than one might expect.

I did not panic down here in the salt waters of this strange landing.

I waited, working to calm mad, gibbering panic threatening in my brain.

40

Soon, the tumult of surging waters lessened and then stopped altogether. I'd closed my eyes because the salt water stung. Now, I opened them despite the stinging and forced myself to think the best I could.

I was in a blurry underworld but the basic shapes helped me act, as it grounded me in a reality, so to speak.

I unbuttoned my heavy sheepskin coat and yanked it off. That meant I had to shed my backpack first. I kept hold of the hollow tube and backpack straps. Then I shed my boots, woolen socks and sheepskin trousers. I shed everything down to my buckskin, until I was naked, in other words. I slipped the pack back onto my shoulders, tightening the straps, and flutter kicked my feet.

Disorientation made this difficult, as the world felt upside down. There was a way to deal with that. If I could just remember it… Oh, right. I exhaled bubbles, although not too many, and watched them float… sideways.

That was strange, the wrong direction. But I knew that bubbles always floated up. Thus, I obeyed logic instead of feeling and followed the bubbles sideways, kicking but also trying to remain relaxed.

That was hard to do but important. The relaxation helped your body retain the oxygen longer. Being tense burned up air faster.

It seemed as if the surface lay at an odd angle to the world.

Think, don't feel, you must reason this out.

Seconds later, my head burst out of the water, and I sucked down gloriously precious air. This air had a different tang and taste than that of Mu. It was saltier and thicker, denser, but it was still precious.

After several heaving gasps, I looked around but I didn't see any land. I saw ocean in all directions.

I hadn't anticipated this landing.

I shivered, but not from cold. I shivered because a wave of water surged along the surface as if a giant sea beast swam just under it toward me.

Then snakes surfaced and wriggled. These rubbery snakes had suckers attached to them.

With a jolt, I realized those weren't snakes, but the

41

tentacles of some giant sea beast that rushed nearer and nearer.

Did the beast want to eat me?

Before I could answer that, a giant creature broke the surface. It took several seconds for my mind to comprehend what I saw.

When I did—

This had to be an ancient kraken as olden seafarers spoke about. It was dark, had an octopus or squid-like main mass and many tree-trunk-sized tentacles. The main body was big like a billionaire's yacht, maybe even bigger. It had hideous eyes and a great maw of a mouth.

Those eyes watched me as the tentacles drew it closer and closer to me, and then a tentacle reached for me.

I should never have left Sky Island to come here. That was undoubtedly the greatest lesson of this experience.

-11-

The giant kraken could have easily broken an ancient galley. Hell, this one could have climbed onto it and submerged the entire wooden craft. Instead, one of its rubbery tentacles with suckers reached for me. I had no doubt it planned to pluck me from the sea and drop me into its maw.

As I trod water in the salty alien ocean, I debated the best course of action. I thought about diving, but that seemed useless. The sea was the creature's element, not mine. Then I recalled that I held onto the fiery staff of Zeus.

Yes! I grasped the metal tube with both hands. I was unsure if it might electrocute me if activated. Or maybe the blue nimbus would cause me to sizzle like bacon in a pan. However, I was as good as dead if I did nothing.

Thus, I aimed the hollow tube at the reaching tentacle and willed it to fire.

I felt the familiar tingle and then fire, blessed fire, hosed from the end of my staff and licked the tentacle just a few feet away and closing in.

The stink of burning flesh was immediate—nauseating yet satisfying.

The kraken snatched its tentacle back, and it cried with an eerie almost subsonic call.

That wasn't the end of it, though. More tentacles sped for me. These did not reach as if to grab, but moved swiftly as if to slap me out of existence.

I continued to hose flames from the hollow tube, washing tentacles with blistering fire.

The giant kraken gave what must have been a whistling call of dismay. It drew back its tentacles and plunged into the sea, disappearing from view with startling speed.

Would it swim beneath me and drag me down to a watery grave?

I felt certain this was the case.

Instead of just waiting for the end like a docile cow, I plunged my head underwater and opened my eyes. I saw blurry images and then spied the great bulk of the kraken. Sure enough, it headed for me. I also saw more of the nearby ruins further behind it.

I have always hated the idea of just waiting for the killing blow. Far better to attack, even if only to bite your opponent or scratch him. In other words, do something aggressive even if it proved futile.

I jackknifed down, flutter kicking with my feet. I was desperately slow, but I moved underwater. Not knowing what else to do, but knowing I should do something, I aimed the hollow tube at the approaching mass of kraken. I willed the tube to fire. I didn't know if this was certain death for me or—

Something flammable bubbled from the tube opening and through the water, jetting at the kraken.

The great beast must have turned aside, though perhaps only temporarily. I kicked nonetheless and swam deeper, reaching the nearest ruin or building. I wasn't sure about my thinking, maybe to put my back to it.

Surprisingly, the structure was only forty or fifty feet underwater. I might have liked to swim inside it, but my lungs were already hurting. I wasn't used to diving. I was tired, disoriented—

A narrow shape shot out of a window in the building. It might have been this world's version of a barracuda, a torpedo-shaped fish several feet in length.

I jabbed with the hollow tube and willed another burst of fire. The air bubbled before the opening and something hot lanced out.

The torpedo-shaped fish darted away.

The need for air had become unbearable. I kicked for the surface and soon broke through, gasping.

My backpack was too heavy and immediately started dragging me underwater.

As I trod water as taught in a YMCA pool in my childhood, I went through the pack and tossed whatever seemed useless to an existence in the ocean. The discarded objects sank out of sight or floated on the waves.

After putting the pack back on, I lay back in the water, holding my breath most of the time. That made me more buoyant. If I exhaled too much, I began to sink.

Kicking my feet in a leisurely manner, I moved away from this section of the sea. From time to time, I lifted up as best I could and looked down.

Soon, I no longer spied any underwater ruins. That included the landing ziggurat.

I had a terrible thought. If the landing ziggurat was underwater, maybe the exit obelisk was as well. Maybe I'd be stuck on this planet for the rest of my life.

Given the size of the kraken, I didn't think that I'd landed on Earth over some sunken Atlantis.

That stopped me.

Atlantis.

Had I reached the planet of Atlantis, just as I'd once reached the planet of Mu?

The legend of Atlantis spoke about a sunken city. Had I just arrived on the greater planet of Atlantis by landing at the old city of legend?

Maybe after all I'd been through, I shouldn't have been surprised. But I got the willies and goosebumps all over my body thinking about this. I'd reached ancient Atlantis. What would the people be like on this planet? Had Omilcar reached here ahead of me?

Thinking about the psi-master reignited my anger.

I shook my head.

I couldn't afford the indulgence of anger or rage right now. I needed to survive and thus start figuring things out.

It had been a few months since I'd traveled last. I'd learned a few tricks during my interstellar journeys. I'd never landed in an ocean before, but I had landed in seas of Ophidian aliens before. I had dealt with mutated snapping turtles. If I kept my wits about me, I should be able to survive this place, too.

Once more, I halted and looked around. Then, far off on the horizon, I saw something unusual—a tiny smudge. Could that be a ship, an island, what?

I exhaled deeply and told myself to relax. It was a destination, but I wouldn't reach it right away, and I certainly wouldn't do so if I drowned.

Thus, I lay back and continued to kick, working on maintaining my strength and energy. I stopped and looked around every so often to make sure I continued to head in the correct direction.

I did.

For now, that was good enough.

I continued my slow swim toward the smudge on the horizon. The next time I trod water to look at it, I felt myself becoming tired and dispirited.

The worst thing was that I realized I could be further from getting home to Earth than ever. How did one find a submerged obelisk? Then, how did one swim down far enough to engage the pyramidion? Was the obelisk in the same general region as the ziggurat? If so, would I have to contend with the kraken first?

That wasn't the end of it. What if Omilcar had tricked me into traveling to this place so I'd never see him again? That seemed more likely the longer I thought about it. He was a psi-master. I'd inadvertently used my mind to see into his. Surely, he could have used his superior mental abilities to insert that lie to trick or misdirect me.

I wasn't a psi-master in any sense of the concept. Rather,

I'd communicated with the pyramidions from time to time when I used the interstellar teleportation machines or devices.

Clearly, I had some sort of ability in this area. Why otherwise had Omilcar severed my beloved's head from her body?

I shuddered while thinking about it again.

I trod water and peered into the distance at the smudge. This was interesting. It appeared to have a shape this time instead of merely being a smudge. I could have sworn it was a ship, although I couldn't be certain.

Then, out of the corner of my eye—

Perhaps my time as a pterodactyl rider had trained me to be alert to what happened in the sky. I looked up, and sure enough, I saw… a floating ship, an airship.

Yes, that vast part was a balloon or dirigible. The craft seemed to be tacking its way toward me.

An airship implied advanced technology, at least compared to wooden sailing ships and swords for weapons.

Actually, if this were a water world, what would be the safest way to hover over a place you wanted to explore? I was thinking about the kraken and storms. It would be by airship.

Did the crew study sunken Atlantis? Surely, I'd arrived on the planet at the ancient city of Atlantis, the legendary city or country that had sunk beneath the waves thousands of years ago. That had happened sometime in BC, Before Christ.

I found that an awe-inspiring thought.

I resumed lying on my back and flutter kicking toward the ship. I didn't use my arms to backstroke because I held on to the hollow staff. I kept the rest of my meager possessions in the backpack.

From this position, I discerned a slowly rotating giant rotor or propeller on the back of the dirigible. The airship rotated gently and began to descend.

What provided the propeller its propulsion or motion? I didn't see any smoke to imply steam power. Steam power would pose an extreme hazard to a dirigible. I doubted they used helium to inflate the dirigible but more likely highly flammable hydrogen.

That meant the propeller's propulsion remained a mystery

to me.

I watched the airship maneuver for a time as I continued my kicking swim. I perceived that the dirigible was much bigger than I'd originally estimated.

That made it more interesting that it was taking such pains to descend to me. That implied I was important in some manner, and that implied two other things. Omilcar could be up there, and he would want to capture me. Or, it could be that any man swimming in these waters was important. Perhaps they knew about Travelers and were coming to pick me up for that reason.

Did the ship and dirigible coordinate or…

Once again, I trod water and looked into the distance. That was a sailing ship. It had two main masts, although I didn't see any sails on the masts. Instead, to my amazement, great oars moved along the sides, turning the craft into a great wooden sea centipede.

This was certainly interesting. It felt as if the ship had turned away from me and was fleeing.

I considered that. Did it mean that those in the airship preyed upon those on the sea? Given primitive weapons, height advantage would surely mean the airship was supreme.

Since it was easier to float and kick than tread water, I continued to head toward the fleeing ship, the giant galley, I suppose.

I continued to watch the airship maneuver, and circle or spiral down toward me. The swinging gondola beneath the great blimp became apparent. I imagined the gondola was constructed of withe or huge woven reeds like someone might weave a basket.

Now, dot heads peered over the gondola's railing. Then it became apparent they used telescopes to peer at me.

I waved at them.

Did I demean myself in their eyes by doing that? Did I have less dignity because of it?

A premonition swept over me. I became certain those in the dirigible had picked up Omilcar several days ago.

What sort of beings manned the dirigible?

I strained to see what sort of being used the spyglasses.

Were they humans, Ophidians?

A chill swept through me. I discerned Draconians, the same kind as the vicious raptor riders of Mu. These wore gaudy feather hats.

Then the worst thing of all happened, although the vengeance driven part of me was glad.

In my mind, I heard, *Bayard, you came after all, you fool. Good. Now I don't have to worry that I left you behind.*

-13-

"Omilcar," I said.

Yes, you fool. It's me. But why not think your thoughts directly at me? Why do you need to vocalize your thoughts in order to communicate with me?

I'd taken the psi-master headband with me, but it was in my backpack. Given my present precarious position, I didn't want to take off the pack and rummage around for it.

In the past, I'd resisted psi-master domination. I believed I could do that now... except I recalled how Omilcar had paralyzed me with his psionic powers. He had become the Great Sark of Mu for a reason, and was far superior to any other psi-master I'd ever met. I needed that headband if I was going to resist him. Still, I knew that proximity was critical with mind power. Like gravity, the effect weakened with the square of the distance... meaning proximity was often more important than size or power.

What are these thoughts, Bayard? They are murky and unclear. I can't quite understand what you're thinking. If you want me to know it, you're going to have to say it aloud because you're a mental midget compared to any psi-master.

I scowled, hating his smug arrogance.

Do you remember the severed head I used to get here? It was familiar to you once. Well, I don't have it anymore. Do you know why? I tossed it to a sea-creature, a beast. It ate the head. Isn't that funny?

My teeth grated against each other as I worked to contain my rage. I realized... no. I was a mite on this planet. I needed my wits, my logical mind, not my seething hatred.

Choking back the insults I wanted to hurl at Omilcar, I asked aloud, "Is this Atlantis?"

Can you think otherwise?

"Just answer the question," I said.

No, I'm done answering your questions whenever you please. Do you know how tedious, how odious it was having to truckle to your whims? You're such an idiot, a buffoon. You think yourself clever. Oh, you know a few historical antecedents, but really, you're a dumb American fool. Yes, I know what that is because I spent enough time on Earth to learn. Do you think you're so tough, you, a U.S. Marine?

"You ran away from me," I said.

Yes, to reach my next venture, the next set of circumstances I need in order to complete my plan. Do you like my crew, Bayard?

"Were they waiting here for you?"

Omilcar laughed in my mind. *Wouldn't you like to know, you idiot? You're soon going to be part of my experiment once more unless you dive deep and drown yourself. Go ahead, Bayard. I dare you to try that. If you do, I'll bring you back up because I'll force the life desire to throb within you. You're far more malleable than you know, though you are a stubborn mule of an ass.*

"Is that a play on words?" I asked. "If so, I find your pun ludicrous and juvenile."

Omilcar didn't respond immediately.

From my back, I watched nets lowering from the dirigible.

Then ropes uncurled toward me. Small Draconian warriors slithered down the lines like commandos.

I studied them, looking for clues. They did not bear any sidearms I could see. Some had crossbows on their backs; others seemed to have daggers or slender swords at their waists. They looked like pirates or Recon Marines flying on the lines of a helicopter.

We're going to take you before the Sea Lords arrive, not that they're heading for you anymore. Did you know about the Sea Lords? Is that why you're swimming for the ship?

"I know all about the Sea Lords," I lied, glad for this little bit of information.

It is almost inconceivable that you know about them. However, if you do, you must realize that the Draconians hunt them in their airships and burn the vessels out of existence. Even if you had reached their ship, it would have done you no good.

Then it struck me—the solution. I was giddy at the thought, and knew I had to think of anything else.

What is that? You're trying to keep something from me.

"You killed my wife and my son-to-be," I shouted, letting rage consume me, even though there was a hidden part in my mind that strove to keep information from Psi-Master Omilcar, the Great Sark of Mu.

What are you hiding from me?

I laughed, with unrestrained glee, vengeance burning in my eyes. I let my emotions flood my mind so I wouldn't give away the wonderful secret.

Come just a little closer, just a little closer.

What do you want closer? Omilcar asked in my mind. *Are you trying to be tricky? Do you think you—?*

Abruptly, Omilcar swore in my mind, and the link between us snapped off.

I could not see what happened next. I could not even sense it, as I lacked that sort of psionic ability. Even so, I knew that Omilcar ran to the captain of the airship. The psi-master must be screaming orders to take the airship higher.

As I watched, the airship continued to lower. The Draconians still slithered down the lines.

Then a Draconian with an elaborate feather headdress, like a Sioux or Cheyenne Indian, leaned over the edge of the gondola. He used a megaphone to shout at the commandos.

They all craned their heads, looking up, listening. Several glanced sharply at me. Then they began to scramble up the lines.

Omilcar had told them the awful truth, at least from his perspective.

I laughed with unrestrained glee, with vengeance burning in my eyes as I raised my hollow tube. Here was my opportunity. I straightened, trod water, and willed my hollow tube to expel a gout of flame like a great bazooka.

This was yet another World War II reference. I'd read a lot of those kinds of books when I was a kid and watched endless World War II movies as a punk.

The gout of flame flew up but arched, not quite reaching them. I fired another, and this fireball reached the gondola. That part immediately burst into flame. Draconians ran to put it out. That told me the gasbag was filled with hydrogen instead of helium.

I trod water and lifted up, willing the greatest shot that I could from the tube. A glob of fire burst forth and sailed up, up and past the gondola. The fireball touched the bottom of the gasbag.

I howled with glee as the gasbag burst into fire and expanded with wonderful haste. This was just like that old-time newsreel when the Zeppelin *Hindenburg* began to burn. With grim satisfaction, I watched the dirigible blaze.

-14-

I enjoyed the spectacle so much that I began to wax poetic in my thoughts. How I hated Omilcar. How I needed this sweet relief to the horrors I'd witnessed on Sky Island.

The vastness of the ocean stretched endlessly in every direction, a sprawling expanse of water that shimmered under the alien sun. The gentle waves lapped against each other with a soothing rhythm. Salt-laden air filled my lungs with each breath, carrying an unfamiliar tang that reminded me this was not home or Mu—this was somewhere else entirely.

Above this watery expanse hovered the burning dirigible. The hydrogen within the gasbag created a mix of orange and blue flames that turned the sky into a vision of hell.

The fire consumed the dirigible with terrible ferocity. The outer skin blistered and blackened, writhing like a living thing in agony. The framework beneath twisted, its structure failing under the intense heat. Within moments, the fabric gave way, and the great vessel began its descent, tumbling awkwardly through the air as though the heavens conspired against its survival.

The sight was beautiful, and I realized I smiled like a madman.

Screeches pierced the air as some Draconians scrambled for survival. They were swift and agile but it didn't help. Their scales reflected the flames as they fought against their impending doom. Some leapt into the void, their bodies spinning against the surreal sky, limbs thrashing against gravity's relentless pull. Others, caught by the flames, became silhouettes in the inferno, disappearing with barely a trace, their existence reduced to ash and memory.

Then I saw a thing that dashed my joy into gloom and rage. I couldn't believe this. It was so dreadfully unfair.

A man appeared in a silver transpar suit, similar to what the Neanderthals and I had used against the Ophidians of Saddoth. He ran through burning fire and leapt like Superman. He soared away from the destruction, leaving behind the fiery disaster.

I had no doubt that was Omilcar. He flew farther away, escaping with his life.

In the ocean where I floated, the airship continued its death spiral, plummeting toward the water. The heat of the explosions reached me so I dove to get away.

When I surfaced, smoke and embers rained down, hissing as they splashed within the alien sea. Each ember created a small circle of steam, like countless fleeting rings appearing and vanishing on the ocean's surface.

What was left of the dirigible and gondola hit the water, sending waves outward. Debris scattered across the surface— wood, charred fabric, and unidentifiable pieces of what had once been a mighty vessel of the sky. The acrid smell of burning hydrogen mixed with the tang of the alien air, creating an atmosphere that seemed appropriate for this destruction.

Many of the Draconians had struck the water in harsh belly and back flops. Those did not move. Some dove cleanly into the sea, and struggled up to the surface, gasping desperately.

It soon became apparent that the Draconians weren't

buoyant like most humans, having to struggle to stay on the surface.

The burning airship that had struck the water hard and the many raining individuals had created commotion. That now brought sharks or other aquatic predators. Soon, huge fins cut the water and Draconians who had been inert disappeared in a flurry of motion and teeth.

I had to get out of here, but I couldn't thrash and expect to get away unnoticed. Instead, I turned over and swam slowly but surely. The hollow tube was secured to my pack, making it easier to swim. From the nature shows I'd watched in the past, I knew sharks were attracted to such thrashing motion. So, I swam as smoothly as I could. Even so, I soon noticed a big fin trailing me, coming up fast.

I retrieved my tube, though I was exhausted and ravenous. That was critical.

I'd learned that powering the tube used up sustenance from me. To hit the gasbag with my fiery glob had taken great emotional effort, berserkergang rage for the loss of Livi and my son. Now, I had little left.

I noted the direction the transpar suit flew in relation to the galley. Incredibly, the galley no longer fled but seemed to be coming toward me at speed as such things went for a wooden ship of that size. The crew must have seen the airship catch fire and crash. Could they realize I had caused that?

I willed my hollow tube to fire again. A weak flame arched out and licked against the fin. In a flash, the fin went down.

I treaded water, ready to stab down with the blunt point of the hollow staff. But nothing attacked or inspected me.

The flame lesson had been a salutary one for the meat-eating fish.

I resumed my slow but steady swim on my back. Finally, it became too much. I would soon slip beneath the waves, unable to keep my head above water.

I worked on holding as much air as I could in my lungs. In that manner, as my mind reeled and hunger gnawed at my belly, after the cries of the Draconians had stilled and all fires were out, I continued to float, hold my breath, and then expel and regain it.

After what felt like an eternity, I could no longer picture Livi. I was too exhausted. I could no longer think of my son squirming in the amniotic fluid. Dully and tiredly, I watched as the behemoth of a galley approached.

When had it gotten so near? I must be delirious.

Wood creaked even as the oars stilled, rowers pulling them in. Men—they looked like pterodactyl riders, which was to say remarkably like Vikings. Big bearded men, Caucasians, the majority, anyway, lowered a net over the side. Several men scrambled down with monkey-like agility, rigging a harness around me. One took the tube; I clutched weakly at it but to no avail. Others pulled me up, up. The wooden side seemed to go on forever, but I was so grateful they had come. Would I be grateful later?

The men deposited me on the deck, where a great giant of a man, not quite of Forkbeard stature but with a great blond bushy beard, stood. He wore leather and woolens, his arms akimbo. He looked at me, and I could see questions in his squinty eyes.

Others crowded behind him, watching me as I swayed unsteadily, staring back at them. Then I collapsed, exhausted beyond endurance. I hit the deck with a thud, and then everything went dark.

-15-

I awoke sometime later in a stiff cot. I had a blanket over me as the giant galley creaked and heaved, my chamber swaying back and forth. I heard the clack of oars but no whips or clinking chains. I did hear a great drum beat the time.

My cabin was surprisingly spacious, although the ceiling was low, with beams overhead. That looked like wood, although I had no idea what kind. There were beautiful, wonderfully carved furnishings, hanging leather jugs, unlit candles and possibly a lantern. It rattled and was obviously metal.

"Hello?" I said.

I heard a feminine sigh and then a woman sat up from the floor beside my cot. She stared at me with surprise.

Had she been lying there, waiting for me?

The woman had a tangle of red hair and a fair, although smudged face. She stood quickly and jabbered a question at me. Her leather garments were on the skimpy side, apocalyptic survival style, although they covered the essentials. They did show that she had beautiful tanned legs.

"What did you say?" I asked weakly.

She cocked her red-maned head, blinking several times. Then she jabbered again in her crazy tongue.

It finally struck me. I didn't understand what she was saying. That was unusual for Traveling. The sending pyramidion always—or nearly always—gave me the native tongue of whatever planet I reached. Why hadn't that happened here?

I'd understood Omilcar's telepathic thoughts. Did one think in the new native tongue, or did the mind merely translate it into speech when opening a pyramidion-trained mouth? I didn't know the answer to that.

"Who are you?" I asked, deciding to try again.

Once more, she tilted her head as if she might understand some of what I said. Then she gave a cry, possibly of despair.

"Does it help if I talk slower?" I asked.

She hesitated for a moment, then whirled around, stepped to a heavy wooden door, opened it, and dashed outside, shouting in alarm.

Oh boy, I knew I didn't have long. I lifted the covers and found myself naked. I leaned over and saw a rug where she must have been sleeping or lying. My backpack was to the side. I wanted to get up and check it, but felt too weak to try. They'd taken my hollow tube. From the cot, I looked around until I saw it. Someone had placed the five-foot tube on pegs, like a flintlock rifle over a fireplace. My tube hung over a glass window that showed the vast ocean beyond. The chamber had to be located in the stern of the galley. Wouldn't this be the captain's quarters then? Did that mean his woman had been taking care of me?

The door opened again, and the big blond-bearded Viking I recalled earlier stooped in. He had to hunch as he entered. He spoke a gruff word that meant nothing to me.

"I don't understand you," I said.

He halted and cocked his head, blinking at me. Did he almost understand me? I had that sense, but couldn't really know.

He didn't wear a Viking's horned helmet, but a leather cap. By his seamed features and ample size, I figured him to be in his forties or even fifties. He didn't wear metal armor, but buff leather and woolen garments, with a long cape trailing behind.

The woman jabbered as she squeezed into the cabin with him. He ignored her, coming forward, picking up a small stool and placing it beside my bed. He sat and regarded me, and spoke again.

"Sorry, chief," I said. "That means nothing to me."

Now the old boy turned to the woman. She shut the door as he tapped his head, questioning her.

The woman answered softly, shaking her head.

Did he wonder if I'd bumped my head or if I was somehow impaired?

The woman tiptoed closer, sliding in front of the bearded guy so the back of her knees pressed against his knees. She leaned over me and ran her fingers through my hair. She focused, perhaps feeling for bumps.

I lay still.

She straightened as the chief placed a big hand on her rump. She didn't complain or swipe the hand off. Instead, she spoke softly to him.

He listened, finally pulling her down on one of his knees. She stayed put as if that happened a lot.

The bearded man cleared his throat and spoke more slowly and loudly than before to me. It didn't help, although there was a glimmer of possible familiarity for a word or two. I thought that strange. Were there some root words to this planet and Earth?

"I still don't understand, sir," I said.

He frowned and then scowled. He patted her back.

She jumped up, moving to the side.

He spoke gruffly.

She watched him with a fearful expression.

He said it again.

She crept to the large glass window and took down my hollow staff, holding it as though it might bite her. She walked over and gave it to him.

61

He took it, holding it a little more confidently, but with some hesitation just the same. Then, he proffered it to me.

"It's mine," I said, without reaching for it.

He spoke again, shoving it at me.

I took it, nodding. "Yeah, this is mine all right."

He frowned in obvious concentration. Did he try to make sense of my speech?

I was finding it hard to follow all this, as my eyelids were becoming heavy. I yawned, wanting to go back to sleep. My stuff was okay, and I seemed to be safe for the moment. It would have been a lot better if we could have understood each other. What if no one in Atlantis could communicate with me?

I closed my eyes with the hollow tube to one side of me on the cot. I needed sleep. That was often the best medicine, a good night's sleep.

When I opened my eyes again, the bearded man was gone, though the stool remained. I leaned over and looked down at the woman lying on the rug staring up at me. I didn't say anything, just rolled onto my back and fell asleep.

-16-

I awoke to a loud hubbub outside the cabin.

The woman was up, peering through the crack of the barely opened wooden door. It let more noise through, possibly waking me.

I sat up on the cot, leaning back against a wooden bulkhead. It sounded like real agitation out there. Were they debating what to do with me?

Despite the predicament, I felt marginally better physically but ravenously hungry and thirsty.

"Hey," I said. "Where can I get some food around here?"

The woman whirled around with a cry of dismay. A second later, she shut the door softly, raising and lowering the latch. She stared at me as if I'd sprung antlers from my forehead.

"Food," I said, mimicking eating.

She continued to stare at me.

"Look," I said. "I'm not going to hurt you. I just want

something to eat and drink." I mimicked doing just that once more.

She didn't move, just stared.

"Fine," I said. "I'll get it myself."

I've never really been that self-conscious, so I whipped back the covers.

Her eyes bulged outward.

I'd like to say it was because I was so well-endowed, but it seemed more like terror on her part. With a jerk, she looked away.

I had enough strength to swing my legs over the cot, lean over and retrieve my pack. I opened it, took out a pair of shorts, and slipped them on for propriety's sake.

"It's okay," I said. "You can look now."

It must have been my voice. She peeked at me, and her shoulders relaxed as she faced forward again.

"Now how about getting me some grub?" I asked, mimicking eating again.

This time, she went to a cupboard, picking up a plate, returning and handing me what looked like the remains of orange-colored cold fish. I set the plate on my lap and devoured the fish. It tasted like salmon. I felt marginally better afterward.

She took the empty plate and handed me a leathery jug. I uncorked it, sniffed, and took a tentative sip. It was grog of some sort, but didn't seem too alcoholic. I assuaged my thirst with it and almost immediately began to feel a little light-headed.

The noise outside had gotten worse, maybe turning into an argument. It was time to peek out the door and make an assessment.

I did notice that no oars clacked, nor did the galley do much creaking. I assumed we had stopped.

Had another dirigible shown up? The Vikings—the Sea Lords, I corrected myself—might want some help against any Draconian airships.

However, I didn't feel like using the hollow tube just yet. I was still too exhausted from my previous ordeal. I sure would have liked to know what everyone was saying out there.

As I debated on my next move, I heard the tread of heavy feet, and then the door banged open. The big blond-bearded chief glared at me with angry, squinty eyes. He took in the scene at a glance before roaring orders.

The woman ran to obey, picking up my backpack and shoving it into my arms. Then she pointed to the hollow tube on the cot.

I looked at it, at her, her gesturing, and picked it up.

The Sea Lord roared more orders. He sounded seriously angry.

The woman jabbered back at him. He raised a beefy hand as if to backhand her. She shrieked, rushed near and began to push me from behind. She steered me toward the open door and the captain blocking it.

I stumbled in surprise. I would have walked smack into the captain, but he nimbly stepped out the door. The woman kept pushing until I stumbled onto the poop deck. Was that the right term, or was it the stern bridge or deck of a galley?

The galley was bigger than I'd originally realized. There was a fair amount of space up here and in the long waist of the galley. I stood forty or fifty feet above sea level.

A lot of big, Viking types milled just below the poop deck in the waist. I estimated fifty or sixty men, but no women. Did they keep the women below deck, or did the captain have the only woman aboard?

Ten or so gruff Vikings were on the stern or poop deck with me. They all had swords belted at their sides. Their leather garments seemed like armor of sorts. Each of them wore helmets as well.

The captain shouted to everyone, pointing at me.

No one cheered. No one booed. They all fell silent and stared at me as if I were an alien. I had no idea what this meant.

Then everyone turned toward the other side of the galley. I'd had my back aimed that way, so I had to turn around. What I saw blew me away, and it helped me understand what the commotion had been about.

A metal-skinned submarine lay in the water approximately fifty feet away and parallel with the galley. The sub had a conning tower and even a big gun forward of the tower, maybe an 88mm gun. It reminded me of the Type VII U-boat in the German Kriegsmarine or Navy when Hitler made his run at conquest. That had been the workhorse U-boat back then—the kind that sank millions of tons of Allied shipping.

The implication of a submarine on Atlantis—

It left me speechless.

After recovering from my surprise, the first thing I wanted to know was the type of occupants of the sub. I dearly hoped it wasn't Draconians, Ophidians and certainly not Krekelens.

I did recall Krekelen submarines on Earth. Those had been more futuristic looking and been able to run circles around Russian or American submarines. This relic of a sub was nothing like that.

Everyone on the galley stared at the submarine. Then a person appeared at the top of the conning tower. He used a bullhorn, shouting at us in the galley.

He was a man in a black military uniform and wearing a military hat. The combo could have easily come from Earth in the middle to late 20th century.

When he ceased shouting, the Sea Lord shouted orders at his crew.

Several strong boys grabbed me, hustling me toward the waist of the ship. No one tried to take my hollow tube or tear off my backpack. My bare feet slapped against the wooden deck as my minders forced me down a ladder.

Were they going to kill me?

The Sea Lords had definitely grown hostile toward me. My minders hustled me to the side of the galley and forced me to climb over the rail and down a net along the outer side.

I climbed into a wooden dingy or launch that bumped against the galley. Several Sea Lords climbed into it with me. A minder forced me to the front.

Others with poles pushed off from the galley as six men took up oars. There were some curses and clacking. The six rowed the launch toward the waiting submarine.

The waiting officer in the conning tower watched us closely. He used the bullhorn to shout something in their tongue at them.

A minder thrust a jacket at me. I slipped it on.

As we approached, sailors in light blue uniforms climbed out of the conning tower and walked on the sea-washed deck of the submarine. They had ropes and wore life vests. All wore military hats or woolen caps. One stood back and held what looked like a submachine gun. He aimed it at us.

Soon, the wooden launch struck the submarine. Sea Lords helped me up and guided me to waiting sailors on the higher sub.

I made the leap between the launch and the sub, and slipped. I would have fallen into the sea, but one of the sailors grabbed my jacket, hauling. He needed help, as I was much bigger than they were. All the sailors were on the smaller side. They weren't puny, mind you, just nothing over five-ten.

"We got you," the first sailor said.

My head whipped up as I stared into his eyes.

"Do you understand me?" the sailor asked.

"Yes," I said.

He grinned.

So did I.

The sailors helped me toward the conning tower. There were handholds or iron rungs on the side. I climbed the conning tower to the waiting officer, who opened a gate.

At the same time, the launch left the submarine and returned to the giant galley.

"He understands us, Captain," the sailor shouted from below.

The officer grasped my hand and helped me into the conning tower. He was the tallest of the lot, although still considerably shorter and lighter than I was.

"You under what I'm saying?" he asked me.

"I do," I said.

"Then welcome aboard the *Triton*," he said.

"I'm staying with you?" I asked.

"Are you a Traveler?"

I grinned, and I nodded before thinking it through.

The officer's face turned grave. "Then you're most certainly staying with us," he said.

-17-

I climbed down a ladder, entering the submarine. It was a refreshing change to return to a technological society.

Perhaps I should preface that. Clearly, the Sea Lords used technology, though theirs was primitive compared to Earth's. The submarine's tech was more in line with what I was used to.

The others came down the steel ladder as well. Interestingly, the last one down didn't close the hatch.

The diesel engines began to throb audibly. Those diesels had been running the entire time, just at idle. I felt motion as the *Triton* began cutting through the choppy waves.

It was not a smooth ride, and I crashed against a protruding piece of metal.

"Careful, Traveler," the officer said.

I looked back at him. His uniform seemed military, archaic in ways and futuristic in others. Under his cap, he had short, sandy-colored hair, brown eyes and could have been in his early forties. He had hollow cheeks that seemed fitting for a submarine commander. There was something stern in his bearing, although he had a pleasant face.

"You need your sea legs," he said.

I stuck out my hand. "I'm Jake Bayard."

"Captain Andros Spiro," he said, shaking hands with me.

For those of you who think it strange that a man of Atlantis should use the word captain, realize that it was a translation of the actual term. I decided early in my travels to use regular English-Earth terms wherever it seemed suitable, even if the aliens used something else. This was such a situation.

"I'm glad to make your acquaintance," I said. "I would like to know, however, if you have good or bad intentions toward me."

An even more serious look transformed his face, giving him a sense of gravitas. "That depends on your intentions toward us."

I debated that for all of three seconds. "Let me tell you frankly then. If you're siding with the Krekelens or psi-masters, we're enemies. If not, we can be friends and allies."

He raised his eyebrows and said a curious thing. "Well then, Mr. Bayard, I'll have to see if any of the men know about Krekelens or psi-masters."

"You don't yourself?" I asked.

"Do you think I should?"

"I do," I said.

He nodded brusquely, motioning down the corridor. "Please, Mr. Bayard, continue down the corridor. We'll go to the mess and ask the chief if he has any spare clothes that will fit a brute like you."

It was my turn to raise my eyebrows.

He chuckled, which help dissolve some of the building tension. "I meant no disrespect by saying that, sir. You're a big man; someone your size could easily pass as a Sea Lord. Those of us from the Project seldom reach your height or girth, as you can see."

That was another curious statement. The Project sounded too much like the Institute of the *Homo habilises*.

I decided to stay quiet for the moment because loose lips

sink ships. I didn't want to sink mine. My position here was precarious enough, as I had no idea of the factions or sides the Project or this submarine represented.

We did not say more until reaching the mess. It was a cramped room with tables, chairs, and a hatch leading to the galley. There were two other hatches leading to different parts of the submarine.

"He's a big one, chief," the captain said.

The waiting chief was thicker and tad taller than the captain, with a puffier, angrier face. He had a bushy red beard and thick red eyebrows.

The chief sized me up, turned away and returned moments later with something more like a peasant's smock than a sailor's uniform.

"This is all we have that will fit you," the chief said gruffly, tossing the garments to me.

I caught them and nodded. "You want me to change right here?"

"Of course not," the captain said, sounding offended. "Go in there."

He indicated a claustrophobically small closet with a curtain. I pulled the curtain for their sake and changed into the smock. It felt as cramped as an airplane's restroom. The clothes were tight and looked like a Russian peasant's tunic and trousers from the 1700s. Still, I suppose they would do for now, as the Sea Lords had my clothes.

I came out, and they both stared at me.

"He's a big one all right," the chief said. "I don't have any shoes that will fit his feet."

The captain nodded. "I don't want him dressed like this among the men. Get Argos. He can sew him something better. Find some galoshes that will fit his feet. I don't want him walking around barefoot."

"Yes, sir," the chief said, exiting the mess in a hurry.

I wanted to ask who Argos was, but found out soon enough that he was a lanky fellow, a bit taller than the captain or chief but still shorter than me. He had a measuring tape, pencil and paper. After using the tape on my arms, legs, neck and chest, he made notes.

70

"I'll get right to it, captain." Argos nodded to me and left.

The chief then left for a second time as well.

I sat down, which made my trousers and tunic even tighter. I tugged at the collar, as it was uncomfortable.

"It's the best we can do in a pinch," the captain said. "You're a Traveler, isn't that right?"

"I've said as much. You don't believe me?" These clothes were beginning to irritate me.

The captain sat across the table from me, and gave me a pensive look. I suspect he didn't like anyone questioning him.

"Do you have any grub, sir?" I asked. "I'm starving."

He came out of his reverie. "Of course." He pulled out a whistle and blew it.

A small, hunched man appeared from the galley and served me stale bread, watery stew, and diesel-tainted water.

I ate without checking the stew too closely, recalling stories of servicemen eating weevil-infested food.

I belched when finished and glanced at the captain, but he didn't seem to mind my manners or lack thereof. The belch did draw his attention back to me.

"What am I going to do with you, Traveler? That is the critical question. I wonder, who do you really serve?"

"Ah," I said, "so you do know about the Krekelens and psi-masters."

He shook his head as a cross look filled his face. "Why would you say that?"

"You're talking about sides," I said.

"Of course," he said. "There are the Draconians in their dirigibles and the Sea Lords with their scattered islands. The two wage an eternal war across Atlantis."

"You're not part of that?" I asked.

He scowled. "Are you suggesting we're primitives? That we've forgotten about the glories we lost in the catastrophe?"

Now we were getting somewhere. What was the best way to proceed? I had an idea.

"I'm a Traveler, which you know. I don't know if you're familiar with the ziggurats and obelisks we use for interstellar teleportation from one planet to the next."

As I spoke, his interest obviously grew so he leaned

forward, avidly so. I believe he tried to hide it, but he was clearly greedy for information. I had the sense those on the submarine lacked knowledge. I mean more than a simple lack of understanding about Travelers, although he had known the term meant something critical.

I smiled and said, "But you certainly know all that."

He grunted, which could have meant anything.

"My only point is that I don't always know what others on the different planets I travel to know about—"

He held up his hand, interrupting me. "You've journeyed to more than one of the Harmony of Planets?"

Okay, he knew about the Harmony. That said a lot. Maybe I was wrong about them not knowing stuff.

"Former Harmony of Planets," I said. "It shattered a long time ago."

"Of course," he said. "I'm well aware of that."

"I see," I said. "I've traveled to a few of the former planets and seen the conditions on them."

"I'm interested to hear exactly what those conditions are," he said.

I sighed and looked away, wondering on the best way to proceed. Did he side with the Institute, with Saddoth Ophidians? I needed to know his allegiance.

"Is this going to be a problem?" he asked. "Are you refusing to say anything about the other planets?"

I regarded him closely. "No, not a problem, but I feel…" I pointed between him and me "…that there should be an exchange of information. It shouldn't all be in one direction."

He frowned.

"Doesn't it seem right that I learn about this world as I tell you about other worlds?" I asked.

His eyes narrowed. Obviously, he didn't trust me. Did he have good reason for the mistrust? Did it have anything to do with Omilcar?

"Are you feeling tired?" he asked.

"Not particularly," I lied.

"That staff. You hold on to it. Does it have any significance?"

"It's mine," I said. "But it's just a hollow tube." "Would

you like to take a look at it?"

"May I?" he asked.

I extended the five-foot tube to him. He accepted it, and studied it from top to bottom.

"There's no switch to turn it on," he said.

"No," I said.

He thought about that and then peered into the hollow area. He held the far end up to a light. Then he got up, grabbed a pen light, clicked it on, and shined the light into the tube. No doubt, he saw some of the electronic equipment in the tube. I'd been hoping he wouldn't notice. He clicked off the pen light, pocketed it, and handed the hollow tube back to me.

"It's an electronic device," he said.

"An ancient device as far as I know," I said.

"From before the shattering of the Harmony?" he asked.

"That's what I've been led to believe."

"Which means it's more than just a staff you happen to have?"

I shrugged.

"Where did this device originate?"

"The planet of Mu," I said.

He stared at me, and I didn't know whether he disbelieved or believed me.

He stood abruptly. "Make yourself comfortable, Mr. Bayard. The others and I have to talk for a bit if you don't mind."

"Not at all, sir," I said.

"Stay in the mess, please."

I nodded.

With that, he left, leaving me alone in the mess.

-18-

The captain, chief, and two bullyboys were in the mess with me. The two toughs weren't anywhere near my size, but they were thicker and taller than the chief or the captain. The two wore holstered sidearms. Whether those were gunpowder weapons or energy-based blasters, I had no idea. A flap covered each. The toughs took up positions by the hatch leading to the control chamber.

This reminded me of when I'd first met Colonel McPherson. In Antarctica, we boarded an airplane for a meeting where Krekelens posed as American high command to conduct the questioning.

I didn't think these men were Krekelens. I was in close quarters and hadn't felt any heat radiating from any of them. Did they think I was a Krekelen or some sort of enemy agent? It seemed more than possible.

The captain and chief sat at the table across from me. The

chief glared at me, occasionally glancing at my hollow tube.

"I'm going to ask that you not touch that," the captain said.

I picked up the tube, set it on the table and rolled it across the table to him. "You can hold on to it for now if that makes you happy."

He picked it up and handed it to one of the toughs. That man leaned it against a bulkhead. Then the captain ordered me to surrender my backpack.

Since they could overpower me by calling in the rest of the crew, resisting would have been futile. Besides, I wanted answers. Cooperation should get me those answers faster. There was another thing. The submarine was small. I would have a chance to get my stuff back later, if I remained free. I doubted they knew how to use any of the important equipment like the fiery tube, Phrygian cap or psionic headband. Therefore, I shrugged off the pack and slid it across the table to them.

The chief took it and set it at his feet.

The captain folded his hands on the table and nodded approvingly to me.

"I've had a conference with my officers," the captain said. "We agreed that we need some information before we allow you to stay aboard with us."

I wanted to ask him why he'd taken me from the Sea Lords. I'd been thinking about that. In the same manner, he must have learned about my destruction of the Draconian dirigible. That had brought him to the Sea Lord galley. He must have given them a command to hand me over. That implied effort. I didn't think he had any plans to release me, which meant he planned to keep me no matter what. Still, I wasn't going to call him a liar. My plan was to cooperate in hopes they would reciprocate.

I nodded, smiled, and said, "Fair enough. What would you like to know?"

His expression grew grave as he stared at me before lowering his gaze. A moment later, he looked up at me again.

"What do you know about Atlantis?"

I shrugged. "I know lots, some false, I'm sure, but some no doubt true."

"That doesn't answer my question."

"It does," I said, "just not to your satisfaction." Okay. That was the wrong way to do this. I needed to keep my smart-aleck ways to myself. I cleared my throat. "Why don't you ask me specifics about Atlantis? I'll answer to the best of my knowledge."

He nodded. "How many Travelers come here each year?"

"I have no idea."

He glanced at the chief before regarding me again.

"How do I know if you're telling the truth or not?"

"You're a captain. I imagine that means you're a good judge of character and men. Certainly, you can tell, can't you?"

He scowled, and he seemed to be growing increasingly irritated with me, which did not bode well. I should be ingratiating for the reasons I'd stated before. And yet, he was beginning to grate against me, the little prick.

"Look," I said, "why don't we do this in a friendly way. We're all friends here, right?"

"I'm chairing the meeting," he snapped.

I stiffened and nodded, and said without thinking, "Suit yourself... sir."

He held himself still, maybe counting to hold his temper in check. "What do you know about the Draconians?"

"They have airships. One tried to scoop me up."

"Indeed. Why?"

"You'd have to ask them," I said. "I didn't let them get close enough to talk."

"You used the hollow tube to eject fire at them. How did you know fire would work so spectacularly against their gasbag?"

I nodded. I'd been right about them knowing about the battle.

"Over a hundred years ago, there were hydrogen airships on Earth. In one of our cities, there was a disaster and the dirigible *Hindenburg* caught fire. It was a famous disaster, as they caught it on film. I figured the primitive Draconians would be using hydrogen instead of helium, and—"

"What?" asked the chief.

"Hydrogen instead of helium," I said.

The chief pulled out a pad and pencil. "Explain both," he

said.

That seemed weird. I told him the little I knew about hydrogen: that it was flammable, easier to produce, and helium was harder to produce but not flammable. I shared what I remembered from my science classes.

The chief scribbled all that down.

I not sure why, but it struck me then. Something I'd been missing until now.

"Hey," I said, "you guys understand me, but the Sea Lords didn't. What gives? How come they couldn't understand me?"

The two men glanced at each other.

"You didn't understand the speech of the Sea Lords?" the captain asked.

"Nope," I said, instead of saying something cheeky.

"The Sea Lord dialect is a derivative of the original speech," the captain said. "In truth, it has deviated to a considerable extent."

"You mean like Latin?" I asked.

The captain shook his head. "I don't understand your reference."

"Do you mean to say that you speak the original Atlantean tongue?" I asked.

Once more, the two men glanced at each other before becoming tight-lipped. The guards in back shifted uncomfortably.

"What the deal?" I said, annoyed. "I don't know why that should be such a big secret. You say the Sea Lords spoke a derivative of what you speak, but I couldn't understand them."

Then I thought back to Earth history. German, French, English, Danish were derived from similar root tongues. But a German wouldn't understand an American these days. However, if you listened long enough, you'd hear similarities with some words. Perhaps that was the case with the Sea Lords. I hadn't listened long enough to catch it. The pyramidion had given me the pure Atlantean tongue, not the butchered dialect.

"Okay," I said, "that's interesting. So the Sea Lords speak a guttural tongue of the pure Atlantean speech. That tells me a lot right there."

The captain and chief's eyes widened, as if I'd touched a nerve. I needed to placate them. I needed to keep my worst habits in check.

"It tells me you guys are more cultured," I said. "It tells me that you're closer to Atlantean technology. The submarine says as much, too."

The captain's lips thinned and he drummed his fingers on the table.

He opened his mouth several times before thinking better of it, I suppose. Then he said, "You have been remarkably reticent telling us what you know about the Draconians."

"Let me change that," I said. "I've faced Draconians on other planets, just as I've faced humans on other planets. Everywhere I've been, the Draconians and humans fight each other. However, I certainly am not on the side of the Draconians. I never have been."

"They are more technologically advanced than the Sea Lords," the captain said.

"What is that supposed to mean?" I asked.

"Don't Travelers necessarily side with those who are more technologically advanced?"

"Whoa, whoa," I said, raising a hand. "You've had Travelers here before, am I right? That's why you asked about the number of Travelers each year. Have those Travelers joined the Draconians?"

Neither said a word to that as both became stony-faced.

"If you're going to distrust me, and if you're not going to answer even the most basic questions, then I'm not going to answer any of your questions."

"We could make you answer," the chief said.

I stared at him, and I stubbornly dug in—one of my worst habits. "Go on, give the order. Then you're going to find out how many broken bones are in your face."

The guards stepped up, drawing their sidearms. Their barrels were narrow, suggesting advanced or unfamiliar technology. They didn't look like ray guns either. I wondered what the devices expelled and how they did that.

I raised my hands. "I don't mean to threaten you guys, but you guys are threatening me. You took me off the Sea Lord galley, and they were treating me pretty well."

"I expect they would," the captain said dryly.

"I have no idea what that means. You're cross with me. You're not telling me anything, and yet you're expecting me to spill my guts. We should implement fair trade. I have new knowledge. You have whatever knowledge you hold. Why don't we agree to tell each other what we know?"

"There have been a few Travelers in the past, and more recently a new one," the captain said. "These Travelers have always joined the Draconians, as you suggested, and we feel they have joined the—"

The captain stopped as the chief grunted and shot an elbow against the captain's nearest arm. The captain turned to the chief and nodded curtly.

"I get it," I said. "You don't want to tell me anything interesting."

"You claim not to belong to the Draconians," the captain said.

"I more than claim that. My actions prove it. Look, the Draconians came down to capture me. Instead, I destroyed their airship, and I would have killed Psi-Master Omilcar, too, if he hadn't had that flying suit."

The captain grabbed one of my wrists. "There, that word. You've used the word psi-master before. What does it and Psi-Master Omilcar mean? Are you speaking about the one who flew away in the transpar suit?"

"You know what that was, huh?"

"Yes, yes, of course I know."

I sighed. "Omilcar was on Mu a few days ago."

"Isn't that where you came from?" the captain asked.

"The same damn place," I said.

"Yet you claim you're not working together?"

"I don't claim it," I snapped. "I hate the bastard."

The captain and chief exchanged glances.

My grief burned through my good sense. "Omilcar killed my wife and son. I'm hunting to kill him, and I almost had him on the dirigible."

Then I calmed down, as everyone else grew tense, watching me closely. I shook my head. "Sorry, sorry."

"This Omilcar killed your wife?" the captain asked.

"Yes!"

"Why?"

"Because he's a traitor," I said. "Because he works for the other side, not our side."

"What side is that?" the captain asked.

"Don't you understand yet? The Krekelens are the masterminds behind so much. They're trying to achieve something bad on Earth."

"Earth?" the captain said. "Where's that?"

"All right, all right," I said. "I'm from Earth. I've traveled to different places for a while. I'm trying to figure this all out. I thought I knew what it all meant, but now I don't know. I don't know because Omilcar lied to me, and I'm going to hunt his ass down, and then I'm going to kill him. And I read the word Atlantis in his mind."

The captain and chief scrambled out of their chairs and away from the table.

"No, no, no," I said, feeling tired. "I'm not a psi-master. I'm not a Mind Worshiper of Mu, but I was using a device to protect myself against the psi-master. For a moment, our thoughts connected as he tried to read my mind. I caught a single word from him: Atlantis. Later, I used the obelisk-pyramidion to follow him to Atlantis, to here. That's why I'm here."

"But you are a Traveler," the captain said. He said it as if to prove that meant I was a psi-master.

"Yes," I said, "Travelers have certain genetics, but that doesn't include psi-mastery. Psi stands for psionics or mind powers by the way. The psi-masters have it. I don't know if the psi-masters created the Krekelens or if the Krekelens created the psi-masters. They seemed to do that on the planet of Mu a long time ago. How that works or worked with Atlantis, I don't have the foggiest. What legends you guys have about mind powers, I don't know that either. That's why I destroyed the Draconians, though. I wanted to kill Omilcar, but he escaped."

"He speaks with passion," the chief said.

"Yes," the captain said. "I almost believe him."

"Oh, whoop-de-doo," I said.

Once more, the captain scowled at me.

"Look, Captain, you do your thing, I'm going to do mine. I've given you my backpack and hollow staff. The staff is an ancient device as you've learned. I can use it because I'm a Traveler, because the same thing that allows me to use the pyramidions, allows me to use the staff. You're welcome to try to use it if you want. Do whatever floats your boat."

"What does that mean?" the chief asked.

"What?" I said.

"Float your boat."

"It's an idiom," I said. "Why, what do you think it means?"

The chief glanced at the captain, and they both fell silent.

"You guys have a great big secret," I said. "Somehow, you're more pure than the Sea Lords are. That's fine, too. At this point, I just want to get back to the obelisk so I can reach Earth."

"This obelisk is where the kraken resides?" the captain asked.

I pointed at him. "So you know about the kraken. It tried to eat me. So I used my staff against it, and it fled. Yeah, I need to go where the kraken lives so I can get the hell off this watery planet."

I was faking that part, as I first yearned—lived and breathed—the need to find and kill Omilcar.

Both men glanced at each other. Then the captain took two steps forward, put his hand out, and shook my hand again.

"I'm still not one hundred percent sure of you, Traveler," the captain said. "But I'm going to give you a bunk. You can bed down there. We will keep these war articles for now."

"Whatever," I said.

"We must reach a place, and then we will make a decision. After that, we will see if we will trade secrets."

"Great," I said, understanding little of that.

But that did end the meeting, and I found myself a certified passenger aboard the *Triton*, heading for who knew where, in a world covered by ocean, except maybe for a few islands that these Sea Lords controlled.

How all this came about and what the crew of the *Triton* was trying to do about it, I had no idea.

The priority now was to recover my strength.

-19-

The *Triton* was cramped, with constantly dripping pipes and old, strained equipment. The submarine traveled solely on the surface, even through rough seas. I puked several times from the harsh motion and bruised myself more than once on a metal protrusion. At those times, I learned it was best to stay in my bunk and endure.

My bunk was in what would have been the forward torpedo room on an old Kriegsmarine U-boat during World War II. There were several tubes here and torpedoes, although they were designed differently from what I'd seen in books and more of them, making it incredibly cramped. I barely had a couple of extra inches above my head as I stared up at a torpedo. Combined with the deck gun, the torpedoes seemed to be the *Triton's* offensive weaponry.

I made it into the control room. There was a periscope and radar screens, or some kind of detection devices, though the captain did not let me look closely at any of it.

After a couple of days, I determined there were about twenty-eight to thirty-three people onboard. That was fewer than the German crews of the Type VII U-boat. If I remember correctly, they had anywhere from forty-two to fifty people aboard depending on the year and model.

The crew was subdued for the most part, although there was an unusual number of conversations during their off periods. I listened in several times. They gave each other history, botany, and physics lessons. It seemed the listeners didn't know anything about what the teacher said, either. Many would take notes, and ask endless questions, most of which it seemed they should have already known.

It felt as if each man held specialized knowledge the others lacked, and they were trading this information to fix the situation.

I listened in order to learn myself, but it was mainly basic information, ordinary things that I already knew. Occasionally, I'd hear something half-interesting. But I must have been too obvious, as the men would notice and move away or stop talking altogether.

I wondered how much diesel we had in the main fuel tanks. I asked the captain in passing. He gave me a searching stare.

"What do you know?" he finally asked.

"Uh. That submarines like this need diesel."

"Do they have diesel engines on Earth?" he asked sharply.

"Some trucks do, and some submarines."

"What are trucks?"

I explained. He listened, and then asked me to explain the concept of highways, freeways and individually controlled land vehicles. The ideas astounded him.

"Are you saying this in order to see how gullible I am?" he asked finally.

"No sir. It's the truth. If you doubt me, you can keep asking hard questions, and compare and contrast them and see that it's so."

"Why would I do that?"

"That's how you stump a liar," I said. "You ask detailed questions."

84

He frowned.

"The liar invents so many details that it's usually hard for him to remember all the lies he's told."

"That's ingenious," the captain said, surprised. Then he must have realized he spoke with a Traveler, to the possible enemy agent. He nodded. "Thank you for the information."

"That one is free, Captain."

He nodded again, and left.

The next day we passed an island—not one in the sky, just a simple, ordinary, in-the-sea island. I saw two big galleys, as the captain allowed me onto the conning tower. I used a telescope, spying black-faced sheep on the grassy island. I didn't see any buildings, though.

"Do the Sea Lords grow their foodstuffs there?" I asked.

"Some. I believe that island is more important for their woolen products."

"Why are we here? Do the islanders have diesel?"

"No diesel," he said, "but something else."

"What's that?" I asked.

"I do not want to say," he admitted.

"At least that's an honest answer. I appreciate that. Can I ask you something else, sir?"

"You can ask," he said.

"Why are you keeping me around if you distrust me so much?"

"You'll find that out soon enough, Mr. Bayard. However, I will say that you have a fund of knowledge that we do not possess. That makes you a treasure."

"I've noticed that."

"What did you notice?" he asked sharply.

"That your crew members are all sharing knowledge with each other. That you guys seem deficient in specialized areas. That seems strange."

"Does it?" he asked.

"That's what I just said, so yeah."

"Why would you think we don't know certain things? Have you heard of that happening before?"

He was testing and probing. Had something happened to them so each had lost knowledge? It seemed like that might be

85

it. But how could such a thing happen?

The captain stared at me, waiting for an answer.

"As a matter of fact, sir, I have not heard of that before," I said. "The situation strikes me as odd, but I'm beginning to think it's an important point to you pure Atlanteans."

He turned pale, and then appeared worried about me. I thought he might call his bullyboys up here to throw me overboard.

Finally, he said, "You have an astute mind, Mr. Bayard."

"A Traveler needs that because he comes across many strange things and has to figure them out fast, or die."

"I wish you would write a book about those oddities so we could read and understand more about our universe."

I bet you do, Mr. Greedy Pants. But I said, "That's a good idea. When I get back to Earth, I'll write a journal about my travels."

He let it drop, and soon, the *Triton* left the island behind until it became a dot and then disappeared altogether. He said the islanders possessed something important, but we hadn't stopped to retrieve it.

-20-

Two more days passed as we continued our journey across the lonely and sometimes choppy surface.

The crew became increasingly tense, filled with nervous energy. No one informed me what was happening or what was going to happen. I spent a lot of time in the mess and learned to play a different version of checkers on this watery Atlantis.

Abruptly, the diesels stopped. They had been chugging away ever since I boarded. One thing about diesel engines is that it's more effective to keep them running at idle than to constantly shut them down and restart them. There were only two real reasons to stop the diesels aboard a sub: one, because we'd run out of fuel and two, in order to dive. A diesel engine needed air to burn the fuel. If we dived with the diesels on, the engines would quickly consume all the breathable air, leaving us to suffocate.

The silent engines created an eerie atmosphere. I found

myself looking around, waiting for the other shoe to drop.

It did in short order as a klaxon blared. Two sailors rushed into the mess, shutting and sealing the hatch they'd come through and moving to the second hatch, no doubt to do the same.

The larger sailor halted and stared at me.

"What's wrong?" I asked.

"Felix," he said, "escort our guest to his bunk." He turned to me. "You are to stay in your bunk for the duration of the dive."

There it was—the magic word, the other shoe.

"You mustn't open a hatch on penalty of death," the sailor added.

"You guys are in a hurry," I said. "Why don't I just stay here so Felix doesn't have to reopen and reseal all the hatches you two have already dealt with?"

The larger sailor frowned, but after a moment, he nodded. "Yes, yes, you can do that. Come, Felix."

They hurried out, closing the hatch behind them.

Soon, from my location in the mess, I heard the gurgle of water, and I felt a lurch as the submarine tilted downward.

They must have been flooding the main ballast tanks with seawater to change the buoyancy and submerge.

Sealing all the hatches now made sense. It was an extra precaution in case there was a breach anywhere. The entire submarine wouldn't flood and sink to the bottom of the sea that way.

I heard ticking sounds all around me, and then groaning, shifting metal. The gurgling sounds continued, more metallic groaning—

Suddenly, a seal burst in an overhead pipe. Water sprayed from it, splashing against a bulkhead and onto the mess deck.

I leaped up and ran to a bulkhead intercom, pressing a button. "Hey, there's a leak in the mess."

No one answered.

I pressed the button again. "Did anyone hear me?"

"Get off the line, Mr. Bayard," the chief said. "We know there are leaks. Now shut the hell up and enjoy the ride the best you can, and do what you can to fix it."

That response was far from reassuring. I tore off my shirt, the new one sewn for me. I approached the spray and wrapped that around the seal and pipe, nearly scalding my hands on the hot water.

That helped for a few minutes. The pressure must have built up again. Water tore through my garment and began to hose into the mess again.

Why were we diving anyway? What were they trying to achieve by it? It sounded as if they already knew this was a leaky old submarine.

A moment later, that struck me. This was an old submarine, and for some reason, that detail felt significant. It must match or fit into the fact that the crew was pure Atlantean and spoke the old tongue. I couldn't put my finger on why, but I think my subconscious had already been working on all this.

I sat back down and watched the water spray in. Soon, fear of drowning began to take hold of my imagination.

Even so, the *Triton* continued on its downward course and then stopped.

I listened. Despite the spray of water, I heard hatches opening somewhere on the sub.

Nothing more happened as time passed.

The water in here was rising. I'd lifted my feet from the deck, putting them on the bench to keep my galoshes from getting soaked.

Then a hatch opened, and three sailors with tools and equipment rushed in. They hurried to the pipe and seal, fixing it in short order.

I immediately felt a sense of relief.

Two others appeared and laid a flexible tube through the hatch into the water sloshing at my feet.

"What's going on?" I said.

They all cast me an evil glance. The three repairmen moved on, exiting through the closed hatch, shutting it behind them. An electric engine turned on somewhere, and the tube began sucking up the water in here.

I'd read somewhere that water in the crew areas would naturally drain to the bilge. That was typical of submarines built on Earth. Did they do it differently on Atlantis? I guess this was a portable bilge team.

The interesting point as far as I was concerned was that the two sailors who had brought the tube departed for elsewhere.

I kept staring at the open hatch. I dearly wanted to know why we'd dived. Maybe I could sneak around and find out.

Finally, I waded through the mess water and crept into the corridor until I reached the hatch into the control chamber.

Thinking about it, I peered through.

None of them saw me. They were all too busy monitoring screens or equipment panels. I could feel their tension.

Then I noticed one of the monitors, a TV screen. It was murky out there, but there must have been bright lights shining. I saw a large, flexible tube snaking from the submarine, attached to an underwater structure. Through the tube were the shapes of several men, moving from the sub to the building.

How had they attached the tube to the building? This reminded me of astronauts moving from their shuttle to a space station. What sort of treasure did the underwater structure hold? How had they known its location?

I eased back from the hatch and turned around, deciding to leave before they caught me. I returned to the mess, thinking hard.

What did they seek? It had to be important enough that they willing risked their lives to submerge in this leaky old submarine.

There was a mystery here. That mystery likely caused the tension between the captain, chief, crew, and me.

It was time to start investigating with focus and determination.

-21-

The *Triton* survived the harrowing submersion as the crew gathered knowledge, equipment or other materials they had collected during the time below. I meant those in the boarding tube who had returned from the sunken building.

The captain had let a word slip when speaking about what had happened. That word was catastrophe. Did he mean the catastrophe that, according to legend, struck Atlantis? If so, at the very least, the catastrophe had taken place in 500 or 400 BC. That was when Plato wrote the story, attributing it to Solon, the lawgiver of Athens, through Critias. Was the story even older, and if so, how old?

I had no idea.

However, a day after our underwater ordeal, the captain summoned me. I followed him through the control room and up the ladder to the conning tower outside.

I wasn't sure what to expect as I spied the sea in all its vast, lonely majesty around us.

"Do you enjoy the fresh air, Mr. Bayard?"

I inhaled for effect and slapped my chest. "I sure do. Is there a reason for this?"

"Look around. What do you see?"

"Water everywhere," I said.

"Yes, water everywhere. Did you know that the entire planet is covered with water? Only the formerly highest mountaintops are above sea level. And a few constructed spires and platforms."

"Oh," I said, cocking an eyebrow, "what are these spires and who constructed them?"

He studied me and finally said, "Are you claiming that you don't know about them?"

"That is what I claim because it's the truth."

He turned away. After a time, he pulled up a pair of huge binoculars. Using them, he scanned in the direction we headed until he seemed to center on something. He adjusted the binoculars, removed the strap from his neck and handed them to me.

I put the strap around my neck just to be safe.

"Good," he said. "That's well thought out."

I aimed the binoculars where he had. Far away, barely visible with these, was a small dot on the surface. I said as much.

"Yes. That is what you should be looking at. Now, what else do you see?"

"Oh," I said. These were harder to find, as they were even smaller. But given their position in the sky… "I imagine those are two dirigibles. Are those Draconian?"

"What else could they be?" he asked.

"Indeed," I said. "I'd like to know."

"They're Draconian."

"Do the airships land at the location, the bigger dot on the surface?" I asked.

"I don't know. I think so."

I lowered the binoculars.

"In any event, we must go there, Mr. Bayard. It is imperative that we reach the location, as you call it."

"Why are you telling me this?"

"I wish to know more about you, and maybe in relation to the location."

He was being coy, and thus confusing. That way often led to mistakes in judgment regarding each other.

"Captain, why don't we set our cards on the table?"

"I don't understand. Neither you nor I hold any cards."

"That's another idiom from Earth," I said. "It's from poker or other card games where we put all our cards on the table so we can see what each other have."

"I understand." The captain appeared thoughtful until he said, "We need to go the location to refuel, as we're running dangerously low on diesel. Unfortunately, I have just learned that Draconians hold the location."

"You're referring to the dirigibles?"

"Yes."

"Why do you fear them?" I asked.

"They have primitive technology compared to us, but... Are you familiar with the term depth charge?"

"I know all about depth charges," I said.

The captain zeroed in on me. "You do? You know all about them?"

I wondered at this sudden intensity.

"Depth charges use a large explosive to create intense water pressure. In Vietnam, my friend's dad used to throw grenades into rivers or ponds. That killed the fish so the soldiers could collect and cook them."

"Is Vietnam another of the former Harmony of Planets?" the captain asked.

"No, it's a country on Earth where a war took place between America and Vietnam."

"Are you familiar with war?" he asked.

"I ought to be. I was a U.S. Marine for many years. I fought in Bhutan, a mountainous country in Asia."

"You have fought in battle?" he asked with some excitement.

"Many times," I said.

"That is good news." The captain rubbed his hands and nodded in approval. "You know about depth charges. Are you familiar then with submarine warfare?"

"Not from direct experience," I said. "I've read some history about it and talked to a few submariners on Earth."

"You of Earth have submarines?"

"That and surface fleets," I said.

"Then you must understand that we cannot do anything against the dirigibles if they fly high enough. They, however, can always drop depth charges to destroy us."

"That makes sense."

"Yet, we must refuel. Do you have any suggestions how we can do that?"

Now I knew why we were talking. The captain was out of ideas and clearly hoped I had one.

"Sure," I said. "You need to either chase off the dirigibles or lure them lower so the deck gun can hit them."

"Do you have any idea of how we could lure them lower?" he asked.

"Oh," I said, growing cold. "Are you asking me to be the bait?"

His eyes widened. Maybe he hadn't thought of that before, but now he did, thanks to my big mouth.

"Not necessarily," he said. "I'm just asking for possibilities."

"Why are the Draconians there?" I asked.

"You'd have to ask them."

"Do you have any antiair missiles or portable heavy machineguns?"

Captain Spiro shook his head. "You used your hollow tube before to destroy an airship."

"That's because the Draconians were stupid and came down low. I don't think they'd fall for the same trick twice."

"I suppose not. As to your question, no, we don't have any devices that can reach high enough."

"Then you've got to do this in the dark," I said. "You submerge from here and come up there at night. Do they tie the dirigibles to the... what is it out there that has this diesel?"

"An ocean drilling platform," he said.

"We have oil platforms on Earth, so I'm a little familiar with that."

94

The captain's eyes gleamed as he studied me. "You may be a greater treasure than I realized. Your knowledge of this and violent situations seems wide. Perhaps you will agree to be my adviser in the assault."

"I'm already doing that, sir."

"You are." His nostrils flared. "I believe the only way to do this, as you suggest, is to arrive at night and hope the dirigibles are low enough for us to hit. Would you be willing to use your special staff to burn them?"

There it was. I thought fast. "First, I'm going to have to know what side you're on."

He became tight-lipped, not liking my answer.

On no account did I want to be helping Krekelens or psi-masters. Thus, I needed to know more about all this.

"We fight against the Draconians and those whose hubris destroyed Atlantis", he said slowly. "I don't know if that event had anything to do with the shattering of the Harmony, as my information about that is slim to none. But I assure you, sir, that our intentions are noble. We do not seek to subjugate anyone, but to free Atlantis from the watery grip that has clutched her ever since the Great Catastrophe."

I almost said, "That wasn't hard to say, now was it?" But I merely nodded instead. That still didn't answer the reason for the submarine crew's higher technology than Draconians or Sea Lords. But...

"All right, I'll use the fiery tube if that helps us in the coming situation. Maybe we won't have to use it. Maybe the Draconians wouldn't be there at night."

"Is it not better to be ready for any eventuality?"

"Yes, sir," I said. "It sure is."

"Then it is time for us to finalize our plan", he said.

This was the first sunset I'd seen on Atlantis, and it was glorious.

The sun was a little larger than ours and perhaps a bit brighter, too. It could be that there was more ozone or some other protective layer in the atmosphere than what protected Earth.

Some Young Earth Creationists have said there used to be a denser water canopy over the Earth, such as before the Flood of Noah. That extra canopy had supposedly protected early humanity from harmful rays, allowing them to live longer. During the Flood, much of that canopy had drained down in the forty days and nights of rain. Perhaps Atlantis still had such a canopy, which might explain this glorious sunset.

Thinking about that made me wonder if there was a connection between Noah's Flood and the Great Catastrophe of Atlantis. Both had supposedly happened in the distant past.

One had come from man's hubris and greed, the other from man's depravity, according to the Holy Texts.

As if to confirm my theory about a thicker, invisible canopy, the stars, when they appeared, twinkled more than they would have from Earth.

I knew enough astronomy to know that stars don't inherently twinkle; atmospheric conditions on Earth create the illusion. Thus, logically, if they twinkled more on Atlantis, it meant the planet had a thicker atmosphere or canopy.

I'm no scientist. These were just the random thoughts of a lonely Traveler who had reached watery Atlantis.

In any case, as night fell, those of us outside the submarine were summoned inside. The last man closed the hatch behind him, sealing it.

The diesels fell silent, and the submarine submerged and began to cruise underwater using its batteries for electric power.

I was with the commando team in the mess. The pipe repairs held, although it still dripped constantly.

Finally, the captain appeared.

"Sir," I said, "I think you should give me all my equipment, not just the hollow tube."

"Tell me why," he said.

"The Phrygian cap allows me to go invisible, and the headband is protection against psi-masters."

The last part wasn't exactly right, but I'd been thinking and wondering about the headband. Perhaps it could help me defend if I focused on that. I wasn't a psi-master, but the headband had given me something. If I focused on a mental wall, perhaps that would be a better use—for me—with the headband.

The captain frowned as he studied me. "Do you need to headband to warn the Draconians about our approach?"

"Just the opposite," I said. "Psi-Master Omilcar might be with them. If so, he might be able to sense our combined thoughts. However, he might be able to sense my thoughts more easily than yours. That would be because he's familiar with mine. The headband functions as a shield against his psionic abilities."

You know what they say: fake it until you make it. Think positively.

"A shield?" he asked.

"I don't have time to explain, sir."

Everyone in the mess was staring at me.

"I don't know if I should trust you to that degree, Mr. Bayard," the captain said. "But we do need your military expertise. I'm going to trust you in this, and I'm not even going to tell these men to shoot you if it looks like you're defecting."

"Thank you," I said. "I'll alert you if I sense the psi-master's thoughts."

The captain nodded, although he glanced significantly to some of the commando team. Despite his statement a second ago, I knew those were silent orders to kill me if it looked like I was turning traitor.

I'd need to remember that.

Soon, I thrust the headband on. Like before, I felt disorientation and a touch of nausea. I couldn't detect anyone's thoughts, nor could I sense Omilcar. I did feel woozy the more I wore it, and disliked wearing the headband.

I stuffed the Phrygian cap in a pouch on my belt and took the hollow tube.

Then we waited as the submarine continued its slow glide. I wouldn't call it the depths, but maybe eighty to one hundred feet down.

After a long wait, a call came down the corridor.

"Get ready," the captain shouted. "We're going to surface soon."

Ten minutes later, we heard blasts of air and gurgling, water no doubt leaving the main ballast tanks. The submarine rose.

What were we going to find up there? How much fuel did we have left, and what would happen if the Draconians drove us from the platform?

I gripped my fiery staff thinking how odd it was for someone claiming to be the metaphorical son of Zeus to go into battle with mere mortals. It was an arrogant thought. Had Omilcar lied when he claimed he was lying to me?

It was confusing. Then I heard a shout, "We've surfaced!

Get ready!"

I ran down the corridor with the rest of the commando team, my stomach tightening with pre-combat jitters.

-23-

I climbed up the ladder behind the others. It was supposed to be pitch dark outside, as there was no moon. The captain had said there were two moons on Atlantis, but this was a rare, moonless night.

I saw a bright light as I climbed up onto the conning tower. The lights shone from the platform in the distance. It was similar to a giant oil sea platform on Earth.

Two dirigibles floated above the highest point on the platform, maybe five stories up. Long lines held the dirigibles in place.

The rest of the commando team and I climbed down into two rubber dinghies. It was something of a miracle that none of us fell into the water. Soon, we began to paddle to the huge derrick about half a mile away.

The submarine remained in the dark, outside the wash of platform light. We wore dark clothing. And because of me, we'd smeared black paint on our hands and faces. Holding ourselves low as we paddled, we scanned the platform with intensity.

Soon, I spied Draconians—just like the little raptor riders we had on Mu. The dinosaurian humanoids were hardly bigger than a *Homo habilis*, which meant barely bigger than a 12-year-old boy. They were leathery-skinned, quick, agile, and ferocious warriors given the right kind of armament. I wanted to know exactly what their armament was out here.

If they had machine guns, we were doomed. Soon, I saw that they had crossbows and long knives or short swords.

I shook my head.

What were crossbow-armed Draconians doing on an oil derrick in the middle of a world ocean on Atlantis?

We continued to paddle. No alarm sounded. Thus, the Draconians must not have seen our darkened dinghies or us.

After considerable effort and some confusion, we reached the bottom of a steel ladder that led up to the first level. We tied each dinghy to a stanchion. One man fell into the water this time, although the others dragged him out in short order. Then the first commando began to climb up the ladder.

My guts clenched as I reached for the first rung. I'd been in combat before, but not like this. Even though I was a Marine, surprisingly, I'd fought in the Himalayan country of Bhutan, which seemed insane when one thought about it. Here, I truly functioned like a U.S. Marine.

I shook my head.

I was a Galactic Marine, as I journeyed and fought on different worlds.

I'd tied a leather strap to my fiery staff, carrying it on my back like a rifle. I'd removed the headband and no longer felt woozy and nauseous. That was good, because I might have lost my grip climbing otherwise.

Luckily, I hadn't sensed Omilcar. That meant neither he nor his transpar suit was here. I waited a second for his mocking thought, but that did not happen.

Soon, we climbed onto the first deck or level.

The commando leader Andrew stepped beside me. He was a tallish Atlantean with sneering features and lank dark hair, looking like a chess-master type of nerd. "This place is bigger than I thought. Should we spread out so we can cover more territory fast?"

"Negative," I replied. "We need to hit them as a group and kill without mercy—mow 'em down."

Andrew frowned.

"You need to get me as close to the dirigibles as fast as possible," I said. "That means we need to scale the heights so I can take them out before they escape."

Andrew looked around, clearly unsure. I was starting to think that he was seriously out of his element.

A combat maxim is to act decisively, even if it's the wrong action, instead of hesitating while trying to figure out the perfect move. It was time to strike.

"Follow me," I said. "When I give the signal—"

"What will the signal be?" asked a commando, interrupting me.

"When I chop my hand and yell 'shoot,' kill everyone. We cannot afford mercy, as we're in too precarious of a position."

"That is unnecessarily savage," Andrew said.

"Savage like a Sea Lord," said another.

"Do you want to survive this fight or not?" I hissed.

"Most certainly, I do," a commando said. "It is our holy mission."

"Then shut the hell up and follow me," I said.

Without further ado, I led our small band of Atlanteans from the old submarine *Triton*. We climbed three more levels until turning a corner into a group of Draconians.

"Shoot to kill!" I shouted, while chopping my hand.

Wouldn't you know it, none of the commando team did a damn thing. That told me likely none had ever been in combat before.

I charged the Draconians as I gripped and aimed my hollow tube. I felt the familiar tingle as the blue nimbus circled me. Willing fire, I hosed the Draconians with it as if I had a flamethrower.

The little suckers screamed as they burned—a foul sound and worse stench. Several ran off and dived toward the water, making a fiery spectacle and surely alerting everyone else on the platform and in the airships.

I whirled around. "What's wrong with you guys? You need to shoot when I tell you."

They looked at me, horrified.

I knew then I was dealing with absolute neophytes. These guys had never been in combat, and had all frozen with buck fever. That was just great.

"Follow me then, and you, give me that." I grabbed a weapon from one of them. Then I charged ahead.

They followed me like frightened teenagers who had just entered a new high school and didn't know anybody.

In the next half hour, I shot and slew 34 Draconians until we reached the highest point on the platform.

A few crossbow bolts had sung at us. One had clipped one of our men. The others presently dragged him along as he moaned and complained.

Someone had freed the tether lines holding the dirigibles. The airships were higher than before. Did that mean they were out of range?

I envisioned Omilcar being aboard one and waited, expecting the bastard's mocking laughter in my mind. The anticipation of that gave me a surge of hatred, just what I needed.

I aimed, holding the fiery staff high above my head. Whoosh! A glob of fire shot up: climbing higher and higher until it hit the gasbag.

There was an almost instantaneous explosion, and then fire began to consume the gasbag like the *Hindenburg* from the newsreels.

The burning dirigible, a little higher than the other, crashed against the second, and then it too burst into a fiery hellscape.

Draconians screamed in their high-pitched, reptilian cry. I watched with avid intensity, seeing if anyone in a transpar suit flew away. No suit left, and the airships burned even as they began to tumble. Neither of the airships, now engulfed in flames, crashed into the derrick, although they landed nearby. From the light of the blazes, I could see the waiting *Triton* and several men on deck watching.

"Come on!" I shouted. "We need to kill all the Draconians

on the platform."

The commando team looked doubtful concerning the need.

"Think of the survival of your world. If you fail in this, if you die, your sub dies."

That brought understanding onto a few faces.

I continued hunting Draconians, and a few of the commandos took potshots at the dinosaur humanoids. I mentally noted which men fired shots and which actually made kills. Despite that, I used the fiery staff three more times.

By the time we stopped, I didn't know if we had cleared all the Draconians from the platform, but the air was thick with the stench of death.

My commando team had the look of shell-shocked survivors of battle. Our only casualty was the man wounded by a crossbow bolt. It was time to bring in the *Triton* and confirm if this place had diesel fuel or not.

-24-

Daylight revealed the wreckage of the airships and shark-like beasts cruising through the water, feasting on the Draconian dead and the debris floating about. Much of the debris sank as Captain Spiro brought the *Triton* to a hidden wharf beneath the platform.

Instead of praising me, the crew held me under guard. At the captain's orders, my team had taken my headband, fiery staff, and Phrygian cap. I sat alone in the shade, on a chair.

Three sailors who had actually shot and killed Draconians stood guard over me. I knew they could kill, so I respected them enough not to provoke them. Instead, I waited and observed.

The sailors of the *Triton* swarmed over the platform facility as if searching for something crucial. Whether they found it or not, I saw others hauling brittle hoses, connecting them to the submarine's fuel tanks. I heard pumps working, and presumably, the *Triton* was being refueled.

German U-boat commanders once used "milch cows"—diesel-carrying U-boats to refill their U-boats at sea. That allowed them to continue hunting without returning to port.

As fascinating as the German U-boats of World War II were to read about, I also loved the stories of the American Submarine Service of World War II. They proved to be canny submariners, perhaps the equals or even superiors of the Germans, as they harried Japan's Merchant Marine and the Imperial or the Combined Fleet of Japan.

According to historical accounts I'd read, America might not have needed to drop the two atomic bombs to end the war. Yes, I know it's a contentious topic. I'm not taking a side, just mentioning that the American submarine blockade might have starved Japan into surrender. There is debate about whether the Japanese would have surrendered. With their Bushido, kamikaze attitude, who knows? The Japanese had given Americans the idea that they would never surrender unless presented with a horror, which we duly gave them at Hiroshima and Nagasaki.

In any case, we had a fully tanked submarine with a crew who succeeded in two desperate missions. One was successfully retrieving, I guess, from an underwater base. This was akin to U.S. submarines extracting men or supplies in the Philippines during WWII. Interestingly, the Japanese had used their submarines as supply vessels at Guadalcanal. But that was another story.

My point is, I waited and watched. After several hours, with no dirigibles or transpar suit sightings, the captain and the chief returned. My guardians remained on duty. The supposed leader of our midnight escapade was here. Andrew looked unhappy and avoided meeting my eyes.

"You got what you wanted, Captain Spiro," I said.

He pointed at me without appearing pleased or enraged. Then he looked up at the sky before facing me. "There's something we must deal with." He turned. "Andrew, it's time."

"Sir." Andrew licked his lips, seemingly afraid of and disgusted with me at the same time. "What I saw last night, sir—I've never witnessed such mindless savagery and butchery in my life."

"Go on," the captain said.

Andrew hesitated and then pointed at me. "He burned them mercilessly and without compunction. He told us to act like executioners, not showing any grace, acting like rampaging barbarians. He even took one of our weapons against our mission's dictates. Instead of using his tainted weapon, he used one of ours to murder our enemies. When the airships fell, burning, he looked on with savage glee. Sir, we are dealing with a brute and a killer. We must be cautious, as he could pose a danger to everyone aboard the *Triton*. I'm not saying we should kill him, but perhaps strand him here on the platform."

"I see," the captain said. "Do you have anything to say in response to that, Mr. Bayard?"

"I find it instructive that the man who successfully led the combat mission, doing exactly what was needed, is now being castigated for doing his job too well."

"You enjoyed it," Andrew said. "It was appalling to witness."

I thought about Omilcar's former words about my one true gift. I was a killer. Sadly, that was the truth. Was that what the ancient Greek gods had been?

I'll drop that line of inquiry for now. I don't know enough about that to be certain either way.

I faced the captain. "I'm not going to apologize for saving all your asses. You guys were too weenie to do the needed killing. If it weren't for me, your submarine wouldn't have been refilled. The submarine would've had to flee and then run out of fuel. Your mission would fail."

"What do you say to that, Andrew?" Captain Spiro asked.

"He may be speaking the truth, sir. I cannot gainsay him."

"Come on," I said. "You led us and did squat. It was all up to me. You should be left on this platform for not performing your duty."

I stopped myself from saying we should kill Andrew to teach the others a lesson. That wasn't what they wanted to hear from me.

"That will be all for now, Andrew," the captain said. "Thank you. Chief, take him aboard the *Triton*."

They left.

My guards had grown tense. They hadn't drawn their weapons, but their hands rested on the grips. That wasn't smart. If I'd gone berserk, they'd probably freeze as before.

I almost felt like charging them to prove it, but I contained myself, feeling a pulse beat in my forehead. Had Omilcar done something else to me? Yes, he had. He'd unleashed something primal and ancient in me. If I had bloodlust and couldn't stop until the fight was done… well, so be it. That was my gift, and I would employ it for worthy goals.

Is that what other killers told themselves throughout the ages? I wouldn't go there in my thoughts, although I had read before that without the coarse, onion-eating Athenian hoplites—the spearmen of their phalanxes—without them beating the Persians, upholding Athenian civilization, there wouldn't have been the luxuries and philosophies. It was the tough men called to do the hard things when needed that saved others. Civilization remained because of those like me, who weren't civilized, who were the wolves. No, scratch the very last part. I was a sheepdog, maybe a savage one, barely controlled, but one nevertheless and not a marauding wolf.

I faced Captain Spiro. "Fighting is hard. As I told you before, I'm a Galactic Marine. I was once a U.S. Marine. Now, I'm fighting for the angels, those who did good in the former Harmony of Planets, not by subjugating others, but by bringing peace and goodness."

"Peace through bloodshed?" Captain Spiro asked.

"How do you deal with a rabid dog?"

"I don't know what a dog is," he said.

"How do you deal with a kraken that attacks every community?"

"You move elsewhere."

"That's one way," I said. "Or you kill the kraken to bring peace. You kill the beasts to build society. But never drop your guard, as someone always needs taming."

"And you're the tamer?"

"I'm the one who fights. If that bothers you, do what you have to, Captain. I did what I had to, and now your submarine is refueled and ready to continue. Will you strand me or take

108

me along and explain what's happening?"

"I'm taking you with us, Mr. Bayard. You have knowledge we need." He looked at my guards. "Andrew shouldn't lead the combat group anymore. But I'm not sure you should lead either."

"The best militaries put killers in charge to get things done," I said. "Do you want to be logical or to feel good? They're not always different, but sometimes hard decisions mean putting a hard ass in the right spot."

"Meaning you?" he asked.

I shrugged indifferently, having already blown my horn enough.

"It's time we leave," he said. "We have more diesel fuel in order to continue our mission. It's been a tough but enlightening night. You were instrumental in our success, but we find the bloody blade hard to praise."

"I get it," I said.

"Come, let's go," he said.

And so we did.

-25-

We left the platform, and the next few days were the loneliest I spent aboard the *Triton*. No one talked to me if they could help it. They left me alone or said the most grudging words. None were rude, but I believed I had the mark of Cain upon me. I had done my task too well for them.

I don't believe they would have gotten the diesel without me, though. The Draconians with their crossbows... would the *Triton's* crew even have fought to defend themselves in the end? Who were the Atlanteans who couldn't even fight to defend themselves, barely understanding combat or its effects on men?

After receiving permission, I sat as close as I could to the bow of the submarine. I sat cross-legged, watching the endless sea as water splashed me.

Once, the chief came and stood behind me.

Sensing something, I turned. "Is anything wrong?"

He appeared to struggle with an idea, finally saying, "You did well for us, and I appreciate it." He shifted uncomfortably. "It's hard for us to accept what you did in our name, and we don't even know who we are."

That final statement was a strange thing to say. What did he mean by it? I looked at him expectantly, waiting.

He shook his head. "I shouldn't have said that. Forget I did."

"Of course I'll forget," I said.

The look on my face or the craziness of his statement caused the chief to snort. He left soon thereafter.

Putting the weirdness behind me, I continued to study the great expanse as the *Triton* chugged through a seemingly endless ocean. Atlantis hadn't always been an ocean-world. Something had happened to it. We had legends concerning that on Earth. What had the ancients done? I frowned for a time. The chief had let a bombshell drop. They didn't know who they were. That meant forgetfulness, didn't it? Yes, it must have something to do with their teaching each other facts.

There had been a great forgetting, fragmented so that some remembered one thing while others remembered another. What would cause men to forget certain facts but not others? Why did these guys speak the pure language of Atlantis—probably meaning the old language—and the Sea Lords spoke the adulterated or corrupted language of Atlantis?

The obvious conclusion was the Sea Lords had been around since after the Great Catastrophe, working, marrying, and living, with the language naturally changing over time. Few people today could understand Old English in its true form, let alone comprehend speech from 700 B.C.

Had the *Triton's* crew been around during the Great Catastrophe? That would make them ancient, far beyond 246 years old, as Omilcar suggested he was.

After some time, I got up and returned into the submarine. I took off my soaked clothes, washed them in non-salty water, and lay in my bunk as they dried. I slept and dreamed.

In the dream, I heard a voice casting about for me like a man shouting at his porch for his stray dog.

That finally got on my nerves. "What do you want?" I

shouted, in the dream. "Who are you? Why can't I see you?"

In dim outline, in the dream-sky, a face appeared. Soon, I recognized it: long-bearded Omilcar wearing the cap of a Sark of Mu. Perhaps I was semi-awake and delirious. I'm not sure. Omilcar spoke as across a great chasm or distance, his voice having an echoing effect.

"What do you want with me, you bastard?" I shouted at him.

His eyes, which had been casting about as if he couldn't see me, now focused as if he finally did.

"So you're alive, are you, Bayard? You've been busy killing Draconians. It's not going to help you, you know."

Was he referring to the Draconians of his airship or the ones at the oil platform? Maybe it didn't matter.

"Sure it is," I said. "It got your attention. I bet you're worried I'm going find you. You should be, 'cause you know what I'm going to do to you, right?"

"Rip off my head and piss down my neck."

It took me a second before the allusion to Livi and her head became obvious. Rage coursed through me, and the connection between us wavered like bad TV reception.

"What are you up to?" I snarled.

"Wouldn't you like to know? But you don't. In fact, you don't understand the situation or you would try everything you could to escape this place."

Yeah, yeah, he was full of threats. How I hated him.

"I'm going to find you, old man, and I'm going to kill you for what you did to Livi."

"I find that doubtful, as your boatload of amnesiacs isn't going to survive much longer."

"Yeah?"

"Don't try to be clever, Bayard. It doesn't suit you. I wondered if you figured it out, but I can see you're still a long way off. There are several mysteries here. You don't even realize yet where the U-boats originated."

"What do you mean, U-boats? This is a submarine."

"Goodbye, Bayard."

"Wait," I said.

It was too late. His mind and ugly mug faded from the sky

and then vanished altogether.

It left me puzzled. I woke soon after that and realized I'd been dreaming.

Or had that been a real conversation with the Great Sark of Mu? I'd been resistant to mind powers before, and likely was to a degree against Omilcar. Yet his psionic questing might have made an impression with my subconscious. That could have broken through to me.

Why would he bother? I felt it was more than just seeking my whereabouts. Thinking back to the dream, I might have sensed fear... but not necessarily fear of me. Could Omilcar fear the crew of the *Triton*? If so, what did he fear about them?

And that word: U-boats. That revelation was significant—it had to be. U-boats meant Germans. Submarines meant everyone else. Had Omilcar implied that Germans with WWII-type U-boats had made it to Atlantis?

The *Triton* was far too much like a Type VII workhorse U-boat of Hitler's Germany. That couldn't just be coincidence, not with the U-boat drop by Omilcar.

I almost sat up fast, but fortunately held myself from doing that. I would have conked my forehead on the damn torpedo just above me. Instead, I carefully climbed out of the bunk and searched for Captain Spiro. He needed to know what I'd learned.

Maybe it was also time to demand some answers, or I might reconsider continuing to help them. Omilcar had referred to them as a boatload of amnesiacs. The chief earlier had hinted at that.

I found the captain and asked to speak with him.

-26-

Captain Spiro and I climbed onto the conning tower, looking upon the wide expanse. The sun was lowering toward the horizon, but it wasn't dusk yet. The diesels chugged in their eternal rhythm, providing some solace.

In some ways, this was like being in a spaceship. We never saw anyone. Without the submarine, we would be dead, as we wouldn't survive long floating in the sea.

"Sir," I said, deciding to get straight to it, "Omilcar says you're amnesiacs, meaning you don't know what you're doing or what you're about. Now, I know you successfully reached an underwater building and sent men to it through an underwater tube—"

"Who told you that?" Spiro demanded, interrupting me.

"No one," I said. "I peeked into the control room when you were attempting that and saw it on a TV screen."

He looked as though he might erupt in anger but restrained

himself, but in the end, he only nodded.

"I'm guessing you got whatever you needed from the underwater structure," I said. "Afterward, you refueled with diesel from the oil platform. But I've been wondering, how in the world do you men have a submarine or a U-boat? And one that's so much like a Type VII U-boat from the German Kriegsmarine of World War Two? I don't believe the *Triton* predates the Great Catastrophe—"

"What do you know about that?" Spiro said, interrupting once more as he glared at me.

"You've spoken about the Great Catastrophe before, and I believe that's exactly what happened. You're likely from that time. But the submarine can't be. I know it's old, a rust bucket, but more like a World War Two museum piece than something from three or four thousand years ago. Now, I don't think the *Triton* originated on Earth, and yet..."

I frowned. There must have been a rebound in my subconscious that finally rattled to a conclusion. There was a legend or conspiracy theory about Nazis in Antarctica. I believe there had been a German expedition to Antarctica from 1938 to 1939. Oh, that's right. The Germans had called the region Neuschwabenland. That detail was historical fact, but the rest was pure conspiracy theory. Some claimed fleeing Nazi scientists and soldiers had escaped from burning Germany in 1945 and gone to Neuschwabenland via U-boats. Could the Germans have used an ancient alien artifact in Antarctica to reach Atlantis? That would help make sense that Type VII U-boats were here.

The subterranean obelisk in Antarctica was far from Neuschwabenland, and how would the Nazis have gotten U-boats through it? They wouldn't have is the answer.

Of course, all this would mean some of the fleeing Nazis had known about Atlantis. That seemed crazy. But it was even crazier to think that Type VII U-boats had been independently developed here.

"Are you a Nazi?" I asked suddenly.

Captain Spiro scowled at me. "I have no idea what that means."

The idea seemed farfetched... except for our submarine, as

I've said. Thinking of Neuschwabenland and the surprising accuracy of some conspiracy theories, like reptilian skin-changers, spurred my imagination. Might there have been another Antarctica portal or teleporter? There had been a portal on the bottom of the Persian Gulf.

"Captain," I said, "the oil platform we reached could have been constructed in the last seventy or eighty years, but not the last three or four thousand. That's stretching things too far. An oil platform wouldn't have lasted that long, certainly not in the condition we found it."

The captain watched me.

"If the oil platform was from the time of the Great Catastrophe, it would have been destroyed or decayed long ago. What's more, it was anchored and not floating. The last point is conclusive regarding its newer age."

"You're sure about the anchoring?" he asked.

"Very," I said.

Captain Spiro nodded. "I concede that is an interesting point."

I watched Spiro as he said that. Would Omilcar have let slip this was a boatload of amnesiacs if that really was the case? Had the psi-master said that on accident or on purpose? How could I find out?

"Look, sir, I appreciate you picked me up when you did. I doubt I would have gotten anywhere interesting if I'd remained with the Sea Lords. I've proven my worth through action, even though I've been condemned for fighting too effectively on the platform. But without me, you would never have gotten your diesel, and would therefore been forced to scrub your mission."

"You may be right, Mr. Bayard." Spiro paused, thinking perhaps, and soon said, "You should know that Andrew will no longer be leading the commandos."

Was the captain hinting he wanted me to lead them? If that were true... Maybe it was time to put some pressure on these blokes.

"I'm not going to lead the commandos either," I said. "I'm not even going to join them next time."

"Unless what?" Spiro asked. "Are you trying to threaten me through this claimed inaction?"

116

"I need to know what's really going on. I have a right. Look, I've warned you that Psi-Master Omilcar is aware of you and the submarine. He called you guys a boatload of amnesiacs. I want to know why he would say that."

The captain became pensive, possibly reflective.

"You once told me you're part of the Project," I said. "What is the Project? What did it entail? What are you seeking? I'm willing to help if you tell me, but right now, I'm in the dark."

Captain Spiro waited, watching me more closely.

It was time to break the ice, time to take a chance. I didn't seem to be getting anywhere with Spiro otherwise.

"I'm going to try something new with you," I said. "This is what it means to act in good faith. We're stuck together, and have similar enemies. I'm about to share knowledge I suspect you don't have. I'm hoping you'll do me the same favor afterward."

The captain still waited, saying nothing.

"Fine," I said. "Here goes. There are many factions or sides in the former Harmony of Planets. There may even be more than that. In fact, I'm sure there are. But here are a few of them. First, there's the *Homo habilis.*"

"Who are they?" Spiro asked.

"Small, hairy hominids, as much ape as human, but they're damn smart, and have cunning plans. They're distinctive from the Draconians, which you know, and from Zero Stones."

"Stones?" he asked.

"Sentient stones with a plan. What that is I don't know. The Zero Stones act like mind vampires or demons, possessing a person and granting certain mental abilities. Then there are the Ophidians. Those are Snake People, upright humanoids, but possessing snake thinking. On their home planet of Saddoth, Ophidians prey on and eat Neanderthals."

"That is incredible. In fact... is that a lie, Mr. Bayard?"

"No," I said. "I'm telling you the truth. I'm telling you what's out there. There's another group, maybe the worst of all, the Krekelens. They're a lizard-like people, but they're shape-changers. They can look like an Ophidian, a human, a Draconian or a Neanderthal. They're on my planet creating

117

chaos, or creating something for an ulterior motive. I don't know if they're the creators or the creation of the psi-masters of Mu. The latter refers to humans with mental or psionic abilities."

Spiro rubbed his forehead as if he had a sudden ache. "You've mentioned these psi-masters before."

I nodded. "I don't know how Atlantis is mixed with all of that or them—the others—but it seems as if the Great Catastrophe was part of the shattering of the Harmony of Planets.

"I believe that some Atlanteans must have escaped to Earth with the news back then, because we have legends about Atlantis sinking. The tale was written around four or five hundred BC, that means Before Christ. That means the Great Catastrophe must have occurred at least twenty-five hundred years ago. I'm not as keen on knowing the timeframes as what happened. Omilcar claims that Sky Island once drifting around on Earth, and beings like me ran the island, beings the local humans worshipped as gods."

"That is all quite astounding," the captain said. "I knew you were a treasure trove, Mr. Bayard. Even with your aggressive tendencies, you are worth having around."

"That's a great big endorsement, and I thank you for it," I said sarcastically. "But sir, now that I've told you all this, you ought to tell me about the Project. Why are we cruising through the world ocean in this submarine or U-boat? What's the plan?"

Captain Spiro looked away and made a show of pulling up his big binoculars to scan everywhere. After ten minutes of looking around, probably to give him time to think, he lowered the binoculars and regarded me.

"You've shared some fascinating information. I wish you would tell the chief and the others this, so we could take notes to help us remember. We are a forgetful group, amnesiacs, as you say. There's a reason for that. Yes, I believe it's time I told you about the Project. Do you have a few minutes?"

"I'll give you ten," I said with a laugh.

"Very well, Mr. Bayard, here is the truth."

-27-

"As far as we know," Captain Spiro said, "we on the *Triton* lived before the Great Catastrophe that destroyed Atlantis. Unfortunately, we don't know what brought about the Great Catastrophe. We don't even know what we did back then, although the chief believes we were scientists working on a special project, hence the name, The Project. That's one of the few things that several of the men agreed upon waking."

"Waking, sir?" I asked.

Captain Spiro nodded. "As we've been able to determine by pooling our limited knowledge, a Great Catastrophe occurred long ago. We do not have an exact time frame either. During the end, we apparently rushed to stasis tubes and—"

"Wait," I said as a chill swept over me. "Stasis tubes, can you describe them?"

Captain Spiro did.

They sounded exactly like the stasis tubes I'd seen in

subterranean Antarctica. Psi-masters and Krekelens had exited them, most of which I had destroyed. That had happened several years ago. My special forte, as I have said throughout these journeys, was putting things down forever. I'd also seen such stasis tubes in the Dark Citadel, where a giant snake had apparently broken them open and devoured their contents.

"All right," I said, "that's interesting, because I've seen such stasis tubes before."

"On Atlantis?" Spiro asked.

"No. On different… on Earth and on Mu," I said.

"Ah, this is interesting. Can you tell me more about that?"

"I didn't mean to interrupt. I'd first like to hear the rest of your tale if I could, sir."

Spiro nodded. "We entered these stasis tubes; we must have, because we exited them less than a year ago. When we exited them, the facility in which we awoke was flooding. We awoke like mindless children, screaming in terror. The chief calmed us down and said, 'What do you guys remember?'

"We each remembered scattered things that the others did not, though a few had similar memories. We believe that during our long internment we forgot much, which included forgetting who or what caused the great disaster. We forgot sciences… we forgot so terribly much. We've been trying to relearn what the others know so we can reconstitute our ancient knowledge. Luckily, we found notes in the stasis tube facility. Those notes led us to believe that we could find the machine that caused the Great Catastrophe."

"Where is this machine?" I asked.

"As far as we can tell, it is deep under the surface."

"Not deep underwater?" I asked.

"No," Spiro said, "under the surface. We believe it has something to do with the core of Atlantis, the molten core, and certain harmonics. The chief believes that the ancient Atlanteans were trying to tap new energy sources by driving magnetic shafts through the mantle so they could breach the molten core. Deep core plants would supply Atlantis with endless power. Some of the others contend there was weather manipulation back then, and that unleashed something horrible."

120

"Ha! That's interesting, sir. Sorry for interrupting again, but according to our legends, Atlantis fell because of the hubris of certain men of Atlantis, that they tried to do too much."

"How fascinating," he said.

"Please, continue," I said. "I'll try not to interrupt you anymore."

Spiro nodded. "Our equipment is antiquated... It is a long and harrowing story how we escaped the underwater facility, but we did. Before it completely flooded, we discovered that others of our kind had already awakened. As far as we could tell, they had taken the better and more modern submarines, or perhaps the older and more ancient ones, the good ones. Through trial and error, we have learned to use the *Triton*. Now, we seek for and search the ancient locations, trying to collect items and learn more so we can gain the knowledge we lost."

That was wild. How could Neuschwabenland Nazis fit into that? If such scientists and soldiers had arrived in 1945, did they know about the ancient core machine or weather control? Were these two independent situations or all part of a whole?

"I hope you don't laugh, Mr. Bayard. We're very self-conscious about this, but if we were the scientists that caused, or helped to cause, the Great Catastrophe, then we want to be the scientists who help reverse whatever occurred then."

"Reverse how, and do what?" I asked.

"I'm not talking about the teleporting obelisks and the ziggurats, as I suspect you are more interested in."

"Can you read minds, Captain?"

"On no account," he said. "I have suspected this about you. We do know about Travelers, as there have been a few in the past. Until you, they always joined the other side or have been captured by the other side."

"Do you know what kind of Travelers?" I asked. Could they have been the Neuschwabenland Nazi connection?

"Just that they were human," he said.

I wondered if Livi had ever been here before. The thought of my dear departed wife brought a severe frown to my face, which I shrugged off after a moment.

"Sorry," I said, "I was remembering..."

121

"I can imagine what you're remembering, Mr. Bayard. I'm not your enemy, nor do I want to be. You are a killer indeed. I almost feel sorry for this Omilcar."

"Don't be," I said. "He's a bastard of bastards."

"I'll take your word for it. The point is we thirst for knowledge. You've shown us that we can refill at the oil platforms. That is critical knowledge we only recently discovered. Your coming has been most fortuitous. Because of that, there are several schools of thought among us regarding our next move."

"Wait a second before you continue," I said. "What rank did you have in the old days? I mean before entering the stasis tubes."

"We have no idea."

"Were your stasis units marked in any way?" I asked.

"Not that we could determine. Why would it matter?"

I frowned. "How did you become the captain and the others their ranks?"

"Oh. I appeared the most qualified at the time and the others have agreed, and still do."

"That's wild. So you could have been the janitor back then for all we know."

I expected Captain Spiro to protest the idea, but he nodded and laughed. "That could be the case. Learning truth is not always a pleasant thing, but that is what we have determined in our hearts to do. None of us was soldiers or Marines like you are, Bayard. We do think we were all scientists. Why else would we have been given the opportunity to enter the stasis tubes?"

"That's a good point," I said. "So what's the next destination?"

"We have several schools of thought on that, as I've said. There is a deep station most of us have agreed is the next place we should search. It is actually nearby. But the others from the Project, those who woke before us, might try to stop us. Whatever the case, we believed we first needed underwater gear to attempt this."

He spoke about that in the past tense. "Did you pick up such gear in the underwater building?" I asked.

"We did. Now we can send men into the depths, using small underwater vehicles and diving suits to achieve this."

"You do know that I am a Marine."

"I do not understand why you just said that."

"Marines operate on land and on and under the sea. We're not UDT or SEALs, but—"

Captain Spiro shook his head. "I do not understand those references either."

"They're Earth military terms. The point is, sir, I'm the most logical person to go down with your group in case you need muscle."

"You mean killing ability."

"Yep, that's what I mean."

"I must think about this," he said. "I'm not sure the others would agree to your joining the expedition. Lately, the one we named Andrew—"

"Wait, those aren't your real names?" I asked.

"We don't know our old names. We have taken these names from various books we read after our awakening. Andrew has started to believe that he was the chief scientist. There are reasons to believe he may be correct, but so far, he has not challenged my authority directly. This last escapade… is going to create trouble among the crew. So it would be better if we could uncover the truth as soon as possible. You have been an element of chaos and a needed element of change that has helped us. And for that, I am grateful."

"Huh," I said. "And you think this underwater base might be guarded by who? More Draconians?"

"Maybe or maybe submarines like ours crewed by those like us who wake up first. That is another reason why I was loath to leave you behind on the platform, Mr. Bayard."

"Yeah?" I said.

"You know something about submarine warfare. We may rely on that expertise in the near future. For we have come to believe that we have the most outmoded and outdated submarine and torpedoes. Therefore, we will need something else to give us an edge."

"I'm supposed to be your edge, huh?"

"Yes, Mr. Bayard."

"What if I do my job too well and kill all your enemies?"

"That would be both good and bad, as I dislike unnecessary killing, but I want to succeed. I want to fix what I broke. I do not want to kill other scientists, but then they shouldn't be siding with the Draconians, who fight against us."

"All right, Captain, thanks for telling me all this. You can bet I'm ready to help you."

"Thank you, Mr. Bayard."

We shook hands, not knowing what the coming revelations would reveal or how they would change everything.

28

After the captain's revelation about their lost memories and likely ancient origins, I spent the next day observing the crew with new eyes. Their teaching sessions took on deeper meaning now. Each man desperately tried to piece together fragments of knowledge, like survivors of some great amnesia collecting scraps of their past lives.

I sat in the mess, watching Felix try to explain basic chemistry to three other crew members. The way he struggled to articulate concepts that should have been second nature to a scientist was telling. These men had possibly been brilliant once—maybe the brightest minds of ancient Atlantis. Now they were like graduate students who'd had most of their education erased, left with only tantalizing glimpses of what they'd once known.

The chief came in while I was contemplating this. He had that perpetually angry look, but now I understood it better.

How frustrating must it be to know you were once part of something great but lost most of it?

"Bayard," he said, "the captain wants you in the control room."

I followed him through the cramped corridors. The constant drip of leaky pipes had become white noise. We passed Andrew in a corridor. He gave me a cold look but said nothing. The failed commando leader still hadn't gotten over our bloody raid on the oil platform.

The control room was more crowded than usual. Captain Spiro stood hunched over charts with several crew members. They were studying depth readings of the area we were heading into.

"Ah, Mr. Bayard," the captain said. "We're approaching the coordinates where buoys we've tapped have informed us of previous submarine sightings. I wanted your tactical assessment of the *Triton*."

I studied the charts. Several days' travel would bring us to a place where the seafloor dropped away sharply, forming an underwater cliff face. According to the charts, there was some kind of structure built into the cliff around 400 feet down.

I recalled stories I'd read about WWII sub combat. I'd been making notes and now referred to them. "That's probably deeper than this sub should go."

"In a pinch, the *Triton* should survive such depths," the captain replied. "However, the underwater gear we recovered, and special diving suits should allow us to reach it."

"Fine," I said. "Do you think this underwater station might have answers about the Great Catastrophe?"

"We believe it was a monitoring station," the chief said.

"Monitoring the sea?" I asked.

"No," the chief said, "something deep in the planet's core."

That must be another reason it was so deep. "Could the station tell you what went wrong? Why the catastrophe happened?"

The chief turned to the captain.

"Perhaps." The captain traced a finger along the chart. "Unfortunately, we're not the only ones interested in this location. The others who woke before us—we have reason to

126

believe they've been searching for this place, too."

I raised an eyebrow. Had Omilcar joined the others? That would make more sense then that the psi-master had sought me.

"We've detected signs of other submarines in the general area," Captain Spiro said.

"What kind of signs?" I asked.

"Sonar echoes. Brief contacts that disappear too quickly to track properly. We believe someone is out there, watching. We're also certain their submarines are more advanced than the *Triton*."

I considered all this. "If they're more advanced, why haven't they reached the underwater station already?"

The captain glanced at the chief.

The chief shrugged.

The captain turned to me. "The chief believes the others lack certain codes or protocols that we might remember. That would mean they need us, or at least need to follow us there."

"So we're bait," I said.

"That is unknown," the captain said. "Andrew wondered whether Omilcar had been trying to read our minds. In truth, there are too many unknowns, and we're running out of time."

"How so?" I asked.

The captain appeared evasive as he said, "The *Triton* isn't going to last forever."

He didn't want to say. Sure, the *Triton* was falling apart, and every dive put more strain on her ancient hull. But that wasn't the real reason.

I thought about that, finally asking, "How long until we reach the underwater coordinates?"

"Two more days," the chief said. "We've been moving slowly to conserve fuel and hopefully avoid detection by any patrolling submarines or Draconian dirigibles."

I nodded. It was wise to remember those dinosaurian rascals, their airships and depth charges. With Omilcar helping them, the enemy would find us soon enough. They might already have located the *Triton*. Would that mean fighting more advanced submarines?

If my Atlanteans were such lousy fighters, maybe the

others were also. Maybe with my help, we could win a submarine battle. However…

"We should run battle drills," I said. "You need the crew as ready as possible for combat operations."

"They're scientists, not warriors," Andrew said from the hatch. I hadn't heard him approach.

It seemed the others in the control room absorbed his words.

"Hey," I said, "they're whatever they need to be to survive. And right now, they need to be ready for an underwater fight."

The captain looked between us. I couldn't believe he was hesitating.

"Remember the oil platform," I said. "My way means the *Triton* is still operational. Andrews' way would have meant bitter defeat. It's no different now."

Captain Spiro looked up at the ceiling before he said, "Agreed." He no longer looked at Andrew. "Chief, begin organizing combat drills. Mr. Bayard, I want you to supervise. Teach us what you can about submarine warfare in the time we have."

Andrew left in disgust.

I spent the next several hours running the crew through torpedo drills, damage control procedures, and emergency protocols. They were clumsy, but their scientific minds must have helped them grasp concepts once I explained it for the fifth time. They were frustratingly slow. I was worried this wouldn't be enough, especially against a more advanced submarine. It wasn't that I was any kind of expert. I'd read—oh, hell, I was far better than any of them were at this. That was the truth.

I could feel the tension building with them. Every sonar ping made the crew jump. Every groan of the hull drew worried glances. We were heading into danger, all of us knowing it but unwilling to turn back.

I thought about Omilcar, wondering how he was connected to the other awakened Atlantean scientists. The psi-master had to know about the underwater station. Was he manipulating events from afar, using these lost souls as pawns in some greater game?

Whatever the case, we had to be ready for anything.

29

A tremor ran through the *Triton*, and this wasn't from one of our numerous leaks. I glanced up from the checkers game in the mess. The guy across from me—Felix—didn't seem to notice anything amiss.

"Did you feel that?" I asked.

Felix concentrated on the board, clearly considering his next move.

Another tremor vibrated through the hull, stronger this time. That drew my attention to the pipes overhead where water dripped steadily.

Felix looked up, his weathered face creased with worry.

A moment later, the chief burst through the hatch. His habitually angry face had paled. "Sonar contact," he said. "All hands to stations."

Felix jumped up, knocking over several checkers pieces as he raced for a hatch. The chief had already disappeared.

I followed at a slower pace, reaching the control room hatch. No one stopped me as I peered into the control room. The crew worked their stations with intensity. Several stood at sonar equipment, although this close it looked more antiquated than what I'd seen in WWII movies.

The captain hunched over someone's shoulder, studying a screen. He straightened and noticed me, beckoning me forward.

"Have you seen anything like this?" he asked, pointing at squiggly lines on the screen.

I studied the readout. "It's another submarine, isn't it?"

He nodded.

A third tremor ran through the *Triton*, and this tremor was accompanied by a distant thrumming noise. The sound raised the hair on my neck. It reminded me of something. Then I remembered.

"That's active sonar," I said. "They're pinging our position with it."

The captain's eyes narrowed. "How do you know this?"

"That's what submarines typically use to locate each other. But most subs use passive sonar—just listening—because active sonar gives away your position too."

"Then why would they use active sonar?"

"Probably because they don't care if we know they're here," I said. "If they know the odds, they must be confident they can take us."

The implications of that sank in. An advanced sub from the faction of scientists who'd woken first, who were now probably working with Omilcar. How long had they been tracking us?

"Captain," one of the sonar operators called out. "The contact is closing fast. Bearing zero-four-five."

I looked at their equipment again. These displays were crude compared to modern submarine tech, but the basics were the same. Sound traveled through water, bounced off objects, created return signatures.

"We need to dive," I said. "Now."

The captain studied me. "Why?"

"Because they're probably going to attack us," I said.

131

A new sound cut through the sub—a high-pitched whine followed by a whoosh.

"Torpedo," someone shouted.

"Dive," the captain ordered. "Emergency dive."

Soon, the bow tilted downward sharply. I grabbed a rail to keep from falling. Seawater gurgled into the ballast tanks. We dived. All around us, the ancient sub's metal groaned under the growing pressure change.

The whine of the incoming torpedo grew louder.

My gut clenched. This was a horrible experience. If it hit, we'd all drown in the depths. It took time for my mind to process that.

Suddenly, "Turn forty degrees to port!" I shouted.

The captain looked up at me.

"The torpedo would have trouble adjusting its course to such a sharp angle," I said. "Now, do it before it's too late."

The captain hesitated only a second longer before repeating my command. The *Triton* heeled over, adding a sideways tilt to our downward angle.

A massive explosion behind us rocked the submarine. I was thrown against a cabinet. New leaks burst out overhead, spraying us with salt water.

"Damage report," the captain shouted, his voice almost breaking.

"Hull intact," someone called back. "But we've got flooding in compartment four."

"Seal it off," the captain ordered. He turned to me. "How did you know to turn?"

"Old torpedo evasion tactics," I said, rubbing my bruised shoulder. "World War Two stuff. The Germans and Americans learned a lot about underwater warfare back then." I'd read far too many of those underwater contests as a teenager. Did I know enough to save us here?

More pinging sounds echoed through the hull. It was quite possible they had us dead in their sights. What was the correct move then? Ah, I had an idea.

"We need to get deep," I said. "There's usually a thermal layer where the water temperature changes. Sound waves have trouble penetrating it. Their advanced sonar might not function as effectively if we can get under the layer."

The captain nodded thoughtfully. "We've detected such temperature variations but never understood their tactical significance." He raised his voice. "Take us to two hundred feet."

The deck angle increased. Pipes groaned.

I watched the depth gauge. One hundred feet... one fifty...

Another enemy torpedo sounded. This one seemed to come from a different angle.

"They must be firing a spread," I said. "Turn starboard forty-five degrees. Keep diving."

This time the captain relayed my suggestion right away.

The *Triton* swung right, as the creaking of the hull grew louder.

"The pressure at this depth will be bad," the chief said.

"The *Triton* can take it," the captain replied.

An explosion rocked us, closer this time. The lights flickered. I heard cursing from the engine room.

"Flooding in compartment six," someone shouted.

"Seal it," the captain ordered. He glanced at the depth gauge. "We're at one hundred ninety feet."

The pinging grew fainter. We must have found and passed through the thermal layer. What do you know; this seemed to have worked.

"Level off here," I said. "We can move more quietly if we're not changing depth. That should make it harder for them to find us again."

The captain gave the order. Slowly, the deck leveled out. The enemy's active sonar became even harder to hear.

"Now what?" the chief asked.

I studied their sonar display. The enemy submarine was still above us, likely confused as to why they'd lost contact.

"Now," I said, "we need to figure out how to fight back. Tell me about your torpedoes."

The captain and chief exchanged glances. The chief nodded reluctantly.

"We have four tubes," the captain said, "two forward, two aft. Fourteen torpedoes total. They're... temperamental."

"Define temperamental," I said.

133

"Sometimes they don't launch properly," the chief said. "Sometimes they don't arm. Sometimes they fail to deploy properly and sink."

Wonderful. We were in a leaky old U-boat with unreliable weapons against a superior enemy. We were thoroughly outclassed in every way that mattered except maybe in fighting tenacity. That meant me.

I had to come up with something, and do it now.

-30-

A new sound caught my attention—a strange warbling tone. "What's that?" I asked.

The captain cocked his head. "I don't know. I've never heard that before."

I hadn't either, and not in any submarine movies.

The *Triton* rocked violently, but it wasn't from a torpedo. The entire sub vibrated as if struck by a giant hammer. What could cause such a thing? Then it hit me.

"It must be some kind of sonic weapon," I said. "They're using it to destabilize the sub."

As I spoke, more leaks erupted around us. Then a pipe burst overhead, spraying scalding water. Two crewmen rushed to wrap it with rubber matting.

"We can't take much more of this," the chief said.

I stared at their ancient sonar display, thinking hard. The enemy knew exactly where we were despite the thermal layer.

Did that mean they were directly above us?

"Can we get a precise bearing on the enemy sub?" I asked.

One of the sonar operators adjusted his instruments. "Bearing zero-one-five, range approximately four hundred yards. Almost directly overhead."

I'd been right. The enemy surely thought they had us. I'd read about this in one of my sub books.

"Here's what we do," I said. "Launch one torpedo, but don't aim at them. Aim it about two hundred yards past them."

"That makes no sense," the chief said.

"Trust me. Then we turn hard to port and launch a second torpedo where they're going to be, not where they are."

The captain frowned. "Explain that."

"My guess is that they're cocky," I said. "They'll dodge the first torpedo easily. But physics and water pressure will force them to turn a certain way to avoid it. If we time it right, they'll turn right into our second torpedo."

"And if we're wrong?" the chief asked.

"Then we've wasted two torpedoes and probably die." I shrugged. "But we're going to die anyway if we don't try something. My way, we're at least rolling the dice against them. What do you say, Chief?"

Another sonic blast hammered us. This one was strong enough to knock pictures off the bulkheads. The whole U-boat creaked as if it were about to split apart.

My stomach tightened, and I felt sick. I could feel my throat thicken. I didn't want to drown.

The captain nodded grimly. "Forward torpedo room, prepare tubes one and two."

This was incredibly risky and uncertain. I'd studied about submarine warfare but hadn't lived it. Worse, these men were clearly inexperienced. Luckily, the enemy had probably never had to fight before either.

"What's the status of tube one?" the captain asked, his voice breaking.

"Torpedo loaded," came the reply. "But sir... the targeting system isn't responding."

Sweat beaded on the captain's face. He wiped it with a rag, blinking rapidly as if in deep thought.

"Can you fire it manually?" I asked.

"Yes, but—"

"That's all we need," I said, forcing calmness into my voice. "Just point it on the bearing I give you and launch when I say."

The captain stared at me, and he said in a squeaky voice, "This is still my boat."

"Yes, sir," I said. "I'm just telling you what I know about submarine warfare. I don't mean any disrespect by it."

He gulped several times and wiped sweat off his face again. "Give them the bearing," he said thickly.

I'd calculated angles in my head. The trick was to predict how a more advanced sub would move to avoid a torpedo. They'd turn away from it, but they'd also try to maintain awareness of our position.

"Bearing zero-three-five," I said. "Fire when ready."

"Firing tube one."

A whoosh of compressed air signaled the torpedo launch. On the sonar display, I watched its track moving away from us. The enemy sub's signature shifted slightly.

"They must see it," I said. "Stand by tube two. Turn to port, bearing three-five-zero."

The *Triton* swung left.

On sonar, the enemy sub began to move. Just as I'd predicted, they were turning away from the first torpedo while trying to keep us in their sights.

I felt a surge of triumph but kept my expression neutral. Instead, I spoke as calmly as I could. "Their arrogance is their weakness. They're so sure of their superiority that they're using standard evasion patterns. Fire tube two. Bearing zero-one-zero."

The second torpedo launched.

"Dive!" I shouted. "Take us deep as we can go."

The captain didn't hesitate this time. "Emergency dive. All hands brace for it."

It took time. Then a massive explosion sounded. The shock wave hit us, doing so like a sledgehammer. That caused every joint and seal in the ancient sub to strain. I was thrown against a console. More pipes burst. Someone screamed.

But under it all, I heard the distinctive and horrible sound of a hull being breached—and it wasn't ours.

"Direct hit," a sonar operator shouted.

I pulled myself up, wiping water from my eyes. The control room was a mess of spraying leaks and steam. But we were alive. That was such a glorious great feeling. I could barely process the relief coursing through me. The enemy was dead, not us. But we could still lose this leaky old U-boat if we didn't do it right.

"Damage report," the captain ordered.

I turned and waited for it along with everyone else.

"Multiple hull breaches," the chief said. "Flooding in compartments three, four, and seven. All sealed."

"What about the enemy?" I asked.

The sonar operator adjusted his instruments. "Contact is descending rapidly. I hear machinery noises. A lot of them."

That meant we'd holed them. I realized my euphoria might have struck too soon. They were probably fighting to keep their fancy systems operational and maybe succeeding. Damn, I needed to think straight, not emotionally.

"They'll have damage control parties," I said. "Better equipment than us to seal their leaks. We need to finish them while we can."

The captain raised his eyebrows. "You want to attack again?"

I couldn't believe it. Here it was all over again. They wanted to show mercy when it was far too early to do it.

"They're wounded and dropping," I said. "This is our chance. How many torpedoes do we have left?"

"Enough," the chief said. "But tube one is jammed. Something broke during that last explosion. We only have tube two forward, and the aft tubes."

I nodded. "That's enough. Their damage control parties will be good—probably better than anything we have. But they've probably never had to use them in combat. I bet they'll be trying to fix everything at once instead of concentrating on what matters."

A new sound echoed through the hull—a weird grinding noise that set my teeth on edge.

"What is that?" the chief asked.

"Maybe they're trying to restart their sonic weapon," I said. "But it's damaged. Probably doing more harm to their own systems than to us now."

The grinding ceased abruptly. On sonar, the enemy sub's descent was slowing.

"They're leveling off," the operator reported. "Depth... four hundred feet."

That was deeper than I'd hoped to go in our leaky boat, but we had no choice. From my reading, I knew Type VII U-boats had gone down to four hundred feet and survived. That was lower than the factory limits, but war made you do crazy things.

"Take us down to three-fifty," I said, starting to get the hang of this. "But swing wide around them first. I want tube two to have a clear shot."

The captain looked at his depth gauge, then at the water still spraying from our pipes. He was no doubt wondering if his ancient sub could take that kind of pressure.

"Do it," he ordered.

The *Triton's* deck tilted as we dove. New leaks appeared almost immediately. The constant background groaning of the hull grew louder.

"Three hundred feet," someone reported.

A pipe exploded off to my left, filling the air with steam. Two sailors rushed to seal it.

"Three twenty-five..."

I moved to the sonar display. The enemy sub was almost directly below us now. They'd stopped trying to run and were possibly turning to bring weapons to bear.

"They're launching," the sonar operator shouted.

I'd been right. Damn it, we could still drown down here. No, I had to pull my head out of my ass.

"All ahead flank!" I yelled. "Hard to starboard!"

The captain repeated my orders. The *Triton* surged forward, heeling into a tight turn. The sound of the incoming torpedo grew louder.

"Keep turning," I shouted. "Tighter."

The metal around us screamed in protest. The deck tilted to

139

an alarming angle.

The terrible, gut-wrenching swish of sound told of the torpedo shooting past our stern, missing by meters no doubt.

"They're too deep," I said. "Their torpedo couldn't turn sharp enough at this angle. But that means—"

"We have the same problem," the captain finished.

"Not quite. Their torpedoes are probably computerized, trying to calculate the perfect shot. Ours are simpler. We can use that."

I studied the sonar display. "Bring us around to bearing one-eight-zero. Ready tube two."

"Tube two ready," came the reply.

The enemy sub was moving again, but slower than before. Our hit had definitely hurt them.

"They're trying to get above us," I said. "Don't let them. Match their depth."

"Three hundred seventy feet," someone called out. The hull groaning was constant now and terrifying. "Three eighty…"

"Fire tube two," I ordered. "Then immediately launch one from the aft tubes."

Two torpedoes shot out. The enemy sub began to turn, but sluggishly. Their damaged systems hindered their ability to react.

"They're launching again."

"Dive!" I shouted. "All the way to four hundred feet!"

"That'll put us on their level," the chief protested.

"Exactly. Their torpedo will pass right over us. But ours…"

Another massive explosion lit up the sonar display. The shock wave hit us a second later, stronger than the first one. I was thrown completely off my feet this time.

New leaks burst everywhere. The hull made sounds no submarine should ever make. We were way too deep for this old boat. I shoved my forearm against my mouth so I wouldn't moan aloud or scream in dread.

"Direct hit!" the sonar operator yelled over the chaos. "Their hull is… wait. Something's happening."

A series of secondary explosions came through the sonar. Then a sound I'd never heard before and never wanted to hear again—the sound of a submarine imploding under massive pressure.

"They're gone," the operator said quietly. "Contact lost."

Silence engulfed the control room, punctuated only by the steady drip of leaks.

I was emotionally drained by this, my clothes were soaked, and my spirit felt drained.

"Surface," the captain ordered. "Get us up before we spring any more leaks."

Soon, the *Triton's* bow lifted. The deeper we'd gone, the more the ancient U-boat had leaked. Now water dripped or sprayed from dozens of places. Sailors rushed around with patches and sealant, but it was like trying to seal a sieve.

The deck tilted sharply upward. That caused waterfalls from the overhead leaks. The very air seemed thick with moisture.

I thought about what had just happened: We'd destroyed a superior sub through cunning, but I wondered about the crew. Had I just killed fellow humans who were only trying to fix their world? Then I thought about my poor Livi and how Omilcar had butchered her. Those people had been working with him, no doubt. They'd chosen their side.

The hull's groaning began to lessen as we ascended.

"Three hundred feet," someone called.

The captain approached me. His uniform was soaked and his face was lined with exhaustion. "That was impressive, Mr. Bayard."

I didn't feel impressive. I was tired, and my shoulder throbbed where I'd been thrown against the cabinet.

"How did you know they'd fall for such simple tactics?" he asked.

"Because they were too sure of themselves," I said, not telling him I'd gotten lucky. "Their advanced technology likely made them overconfident. They'd also probably never been in a real fight before."

Spiro nodded slowly. "Unlike you."

I gestured at the sonar. "War is war. The tech changes but the principles stay the same."

"Two hundred and fifty feet," someone called.

"You saved my boat and my crew," the captain said.

"Thank you."

We shook hands as the *Triton* continued heading for the surface. We'd won. We could continue the fight. And I could keep hunting for the Great Sark of Mu so I could rip off his head and piss down his lousy neck.

-31-

The battle was over, but now came the real test of survival. I stood in the *Triton's* control room with Captain Spiro and the chief as they studied a diagram of the U-boat. Red marks covered it, indicating significant damage from the battle.

"Compartments three, four, and seven were partially flooded," the chief said, pointing. "We've pumped them out, but the electrical systems have failed due to saltwater damage."

I watched crew members carrying damaged equipment through the corridor. Everything reeked of seawater and burned metal.

"What's the status of the pressure hull?" Spiro asked.

"There are three major breaches, all sealed now. But I wouldn't trust those patches below fifty feet." The chief wiped sweat from his forehead. "We need a proper yard and weeks of repair."

"Which we can't get," I said.

143

The chief nodded grimly. "The best we can do is to make her surface-worthy. Maybe give us a shallow dive capability if we're desperate enough."

We toured the damage, moving through compartments that looked like war zones. The explosion that had destroyed the enemy sub had nearly taken us with it. Depth gauge panels hung loose, their glass shattered. Tools and equipment knocked loose during the battle lay scattered.

In compartment four, sailors worked to bypass damaged control lines. The deck was still wet from flooding, and the air had that sharp electrical smell of fried wiring.

"We've rerouted the main hydraulics," one reported. "The secondary systems are dead, but we can still operate the dive planes."

"How are the torpedo tubes?" I asked.

"Forward Tube One is jammed," the chief said. "The aft tubes still work, and forward tube two. Not that we have many good fish left."

That was another worry. We'd used most of the good or sound torpedoes in the fight. The ones we had left might not work. Their mechanisms were delicate as well as old, and the flooding could have damaged them.

In the engine room, the main diesel mechanic gave his report. "The engines are running, but that last explosion knocked the mounts loose. There's too much vibration now. And we're losing oil pressure in number two."

"Can you fix it?" Spiro asked.

"Sure, if we had the spare parts." The mechanic gestured at the engines. "These old girls weren't in great shape before the battle. Now..." He shrugged.

I watched the crew work as we continued our inspection. One thing was quite noticeable to me. These weren't the scared scientists who had frozen in the firefight during the oil platform raid. They moved with purpose, applying their technical knowledge to save their boat. Maybe they weren't soldiers, but they knew how to fight the sea.

The final tally was grim: multiple hull patches unlikely to hold under pressure, damaged electrical and hydraulic systems, and engines at risk of failure. The *Triton* had won her battle, but the victory had nearly broken her.

"How far are we to the facility?" I asked Spiro.

"More than a day's travel." He stared at the diagrams, as we'd returned to the control room. "We'll have to stay on the surface as much as possible. No diving unless we absolutely have to, and that will be shallow dives only."

I thought about the Draconian dirigibles. They hadn't ever found us while we were at sea, but that was partly because we'd dived at the needed times.

"I don't know that I think we should ever dive," the chief said. "It's iffy if the patches will hold or not."

The captain didn't reply to that.

We stood in silence, listening to the creaks and groans of the damaged U-boat. Somewhere out there, Omilcar and his allies waited. And beyond them was the ancient Atlantean deep core system.

The question was whether this broken U-boat could get us there alive.

Later, we ran on the surface through darkness, the diesels thrumming beneath us. I stood in the conning tower with Captain Spiro as he scanned the night sky. The damaged U-boat wallowed in the waves, riding lower than she should, making everything more difficult.

"The patch in compartment four is holding," the chief reported from below. "But she's still making water. We have to run the pumps every hour."

"I see something." I was scanning the stars with a big pair of binoculars. I lowered them long enough to point it out.

Captain Spiro raised his binoculars, searching the horizon. After several tense seconds, he said, "It's a dirigible. It seems to be moving parallel to our course."

I studied the distant shape through my glasses again. The airship was running without lights. Did it even have any to run? It was a darker blot against the stars. Earlier, I'd concluded the Draconians didn't travel much at night. It looked like I'd been wrong about that. I wondered if their big propeller could match our reduced speed.

"Do you think they spotted us?" I asked.

"I don't believe so," Spiro said. "I think they'd be trying to work toward us then and put us under depth charges."

Even so, Captain Spiro kept watching the dirigible.

These Draconians didn't seem as primitive as the ones we'd fought at the oil platform. These struck me as more professional, using modern tactics to hunt a wounded U-boat.

For an hour, we tracked the airship as it quartered the sea ahead of us but off to the left. The *Triton's* wake might be visible from above—a possible phosphorescent trail pointing right to us. But diving wasn't an option unless absolutely necessary.

"Second contact," a lookout called. "Bearing two-seven-zero."

"Not good," Spiro said quietly. "They're hunting in pairs now."

The chief appeared in the hatch. "Captain, engine room reports increasing vibration in the diesel mounts. If we don't slow down, it could get ugly fast."

"We can't slow down," Spiro said. "Not with them up there."

I remembered stories about U-boats running the gauntlet in the Atlantic, trying to reach friendly ports while aircraft and destroyers hunted them. Now I understood a little better the horrible tension they had faced.

The first dirigible turned, cutting across our bow, if far in the distance.

"That's not good," I said. "They must know we're out here or have spotted us and are trying to be cagey."

Captain Spiro studied the airship through his binoculars. He must have seen something that scared him. He lowered them sharply. "Sound the diving stations. We'll have to risk it."

We all slid down the ladder, the last man closing and sealing the conning tower hatch.

The klaxon rang through the boat. Men scrambled to stations to get ready.

The chief entered the control room, staring at the captain. I could feel the tension, the war of wills between them.

It twisted my stomach. This was so different from a direct fight, facing a man or many enemies as you attacked or defended. This was harder, as you had to wait and take it.

146

Finally, the chief looked away, stepping to a console.

The captain exhaled, glanced at me and nodded to someone else.

Soon, the *Triton's* bow tilted down as seawater gurgled into the ballast tanks.

I found myself clenching my fists too tightly and eased my fingers loose.

"Twenty feet… thirty…" the depth keeper called out our descent.

The hull creaked ominously. Even this shallow, the patches were being tested. I heard pumps kick in, fighting the seepage.

The chief stared at the captain again.

"Level at forty feet," Spiro ordered softly.

We hung suspended in the dark water, running on batteries now. These dirigibles were silent. We wouldn't know if they were right above us unless they stared to drop depth charges on our heads. By then, of course, it would be too late.

Minutes stretched into hours. The crew spoke in whispers, as if the enemy might hear us through the hull. This seemed like too much precaution. Still, who knew if the other scientists, the ones who had woken up first, had transferred modern equipment onto the dirigibles?

It would seem the Draconians were much more useful allies for the other side than the even more primitive Sea Lords were for us.

This proved to be a hideous experience. Every groan of stressed metal made us wince. The chief moved from compartment to compartment, checking his patches, adjusting his pumps.

Then a new sound echoed through the water—the horrible and distinctive splash of depth charges being dropped.

Those bastards had seen us after all. They'd been playing games. The captain had been right to wait it out this long.

The captain and I stared at each other.

"They could be hunting blind," I said.

"You mean covering the area?" he asked.

I nodded, waiting for it as my gut tightened with anticipation.

The first explosion was distant, more felt than heard. The

second came closer, making the hull shudder. Water sprayed from a seam in the overhead.

This truly sucked. We couldn't go deeper to escape. We couldn't run faster to outrace the slow dirigibles. All we could do was inch along in the dark while death probed for us.

The third explosion nearly did it. The patch in compartment four started to give. Men rushed to shore it up as water poured in.

I admit it. I wanted to howl just to release the tension that had built up so tightly in me. I bit my lower lip instead.

Fortunately, the patch held just enough so we didn't drown.

Finally, no more depth charges hit the water and thus no more exploded.

Captain Spiro kept us down another hour to be sure. When we finally surfaced, the starry sky was empty. The hunt had moved on.

I panted as I stared at the stars. I couldn't do too many more dives like this.

Even so, we'd learned something crucial. It would be even greater madness to risk another dive. The next time the dirigibles found us, we'd probably have a better chance at survival if we fought on the surface. That would mean luring them low enough so I could use my hollow tube.

I straightened and looked at Spiro. "How much further is this place?"

"We should reach the coordinates by dawn." He stared into the darkness. "Assuming the engines hold out."

I thought about that. This leaky old U-boat was just part of the story. It might be enough to get us to this underwater entrance to the great Atlantean facility. I thought Omilcar must want something there. These amnesiac scientists hoped it held answers to ancient questions. The problem was, how could we get the entire crew down there if the U-boat couldn't submerge, or not more than 50 feet?

Even now, with everything else going on, mechanics and engineers worked on the Underwater Delivery Vehicle (UDV) they'd acquired in the last submerged building. They'd transported the pieces through the flexible tube leading to the aft section. The chief and his boys welded together parts in the

148

aft torpedo room.

I needed sleep. So did everyone else; we were exhausted from everything. What would the morning show us?

"Good night, Captain," I said. "I'm getting some rest. I suggest you do the same."

He nodded without moving.

I headed down the corridor, thinking how crazy it was that we were traveling in a WWII-era U-boat, seeking to unravel the great mystery of Atlantis.

-32-

It was time to do this, thirty-nine hours since the terrible submarine battle.

The men had needed a rest after the grueling struggle of repairing and resealing everything. That had been an endless job, with everyone pitching in, including me. The Draconian depth charges hadn't helped either.

The torpedo explosions had caused more damage than I'd realized. Sure, it hadn't been enough to sink us during the battle, although only just barely. But if an immediate overhaul hadn't commenced, we would have ended up on the ocean bottom soon enough.

In truth, this boat needed a dry dock and weeks of repairs, as the chief had said before.

Despite everything, given what was at stake, Captain Spiro was currently cruising at forty feet.

I discovered this upon waking. I couldn't believe he'd

taken the risk. I thought the creaks and groans around me had given me nightmares.

When I entered the control room, Captain Spiro looked utterly beat, with circles around his eyes. He glanced at me as I walked in.

"Did you spot the enemy?" I asked.

He shook his head.

The chief whispered to me that we'd maneuvered in the shallows for nearly two hours.

"Yes," the captain said. "But now we're here and hopefully without anyone knowing that. Take her up."

The *Triton* surfaced. I was stunned to discover that it was an hour after sunset. I'd slept the entire day away. The stars looked glorious overhead, and I couldn't spot any dirigibles. Maybe the captain had made the wise move, or maybe he'd just gotten lucky.

Given that I felt so refreshed, I helped the crew manhandle pieces of the Underwater Delivery Vehicle from the aft torpedo room onto the deck. The chief had insisted we do the final assembly up here. The fumes from welding inside the aft torpedo room had nearly asphyxiated two men earlier.

The mechanics and engineers had been assembling the pieces from the underwater building they'd looted a week ago. They had done the assembling in the aft torpedo room, at times welding the pieces together. Now, it was time to finish this in the open.

I studied the UDV components laid out on the *Triton's* outer deck. It looked like a giant metal jigsaw puzzle in the darkness. The torpedo-shaped hull sections were surprisingly light, made of a unique Atlantean alloy unfamiliar to me. Twin cockpit windshields caught what little starlight filtered through the thick atmosphere.

"Hand me that welding torch," Felix said. He crouched by the main hull section, checking the battery compartment connections. "These power couplings are interesting."

I passed him the torch, watching as he carefully fused the housing shut. Sparks cascaded across the deck. That was a risk out here, given Draconian dirigibles, but this was the final mile, right?

The batteries were sealed units about the size of car batteries but much lighter. According to the chief, they held enough charge for eight hours of operation at full power.

"You're sure these batteries will work?" I asked.

Felix nodded without looking up. "The chief says they're some kind of chemical cell. They're self-charging, apparently. Our ancestors were highly advanced."

That was an understatement. The UDV's design was decades ahead of anything I'd seen on Earth, despite looking somewhat primitive. The twin-seat setup reminded me of the underwater craft McPherson and I had used in the Persian Gulf, but this vehicle was more sophisticated.

"Those linkages must be perfect," the chief said, "or the whole thing is worthless."

I helped guide the section into place. The chief had been obsessing over every detail of the assembly. Given that our lives would depend on this craft working perfectly at crushing depths, I couldn't blame him.

"The original builders did most of the hard work," Felix said, moving to weld the control assembly in place. "We're just putting it back together like they designed it."

A wave slapped against the *Triton's* hull, making the deck shift. Felix paused in his welding until it steadied.

"How many pieces did you say you found?" I asked the chief.

"There were seventeen major sections, plus all the internal components." The chief supervised as more sailors brought up the twin propulsion units. "The ancient facility had it stored like a kit, waiting to be assembled. Almost like they knew someone would need it someday."

That was another mystery about these Atlanteans. They'd prepared for something and stored their technology away carefully. But what had they been preparing for? And why had it apparently failed to prevent the Great Catastrophe?

We worked through the night, connecting power systems and control linkages. The chief insisted on testing every weld, every connection. I had to admire his thoroughness, even if it meant we've been exposed on the surface for too long.

"Last section," Felix announced. The front viewport

152

assembly slid into place with a satisfying click. "Just need to seal it and run the final checks."

I helped him make the last welds while the chief tested the battery connections one more time. The UDV was really taking shape now. Its sleek form looked deadly serious in the starlight, like some kind of mechanical predator.

"According to the specs, she should do eight knots underwater," the chief said. "Depth rated to five hundred feet, though I wouldn't push it that far if we can help it."

I hoped we wouldn't have to, but given what we were likely to face at the underwater facility, I wasn't optimistic.

Dawn was approaching by the time we finished. This had taken a lot longer than anyone had expected. The completed UDV hung from the *Triton's* crane, ready to be lowered into the ocean for testing. Looking at it, I couldn't help but think of Livi and what Omilcar had done to her. The psi-master was out there somewhere. This would probably bring me closer to reaching him.

"Let's get her in the water," the chief ordered. "We've been exposed on the surface for too long."

I nodded, helping guide the UDV as the crane swung it out. Now we finally had a way to reach the mysterious facility.

The sun was just starting to lighten the horizon as we lowered the UDV into the endless ocean of Atlantis. Time would tell if we'd assembled her correctly. The lives of the three of us going down would depend on it.

-33-

I trod water beside the UDV, inspecting the torpedo-shaped craft as it bobbed gently in the waves. The *Triton's* crew had tied it off with a stern line, keeping it close to the U-boat's hull. Through my diving mask, I studied the twin cockpit setup with its reinforced Plexiglass windshields and the motorcycle-style controls for piloting.

The sight brought back memories of the Persian Gulf, when Colonel McPherson and I had taken Philip, the small *Homo habilis*, down to find his portal to the supposed Institute Planet. We'd found a shark-patrolled, underwater Krekelen base as well, and they had held McPherson captive while Philip and I used the portal. That hadn't taken us to the Institute Planet, but that's another story entirely.

That had been a costly mission; one I'd rather forget.

"Is the equipment satisfactory?" Captain Spiro called from the conning tower.

He looked marginally better. The circles around his eyes weren't as red as before. He must have gotten some sleep.

I'd been swimming around the UDV for twenty minutes now, checking every seal and connection. The batteries were housed in waterproof compartments, ready to power our descent.

I gave him the thumbs up sign.

Andrew appeared behind the captain, already wearing most of his diving gear.

The hardhat diving suit was a hybrid design—traditional canvas and rubber construction but reinforced with modern composites. A network of small tubes ran through the material, circulating warm water from a battery-powered heater to prevent hypothermia at depth. The helmet was compact compared to old-style diving bells, with a professional-grade communications system built in. We, of course, would have our own air supply on our backs and not use a hose that led up to the surface.

Spiro climbed down the conning tower to the outer deck.

"This is the right location," he told me, speaking through a helmet communication device. He held the helmet in his hands. "According to the ancient records, the facility entrance is at four hundred feet. These suits can handle the pressure with their advanced regulators."

"According to ancient records," Andrew muttered skeptically behind him.

I checked my own suit's gauges. The depth rating was good to five hundred feet, though I hoped we wouldn't test that limit. The mixed-gas system would help prevent nitrogen narcosis, while the emergency bailout bottle provided twenty minutes of backup air.

"This reminds me of the Gulf," I said. "The water was different there though—warm and cloudy. Here it'll be clearer but colder."

"You've done this kind of mission before?" Andrew asked, showing the first hint of interest in me.

"Yeah. The Krekelens maintained an underwater base off Earth's coast. We used a UDV to reach a portal near there." I paused, remembering. "Colonel McPherson was never the same after that."

"What happened to her?" the captain asked sharply.

I shrugged inside the suit. "That was a long time ago." Maybe not in time, but in my understanding about all this.

The chief emerged onto the top of the conning tower, carrying our weapons. My hollow tube was among them, along with several of their strange pistols.

"We think the ancient facility extends deep into the mantle," Captain Spiro said, accepting his pistol from the chief. "What we can reach is only the entrance, a gateway to something far larger."

Andrew checked his suit's seals one final time. "We should get moving. The longer we stay on the surface here, the more likely airships will arrive to see us."

He had a point about that, one we'd all been telling each other.

I hauled myself onto the UDV, running a final systems check. The craft was designed to be piloted from either position, with room for a third person in the middle. A small cargo compartment held our extra gear.

"I'll take rear position," I said through the helmet radio. The captain had now donned his suit with help from others. "I've got the most experience with these. Captain in front, Andrew in the middle."

Andrew started to protest but the captain cut him off. "Agreed. Mr. Bayard's experience is invaluable here."

The chief handed down our emergency supplies—extra air bottles and tools. The routine felt strange, like reliving an old nightmare. I desperately hoped we wouldn't find any Krekelens down there.

"If you're not back in eight hours, we'll assume the worst," the chief said.

I doubted the *Triton* would last eight hours if it remained in one place on the surface. But that wasn't my department.

Once the captain and Andrew were aboard, I did a final radio check. The short-range system was clear enough, vital for communication at depth.

"Ready?" I asked.

"Ready," the captain replied.

Andrew just grunted.

The chief untied the stern line, tossing it over. The captain stowed it in a forward compartment.

The chief saluted us.

We saluted him in return.

Then, as the UDV turned away from the *Triton*, I thought about Omilcar. Would I find him down there? Was the facility truly why he had come to Atlantis?

I imagined I was about to find out.

-34-

The salt water closed over our helmeted heads, and the world became a silent, blue-green expanse.

I adjusted the descent rate from the rear controls, watching the depth gauge tick steadily downward. The water clarity was amazing, much better than the Persian Gulf had been. Shafts of sunlight penetrated deep, creating shifting patterns around us.

"Twenty feet," I said. "All systems normal."

"This is remarkable," Captain Spiro said from the front seat. His voice came clearly through the integrated communication system in our helmets.

Andrew shifted uncomfortably in the middle area. The chief had rigged straps around that section of the craft, giving Andrew stirrups and handholds. Still, he was the most uncomfortable of the three of us.

The UDV's electric motors hummed quietly as we continued down. So far, so good, as everything was working.

At fifty feet, I saw our first sea life—something like a shark but more serpentine, watching us from the distance. Schools of silvery fish scattered before us like coins cast into water.

"Seventy-five feet," I said a bit later. The *Triton* was becoming harder to see, just a dark shape up against the bright surface. But something else caught my eye—movement in the distance.

I adjusted a rear camera and felt my gut tighten. Another submarine was approaching fast, sleeker, bigger and more modern than the *Triton*. They were running silent, and the *Triton's* crew likely hadn't spotted it yet. How much could the *Triton's* crew do if they did see?

"Captain," I said. "We've got company up there."

Spiro twisted around to look. "What? Where?"

"Nine o'clock, coming in fast. They don't look friendly." The last was obvious but I said it anyway.

"We have to warn the *Triton*," the captain said. "We need to go back."

"Negative," I said. "We're too deep already. We'd never reach the *Triton* in time." I didn't want to add, "And what could we do about this anyway?"

I heard a noise. No! The attack had already begun. Above us, the first torpedo streaked through the water.

The *Triton* must have spotted the torpedo because she started to move, her screws churning the water. But she was old, too old, slow, and wounded. After helping with all those repairs, I understood the *Triton's* severe limitations.

"No," Andrew whispered. "All our friends..."

I thought about that, too. I could see the chief, Felix and the others in my mind's eye. This was a sickening sensation. The chief had said he'd wait eight hours. They weren't going to have eight minutes.

I hoped for something different to happen. Then the torpedo struck dead on. Even at our depth, we felt the shock wave. The UDV rocked as I fought to keep us stable. The *Triton's* hull breached, with air bubbles streaming out like silver blood.

"Take us back up," Captain Spiro said in a hoarse voice. "Do it now! I order you."

It was over. The others on the *Triton* weren't going to survive this.

"We can't help them," I said. It was a vicious feeling, especially after living and working with them these past days. I pushed us deeper so we could survive. "We'd just die with them, Captain. What good would that do?"

As if to punctuate my words, a second torpedo hit the *Triton*. The old U-boat's back broke with the explosion, her hull splitting in a horrible display of twisted metal. The sea rushed in to claim her as she began her final descent, taking all those scientists with it.

"My friends," the captain sobbed. "The last of us…"

"You don't know that," Andrew said in a high-pitched voice. It sounded as if he was losing it bad. "There could be other stasis tubes, other survivors somewhere—"

"Enough!" I said. The chief, Felix and the others were gone. The grief was raw, more so for my two companions than me. These were just more tally marks against the other side, those that had psi-masters, Krekelens and Neanderthal-eating Ophidians. Omilcar had called me a killer. Well, I was going to square this someday by wading in enemy blood. When I did, I'd say a prayer of farewell to the chief, Felix and the others.

"We need to focus on staying alive, gentlemen," I said. "The sub up there might come looking for us next."

"What do you suggest?" Andrew shouted. "We're trapped down with no way back to the surface."

He was wrong about one part. We could go up again. There just wouldn't be any point to it. This felt eerily similar to the destruction of the *Duke Harry*. That had been the research ship that had taken us to the point in the Persian Gulf back then. This felt like deja vu. The *Duke Harry* had been gutted, ship parts sinking around us. Back then, we could have swum for many miles and eventually reached a shore. That option didn't exist in the endless waters of Atlantis. We had to go down to survive. There would be no other way… except perhaps if a Sea Lord galley picked us up. That was worse than a long shot, though.

"I know this is bitter," I said. "It's hard. We'll mourn them later. Now, we do what we came for. We find that facility and get inside. It's our only chance for living, and maybe if you're lucky, you can fix what you broke long ago."

Andrew was breathing hard, with a sob breaking out now and again. Even so, I think he worked to contain his grief.

The captain was silent for a long moment, perhaps watching the *Triton* pieces sink. What was he thinking? Who would he miss most? Finally, he said in a harsh voice, "Mr. Bayard is right. We've lost too much to turn back now. We must finish the task for their sakes."

"If you're wrong about this facility," Andrew said, "we're going to die down there."

"We're going to die up there if we try to surface," I replied. This was no time to coddle anyone. Andrew had to face harsh truths, and do it now. That's just how it was. "At least this way we might uncover something meaningful."

Andrew's hard breathing lessened. I think he was starting to get it.

All the while, I kept descending, watching the depth gauge tick past one hundred feet. The water was darker now, the sun's reach fading. Our equipment groaned under the increasing pressure.

None of us spoke for a while. What could we say? We'd just witnessed our only link to the surface destroyed, with many good men lost in the attack. We were committed, whether we wanted to be or not.

The water around us darkened as we descended into the abyss. Somewhere below, an ancient facility waited—if the captain had read the coordinates right. I just hoped it would provide answers that justified the cost of getting here.

The facility emerged from the darkness like a sleeping leviathan. In places, massive floodlights still functioned after thousands of years, illuminating large sections of the structure. Great archways large enough for submarines to pass through punctuated a facade that stretched for what had to be miles. Huge pipes and conduits snaked across its surface, some still pulsing with faint blue energy. The whole thing disappeared into the cliff face, extending who knew how deep into the planet's crust.

"This is impossible," Andrew said in awe.

For once, I agreed with him. This was truly awe-inspiring. Could the Atlanteans truly have constructed it so long ago? Was this place built before the Great Catastrophe?

"No," Captain Spiro said, "not impossible, Andrew. This is what we were capable of before the Great Catastrophe."

This was more impressive than the pyramids in Egypt.

Hell, it might have been as impressive as the interstellar teleporting obelisks and ziggurats on the distant planets I'd seen. No... After a moment of consideration, I took the last thought back. Those had been an even greater achievement. Still, this was crazy cool.

I heard mocking laughter in my head. It didn't take long to figure out why.

Are you enjoying the view, Bayard? I knew you'd come here. The ancient toys of Atlantis are impressive, are they not?

I gripped the controls tighter, trying to shield my thoughts from Omilcar.

Oh, don't bother trying to hide. I can taste your fear, your anger, and your grief for poor, sweet Livi.

"Bayard?" the captain asked. "What's wrong with you? Why are you growling?"

Before I could answer, something big moved in the darkness beyond the facility's lights. I thought it might be a small sub. That Omilcar might be piloting it. As the creature emerged into the light, I saw reinforced skull plating, what might have been an extra set of gills pulsing with an eerie blue glow. This didn't strike me as an ordinary deep-sea shark. Yes, it had a shark's shape, although bigger than any Great White I'd seen before. The creature seemed bioengineered for these crushing depths.

Two more shapes just like it appeared, each easily twice the length of our UDV. Their enhanced bodies were streamlined but angular, with hardened cartilage structures visible through nearly translucent skin. What seemed like specialized muscles rippled beneath, possibly designed to maintain power even in this cold, high-pressure environment. Each creature's modified eyes tracked us with terrifying intelligence, emanating the same blue light as their gills.

Say hello to the improved megalodons, Omilcar's thought-voice purred in my mind. *They've been extensively modified, as I sense you understand. The ancient Atlanteans knew how to engineer flesh as well as metal.*

The first megalodon attacked without warning, its reinforced skull aimed straight at us like a battering ram. I yanked the controls hard over, barely avoiding the monster

163

shark's charge.

"What are those things?" Andrew shouted.

I reached back and grabbed my hollow tube. As another shark charged, I aimed and willed the weapon to fire. I felt the tingle of power up. Then, instead of flames, a stream of superheated plasma burst forth, cutting through the water like a lance. It struck the attacking creature in the head, boiling through its armored plates. The monster convulsed, its engineered flesh literally cooking off its enhanced skeleton before our eyes.

It might have reached us anyway, but the captain had taken over the controls from his seat and steered us away from its blind charge.

Unfortunately, there were two more of them left. Their black eyes showed cruel cunning as they circled our UDV, their modified bodies allowing them to accelerate and turn in ways that no natural shark could do at this cold depth.

Again, this was just like the Persian Gulf. Psi-masters had controlled the sharks then. Surely, psi-masters did that here as well, or one at least.

Impressive, Omilcar mocked in my mind. *What I want to know is, how long you can keep it up? The tube drains your energy, doesn't it? And there are so many teeth in the dark.*

I shut him out, focusing on survival. The sharks came in fast from below. I fired the tube again and again, sending streams of plasma scything through the water. One shark died, its head vaporized under the fusillade. The other continued despite burn marks along its sides, driven by programming or rage. I think it slowed, though. Otherwise, we'd never have survived what happened next.

Its armored head slammed against our underside, throwing us into our restraints. I heard Andrew scream through the radio as he was nearly thrown from his seat.

I kept firing as the tube drained my strength. Each blast of plasma lit up the depths like lightning, revealing glimpses of the massive facility beyond and the deadly shape circling us.

Are you tiring already? Omilcar's thoughts slithered through my mental defenses. *Perhaps I'll let him bring me pieces of you. Would you like that, Bayard? To join Livi in*

164

pieces?

Was he trying to enrage me? It gave me new strength. I triggered the tube again and again, filling the water with killing light. The creature was nimble, and swam aside time and again, although I wounded him.

Then the bleeding megalodon pressed his attack with desperate fury. He came with his jaws wide, his armored hide gleaming in the facility's lights.

I used up the last of my strength into the tube. Plasma burst forth, catching the shark as it zoomed closer. The bioengineered creature died thrashing, its flesh splitting open as the superheated energy boiled it from inside.

I sagged in my harness, drained. The hollow tube weighed heavily in my trembling hands.

"Is… is it over?" Andrew asked.

"For now," I managed to say.

Captain Spiro pointed. "Look at that."

Ancient lights blinked as if trying to guide us in. Around us, the bioengineered carcasses of the sharks drifted down into the abyss, their flesh still glowing faintly blue in death.

Well done, Omilcar's thoughts came one last time. *You've won entrance. But what will you find—*

"Shut up, you devil!" Andrew screamed. He had curled his gloved hands into fists, shaking them.

Did I hear something on the telepathic plane? I winced as if something thunderous came near.

Andrew slumped limply after that, breathing hard and making little hiccups as if he'd been crying for a long time.

What had the ancient Atlantean just done?

Omilcar's telepathic presence was gone, leaving only the hum of our electric engines and the vast, ancient structure before us.

Did Andrew possess telepathic power? He had said "Shut up." Could Andrew have mentally heard Omilcar before that?

I was too weary to ask him, barely able to keep my eyes open.

"I am beat," I whispered.

"I understand," Captain Spiro said. "I'll take us in. We've come too far to stop now."

"Do you know where to go?" I whispered.

"I think so," he said.

That was interesting, real interesting. I sat hunched in the last seat, enduring as the UDV headed for the giant undersea facility.

-36-

The entrance resembled something from a Jules Verne novel—a great underwater moon pool stretching into the facility. Ancient guidance lights still functioned, leading us through a water-filled shaft that angled deeper into the cliff face.

"Look at the construction," Captain Spiro said, pointing at the perfectly smooth walls. "No seams, no joints. It's as if the whole thing was somehow grown rather than built."

The UDV's instrument panels showed decreasing pressure, which seemed impossible as we ascended the shaft. That seemed impossible given our depth, but this whole facility was impossible.

"There's a surface up ahead," I said, looking straight up, spotting a change in the water's texture.

"I see it," Captain Spiro said.

Soon, we broke through into an enormous chamber. By

that, I mean our heads broke through the watery surface. The pool we emerged from was circular, maybe fifty feet across, with a broad deck area surrounding it. Bright light came from panels in the ceiling far above, however, it wasn't the harsh glare of floodlights. This was softer, more natural, resembling sunlight.

"It can't be this bright down here," Andrew said. "Not at this depth."

He sounded almost normal now, but I didn't think Andrew was normal. Was he remembering more of who he had been before entering the stasis tube? I was certain he was a telepath, although he didn't seem to be able to read my thoughts.

Captain Spiro guided our craft to a mechanical docking arm that extended from the deck. It looked sized for exactly this purpose, as if the ancient Atlanteans had used similar vehicles.

The moment we secured the UDV, I felt an icy tingle at the base of my skull. I had no idea what it might be. Maybe Omilcar had returned in telepathic power... but I didn't think so. Whatever it was, I thought it might mean more psionics.

I reached for my pack and pulled out the psi-master headband.

"What are you doing?" Spiro asked.

"Omilcar is here somewhere," I said, removing my helmet and slipping the headband on. The familiar wooziness hit immediately, but I'd take that over mental invasion. "I can feel psionic energy or something way off in this place."

Andrew surprised me by checking his weapon. Did he think he'd use it this time? He looked up with his helmet still on. "We shouldn't stay in the open." His voice sounded as if it was far away due to the helmet.

Then I realized how stupid I'd just been. I'd ripped off my diving helmet, assuming the air would be breathable inside the facility. It was, though, cool and slightly metallic tasting, but clean. There was no burning sensation in my throat or lungs, or dizziness in my mind. I'd gotten lucky even though I'd been rash.

"The air is breathable," I said. "Some kind of ancient air circulation system must still be working."

The others removed their diving helmets, breathing deeply

168

of the facility's air.

"How is this possible?" Andrew asked. "After all this time, there shouldn't be any breathable air?"

His eyes looked red as if he'd been crying recently. He didn't seem to be sniffling anymore though. His features seemed... harder, firmer, as if he'd gotten tougher.

I wanted to interrogate him about possible telepathy, but something about him held me back.

"It's the same way the lights still work," Spiro said in reference to an earlier comment. "The same way the structure survived the pressure all this time. Our, or our ancestors' engineering, was far beyond what we remember."

I heard the pain in Spiro's voice—grief for the *Triton's* crew possibly mixed with awe at what his people had once achieved. These men had lost everything twice now: once in the Great Catastrophe, and again today watching their last companions die.

"We need to move," I said. "We need to find defensible positions and determine what we're dealing with."

I didn't feel as if I'd faint, but I was still woozy from using the tube and wearing the headband.

"You're not in command," Andrew said.

I glanced at him.

What do you know? The punk actually rested a hand onto the butt of his holstered weapon. This was a different Andrew from the oil platform. He even gave me a cold, imperious stare, as if he was daring me to challenge him.

"You're wrong," Spiro said, cutting in. "He is in command for the moment." The captain looked around the vast chamber. "We're in a war zone, whether we like it or not. Mr. Bayard has the combat experience we need for that."

Andrew looked as if wanted to spit a lemon out of his mouth. He gave me a visual going over, as if to say, "This isn't finished."

My instincts were warning me. I could actually feel it. This definitely wasn't the same Andrew as on the oil platform. This wasn't the same Andrew that had climbed onto the UDV on the surface thirty minutes ago.

Could this be more like the Andrew that had entered the

stasis tube back when? Could that have really been before the Great Catastrophe, say, in 500 B.C. or even before that?

"Our first priority is finding another way out," I said. "Given what we've seen, we can't count on that moon pool being clear if we need to escape."

"How does escaping to the surface help us any?" Andrew asked in a mocking tone.

The crazy thing was that the man had a point. It wouldn't help. It would possibly let us survive a little longer, but no more than that.

"You know what, your logic is sound," I said. I'd give the sucker a point. Maybe that would help him feel better so he'd back off.

Andrew turned to me. I could feel the contempt in his eyes.

It made me want to burn him down. I was too tired, though, to power my hollow tube again so soon. Was this psi-headband making me weak-willed somehow?

"We need to figure things out down here as fast as we can," I said.

Spiro grunted agreement.

Andrew looked as if he wanted to take this further. Then he shrugged and glanced around. "What about there?" He pointed to a massive doorway across the chamber. Symbols emitted a soft light above it.

"Can you read those symbols?" I asked Spiro. I knew I couldn't, and I didn't want to ask Andrew.

The captain walked toward them, squinting. He stopped suddenly and turned to me with surprise. "I remember their meaning. Those aren't like the tech manuals on the *Triton*. Those are different, and they're starting to come back to me." He faced the symbols. "That's a warning. Beyond is restricted access."

"That's our direction then," I said, "unless anyone else has a better idea."

If Andrew did, he kept it to himself.

We gathered our gear from the UDV and then took off the diving suits. We stowed them near the dock. As we moved away in our regular clothes, I noticed that the chamber's acoustics distorted sounds, creating eerie echoes.

"Maybe we should establish some ground rules," I said.

"That would be wise," Spiro said.

Andrew merely waited.

"Let's not wander off alone," I said. "We need to stay close together. Watch the shadows or anyplace that might hold automated defenses."

"Do you mean like the megalodons outside?" Andrew asked.

I wanted to tell him no, those had been biological, not automated. Instead, I said, "Among others."

A wave of nausea struck me then. I adjusted the headband so the nausea dissipated. How long could I keep wearing this thing? Was it really necessary?

I thought it might be, not only to keep Omilcar's thoughts out, but now maybe Andrew's as well.

Whatever the case, we moved cautiously, our footsteps echoing off the ancient bulkheads. The air grew warmer as we approached the doorway. Its massive frame looked sized for moving large equipment, not people.

"Could this have been the main site for the Project?" Spiro asked.

"That's what we're going to find out," I said.

Andrew walked up and tried the huge doorway. It opened. He pushed and stepped through.

Spiro and I hurried after. The glowing symbols above the large doorway cast shadows on us as we passed under them.

The next chamber was big, although not as large as the first. There were pillars like in an ancient Grecian temple.

"Look at the markings," Spiro said, studying symbols etched into the nearest pillar. "They remind me of something, but…" He shook his head in seeming frustration.

I moved closer to examine the pillar and the symbols. They seemed to shift when viewed from different angles. That was weird.

Then a sensation itched between my shoulder blades. I looked around fast, expecting something off, trouble.

Andrew had wandered a few feet away and stared at a blank section of wall or bulkhead. He was rubbing his temples as if they pained him.

Not seeing any immediate trouble, I asked, "Are you okay?"

"Headache," Andrew muttered. "And... I don't know. Something feels wrong down here."

I studied the chamber more carefully. We both felt something. Despite the age of the facility, some areas showed signs of recent activity. There were scuffed marks on the floor and equipment that had been moved. That reminded me of the chamber in the Dark Citadel with the relocated computers. Someone had definitely been here, and not too long ago.

A distant sound echoed through the facility. It sounded like metal grinding against metal, then silence.

The bad feeling increased in me. Ever since Bhutan, I'd learned to trust that instinct.

"Take cover," I said, clutching my hollow staff. I still felt too beat to use it, but I hurried behind a machine.

Spiro and Andrew ducked behind different equipment.

We waited, listening. The grinding sounds came again, followed by a low hum that seemed to emanate from deep within the facility's bulkheads. The sound gave me the willies.

"That noise," Spiro whispered. "I've heard it before. In my dreams, maybe..."

Andrew gasped, pressing his hands against his head. "The walls," he said through clenched teeth. "They're trying to tell us something."

I was about to ask what he meant when the lights flickered. Just for a moment, but in that instant, I saw something. Yes. Shapes moved in the shadows, but too quick to identify.

"We need to move," I said as a sense of fear filled me. "We need to find a more defensible position and determine what's going on down here."

"There's a corridor over there," Spiro pointed to an archway. "It leads deeper into the facility."

"How would you know where it leads?" I asked.

He frowned. "I... I'm not sure. It just feels like it should."

I didn't like any of this. Spiro and Andrew seemed different down here and the sound... Whatever was down here with us, we needed to be ready when we met it.

"Stay alert," I said. "And Andrew—if your head starts

172

feeling worse, tell me immediately."

He sneered at me, even though he looked pale.

As we moved toward the archway, I couldn't shake the feeling something was watching us. I didn't think it was Omilcar, unless he'd faked leaving before.

I felt bile rise in my throat as I hurried. Screw this. I tore off the psi-headband, stuffing it away. The nausea left immediately, although I felt bare-ass naked.

I looked around, but I didn't see any more shifting shadows. It felt as if things were definitely starting to heat up, though. Was that good or bad?

I suppose I'd find out soon enough.

-37-

We followed the corridor deeper into the facility. Even though my throat was tight with tension, at least the air remained breathable.

Behind me, Andrew moved with less confidence than earlier. The grinding noises in the distance came and went as if the facility was shifting about. I think the grinding noises bothered him.

Ahead, a glint of metal on the floor caught my eye. I held up my hand, stopping the others.

"What is it?" Spiro asked.

I pointed at a brass shell casing, green with corrosion. It was old compared to me, but new compared to this place. I went to it and picked it up.

"Eight millimeter," I said.

"What does that mean?" Spiro asked.

I studied the bulkheads around me more carefully. There—

bullet marks scarred the material. Something had happened here, something violent. I didn't like the obvious implications of a firefight.

8mm would likely indicate German WWII weapons. I believe 8mm was used in their main service rifle, the Karabiner 98k and in machine guns like the MG34 and MG42.

This shell casing would lend credence to the idea of some Neuschwabenland Nazis having reached Atlantis, possibly back in 1945 or even earlier. That would account for the *Triton's* Type VII U-boat specs as well.

Occam's razor suggested as much. The idea being that the simplest or easiest explanation usually was the correct one.

In any case, the corridor opened into a broader chamber. Unlike the clean precision of the moon pool area, this place showed signs of human occupation. Tables had been pushed against walls. There were chairs, metal cabinets, and possibly an old cooking area.

"Someone lived here," Andrew said.

"And recently, too," I added. There were newer items mixed in with old equipment. If I had to guess, I would say that someone was maintaining this place.

A clatter echoed from a side passage. I spun, raising the hollow tube. "Get behind me."

Boots scraped on metal. Then a figure appeared in a doorway—a woman who instantly stole my attention. She was tall with an athlete's build, maybe early-thirties. Her face caught my breath: high cheekbones, full lips, and eyes so piercingly blue they seemed to glitter even in this dim light. Her blonde hair was pulled back from her face, revealing a graceful neck. She wore practical clothes—cargo pants and a fitted black shirt—but they couldn't hide her curves. She carried a rifle I didn't recognize, with the easy confidence of someone who knew how to use it.

Even with a weapon pointed our way, she moved with effortless grace that reminded me of a dancer. But there was something else too—a hardness in those beautiful eyes, a tension in her jaw that told me to be careful.

"That's far enough," she said, her accent giving the words an exotic lilt.

"We're not looking for trouble," I said.

"No?" She studied us with cold eyes. "Yet you bring weapons into my home."

"Your home?" I asked.

She hesitated, and some of the tension in her jaw lessened. Suddenly, she seemed uneasy and possibly afraid.

"You have no idea how long..." she said, shuddering afterward.

I took a step toward her.

She raised the rifle, aiming it at my center mass. "Are you real?"

The question and the rifle stopped me cold. "Yes," I said, as I grasped the nature of the question. "We're quite real."

She gave a harsh laugh even as her amazing eyes filled with tears.

"Look," I said, "we're not going to harm you. We're friends."

She laughed harshly again.

I could almost feel a bullet from her rifle smacking me in the chest.

"You've been here alone for a long time?" I asked.

She glared at me, but not for so long that she forgot to take in Spiro and Andrew.

"How do I know you're real?" she demanded.

"Uh... you're talking to us."

"That's not good enough," she said tightly.

"Shoot him," Andrew said. "If he dies, he's real. If he vanishes, he's just an illusion."

I half turned to Andrew. "What's your problem, man?"

"You're one of them," Andrew said, his voice sharp with accusation.

"Why is he a problem?" the woman asked Andrew.

"I'm not," I said.

"I'm not asking you," she said.

"He's a killer," Andrew said.

"And you're an ingrate," I told him.

"How does he kill?" the woman asked.

"With his hands," Andrew said, "and with weapons."

"Not with his mind?" she asked.

176

"Can anyone kill with their mind?" Andrew asked.

She focused on him, and then swiveled her rifle so it aimed at his center mass. Her gaze lingered, finally moving onto Captain Spiro. Something flickered across her face, recognition perhaps.

"You're like the others," she said. "He's not. He's different."

She meant me.

"What others?" Spiro asked.

She ignored him and focused on me again. "You lead them, but you're not one of them."

"Lady," I said, "I don't know what you're talking about."

"No?" She took a step forward. "Then why are you here? What do you seek in the deep places?"

Before I could answer, Andrew gasped. He pressed his hands against his temples as his face contorted with pain.

The woman's rifle swiveled to him again. "Stop him! Before it—"

The grinding sounds came again, closer this time. The lights flickered, and for a moment, I saw something in the shadows—a writhing darkness that vanished when the lights steadied.

She swore in German. I recognized that from old movies I'd watched as a kid. Her eyes tightened as options clearly ran through her mind. Her lips thinned, and for a moment, I thought she would shoot down Andrew and Spiro.

Something changed, though. Maybe she realized we were real, people. I had a feeling she'd been alone for a long, long time. Her shoulders deflated just a bit, and she lowered the rifle.

"Inside," she said, gesturing with the rifle toward a heavy door. "Do it quickly or you're dead."

"Why should we trust you?" I asked.

"Because in thirty seconds, your friend will start screaming," she said. "In forty-five seconds, blood will pour from his nose. In sixty seconds..." She shook her head. "My room is shielded. It will help."

Andrew moaned. Then, faster than she'd said would happen, blood started trickling from his left nostril.

177

"Damn it." I nodded to Spiro.

Together we converged and helped Andrew toward the door. The woman backed away, keeping her rifle ready but letting us pass.

The door was open and the room beyond looked like a combination of bunker and laboratory. The walls were covered in copper mesh and intricate, unfamiliar symbols. The moment we crossed the threshold, Andrew relaxed slightly.

"That's better," he gasped.

The woman entered and closed the door behind us. "I'm Dr. Ava Kraus. Sit. Your friend needs time to recover."

I helped Andrew to a chair as he practically collapsed into it. "Do you know what's happening to him?"

"I know many things." Ava leaned her rifle against a table. "The question is, how much do you want to know?"

I studied her more carefully, noting the haunted look in her eyes and the tension in her movements. Whatever she knew had come at a bitter cost.

"Start with why you're here," I said.

"No." She shook her head. "First you tell me how you found this place. Then perhaps I will explain why I can't ever leave."

-38-

The shielded room was larger than it had first appeared. Bunker wasn't the right word. It was more like a combination of laboratory and living quarters. Copper mesh covered the walls, with strange symbols etched into dark metal plates placed at regular intervals. The air felt different in here, cleaner, with an almost metallic sharpness.

Andrew sat slumped in a chair, eyes closed, but his breathing had steadied. The nosebleed had stopped, though streaks of dried blood remained on his upper lip. Whatever had affected him seemed blocked by this room's defenses.

I kept hold of my hollow tube, watching Ava as she moved around the space. She checked monitors and adjusted dials, her movements economical, without any wasted motion.

The rifle rested within easy reach against a table. I studied the weapon more carefully. It resembled a hybrid design, combining modern components with an older framework. Like

179

everything else about her, the rifle spoke of someone who'd adapted to survive.

Ava must have felt my gaze and turned, those striking blue eyes meeting mine. A slight smile played at the corners of her mouth. "See something interesting, soldier?"

"First, I'm a Marine, not a soldier," I said.

Her eyebrows lifted.

"Second, yeah, that's a modified Mauser bolt action, isn't it?" I asked, nodding at her rifle.

"You have a good eye." She seemed pleased by the observation. "It was my grandfather's design, updated for current needs."

While we talked, Spiro had gravitated to the laboratory equipment. He ran his fingers over strange devices. They seemed like a mixture of old and new technology. Some of that looked like it came from the Third Reich. Others could have come from a modern research facility.

"This configuration," Spiro muttered, studying one particular machine.

"You recognize it?" Ava asked sharply, turning to him.

Spiro blinked, drawing his hand back from the machine. "I'm not sure. It seems familiar, but..." He shook his head.

I took the opportunity to survey the living area more carefully. A narrow bunk was built into one wall, neatly made with military precision. A small kitchen area occupied one corner, the shelves stocked with what seemed like preserved goods. Books filled another shelf. I couldn't tell from here what they held, the books, I mean. I did see German script along some of the spines.

Photos were tacked to what might have been a corkboard. They were faded black and white images of men in Nazi uniforms. One showed a younger Ava with a very elderly man, both wearing diving gear, standing beside what looked like a small submergible.

"Was that your grandfather?" I asked.

Ava turned back to me, glanced at the photo and nodded. "That was the last picture before..." She trailed off, with a haunted look returning to her eyes.

Abruptly, the grinding sounds came again. They were

muffled but still audible through the shielded walls.

On the chair, Andrew stirred, opening his eyes and grimacing with fear.

We all waited until the grinding sounds ceased.

I was going to ask what that was, but didn't for some reason.

Andrew settled back in his chair, closing his eyes again.

"How long have you been down here?" I asked.

Ava studied me, and I wondered if she was going to laugh again. "You are not like them in more ways than one."

I knew she meant Spiro and Andrew. I shrugged in lieu of an answer.

"I'm right, aren't I?" she asked.

"Yes."

"Why is this?" she asked.

I decided to take a chance. "I'm from Earth like your grandfather."

"You lie!" she said, sounding angry.

I shook my head, waiting.

She finally asked, "How did you reach Atlantis?"

"Do you know what a Traveler is?"

For a second—maybe even shorter than that—shock appeared on her face. She smoothed that away almost instantly, acting as if it had never happened.

"One who makes a journey," she said in an offhand manner.

"That's one definition. Another is a person able to use ancient obelisks and ziggurats to teleport to former Planets of the Harmony."

She eyed me closely. "Do you expect me to believe such nonsense?"

"I'm an American. Well, I was an American. I used to be in the United States Marines. Now, I battle… well, among others, the shape-changing Krekelens on Earth."

She paled and swayed, finding a chair and sitting on it. She rubbed her forehead before looking up at me again. "You're really an American from Earth?"

"Sure am."

She smiled briefly, wistfully. It transformed her face into a

181

vision of beauty. Then she changed back to her neutral look. "You asked me how long I've been here. I'm going to take that to mean here below. The answer is three years, two months and twelve days." She said that without hesitation, adding, "Time becomes precise when you're alone in the deep."

"Not entirely alone, though," I said.

Her lips thinned. "What are you implying?"

"You've seen their kind before," I said, jerking a thumb at Spiro. "I suspect that means you've had interaction with them."

She nodded. "You're correct, not entirely alone." She got up and moved to Andrew, checking his pulse at his throat, her fingers gentle but clinical.

Even so, Andrew jerked as if pinched, his eyes opening as he stared up at her. Then his eyelids drooped and shut as he returned to his semi-delirious state.

"Your friend is stabilizing," Ava said. "The shielding in the walls helps, but unfortunately, it's only temporary. Everything here is temporary."

Ava moved away from Andrew and pulled up a stool, sitting with her rifle within easy reach. "So, let us get to it, Mr. American Marine. You evaded the patrolling U-boat and battled the megalodons." She crossed her legs, her movements graceful despite the practical clothing. "That's more than most manage."

"You saw that?" I asked.

"I monitor everything near the facility." She smiled slightly. "That was an impressive use of an Atlantean sled and an ancient, off-world weapon."

I didn't rise to the bait about the hollow tube. If she wanted to ask me about it, she'd have to do it directly. Then I wondered if Omilcar might have contacted her. The psi-master knew about the weapon's origin. Was that a giveaway on her part? She must be party to one side or another. It probably meant something ominous that her grandfather had been a Nazi.

"You say the U-boat patrols," I said. "Who crews the vessel?"

"Those who fear to enter my station," she said.

"Yours?"

"The Fourth Reich if you wish to be technical."

"The U-boat isn't part of that?" I asked.

"Not any longer," she said.

I thought about that. She was being evasive about the U-boat and its crew. Should I push it or let her lead the conversation for now? If she'd really been alone here for over three years, she might have a screw loose, maybe more than one. I didn't want to set her off. Maybe I should come at this from a different angle.

"The megalodons were clearly bioengineered," I said. "Do you know who did that?"

She studied me with those striking eyes. "Even though you've told me you're an American—and a Traveler—you haven't explained why you're here. I've taken you into my home. I believe I deserve to know your intentions."

I glanced at Spiro, who had turned to listen to us. He now nodded slightly.

I regarded Ava, and despite my fatigue from using the hollow tube, it was time to play a game of wits with her, possibly a deadly one.

We had walked into something bigger down here. Omilcar had told me on Sky Island that there were factions on the Krekelen Psi-Master side. The Great Sark of Mu had used his psionics when we'd been outside, and Andrew had chased him away.

How did Ava play into all this? She obviously knew many things I did not. I sighed inwardly. It was time to play a delicate game of words, and to do it right or risk...

That was the thing. I didn't know all the gambles, odds, and the risks. I wanted to kill Omilcar, and I didn't even know if he was on the station.

I regarded Ava, and began to talk.

-39-

"You must be aware that some Atlanteans entered stasis tubes at the beginning of the Great Catastrophe," I said.

Ava nodded.

"Some of those have finally woken up."

"Yes," she said.

"You surely know then that Spiro and Andrew are such Atlanteans."

"I do, but I didn't know if you knew."

"They've been searching for this place in the U-boat *Triton*."

Something flickered across her face, but I couldn't determine what it meant. "The *Triton* is not the first such vessel to visit here. Most don't make it past the outer defenses."

"What happened?"

"What happens to anything that descends too deep?" Ava leaned forward. "The pressure crushes it."

Was she trying to be funny?

I'd meant any others that had made it into the facility. Had she known that and deliberately changed the subject?

I noticed that her hand was closer to the rifle. Despite her casual pose, she seemed tense, ready to react hard against us.

In fact, I felt that if I asked the wrong question, she'd explode into action against us.

I'd read a book once called *The Gift of Fear*. It had spoken about the positive uses of fear. One of the more interesting stories had been about a police detective questioning a victim of assault. She'd told the detective that it was funny, but her dogs had known the perpetrator had been a bad man, as they hadn't liked him. The detective shook his head. "The dogs didn't know. The dogs knew you knew he was bad. They read you."

The book's point was that we often know something is bad, even though we don't know why. Our gut or instinct realizes it. Our subconscious picks up on cues that our conscious mind overlooks. The subconscious realizes things aren't right with the situation and tries to inform us through vague feelings of fear.

The book's point was this: listen to your fear, your subconscious, when you feel that something is off. Most times, just get the hell out of there.

I felt that here with Dr. Ava Kraus. Something was definitely off, but my conscious mind hadn't grasped what that was yet.

It was time for another approach with this blonde-haired beauty, this possible hair-trigger lunatic that pretended to hold it together.

"You strike me as a sentinel," I said, "watching and waiting for something."

It took Ava a half-beat, as if she needed time to switch mental gears. Three years alone might have caused that. Frankly, I was surprised she was doing as well as she was. Most people would have become mentally unstable in her position.

"Someone has to watch." Ava gestured at the laboratory equipment. "Grandfather understood the station's importance.

185

After he was gone, I continued his work."

"What kind of work?"

Her smile became sad. "The kind that keeps things contained." She rose abruptly and moved to a cabinet. "Would you like some coffee? Real coffee—I insist on certain luxuries, even down here."

She was being evasive and cryptic, both qualities I abhorred. Yet, I hadn't had a cup of java for an insanely long time.

"I'd love a cup."

"Your friends," she said shortly, "they're like the others who came before, the ones who remembered."

"Remembered what?"

She handed me a cup of coffee.

I held it reverently and actually trembled as I took the first sip. This was even better than I remembered.

"Very good," I said.

"Thank you. That's the question, isn't it?"

"Excuse me?"

"What did your two friends remember that drove them deeper to here?"

I glanced at Spiro. The captain seemed absorbed with the lab equipment. Andrew was out on the chair, snoring softly.

"They remembered the Great Catastrophe," I said. "They also wish to fix what they might have caused."

"Fix?" she asked.

I nodded, taking another sip.

"How interesting," she said.

I was going to ask why. Then the grinding sounds came again.

Andrew stirred but didn't wake up this time.

Then the awful sounds ceased abruptly.

"What is that?" I asked.

"You'll know soon enough." Ava sipped her coffee, watching me over the rim. "I wonder, however, if you'll survive the knowledge."

I was growing frustrated with these cryptic comments and evasions, although the coffee helped.

"How many others have made it into the facility?" I asked.

"Since Grandfather?"

"Sure," I said.

"There have been three expeditions. There's also one called Omilcar seeking permission to enter."

Despite myself, I stiffened.

She noticed. "Ah. There's history between you two."

I said nothing, and I wondered how the psi-master sought this permission and how Ava could enforce a negative response. Had the megalodons been hers? Why hadn't she shot us out of hand then earlier?

Ava set down her cup. "I have no doubt Omilcar seeks the helmets like the others before him. But the deep places require preparation and understanding." Her eyes lingered on mine. "And sacrifice."

What had she sacrificed to survive down here? What did these helmets do that Omilcar wanted one?

The grinding noises came yet again, closer this time, and different—more like metal being twisted. Even through the shielded walls, the sound sent a shiver down my spine.

Andrew jerked upright, his eyes flashing open. "Something's changing," he said in a high-pitched voice.

Ava's head snapped toward him as her casual demeanor vanished. "What do you sense?"

"More pressure." Andrew pressed his hand against his temple. "It's searching and reaching out."

Ava's lips tightened. "We should move. Given the new situation, the shielding won't last much longer."

As if to emphasize her words, the lights flickered, and the symbols on the walls pulsed with a sickly blue glow.

Ava rushed about, checking readouts on various instruments. She turned to me. "Your friend's heightened sensitivity is creating a pathway. We have less than an hour before the configurations shift."

"Configurations?" Captain Spiro stepped closer to her monitoring equipment. "These readings…" He reached out.

"Don't touch that!" Ava shouted.

But it was too late. As Spiro's fingers brushed the display, every light in the room surged blindingly bright.

Andrew let out a piercing cry, his face twisted with fear.

Ava slammed her hand down on what looked like an emergency switch. The lights dimmed to normal, but the damage was done. I felt it now—a subtle vibration in the walls, in my bones, like something massive was stirring outside.

"There's no more time." Ava rushed to a locker and began pulling out equipment. "We need to reach the lower chamber before whatever is stirring fully awakens."

"Before what fully awakens?" I asked, tired of these cryptic comments.

Ava turned to me. "You'd better pray you never find out. Now help me with this gear. We need to move, and we need to move now."

"Take these." Ava removed what looked like modified diving helmets from the locker. They were old—possibly World War II vintage—but someone had extensively reworked them. Dark metal plates had been grafted onto the sides, marked with those same shifting symbols we'd seen in the corridors and on these walls. The faceplates were covered in copper mesh.

The grinding noise returned as I studied my helmet. I didn't like how the vibrations of the grind were changing.

"The helmets will provide some protection," Ava said, handing them out. "Not as much as this room, but enough so we can keep moving. We're going to dare the deep, which should distract it long enough for us to proceed."

Andrew was barely keeping on his feet, leaning against a workbench. Blood trickled from his nose again. Even Spiro looked pale, rubbing his forehead as if fighting off a headache.

"How do the helmets work?" I asked, examining mine.

"The dark metal acts as a barrier against certain energies." Ava was already pulling more equipment from storage. "Grandfather found the metal in the lower chambers. It absorbs... certain energies."

She hesitated on the last part, as if deciding how much to reveal. Before I could press her, the lights flickered and Andrew stumbled.

"Take this." She tossed me a harness with various devices attached. Some appeared Atlantean; others looked Nazi-made. Still others were modern. Like everything else about her operation, she appeared to use whatever worked. "The meters will warn you if the field strength drops."

I'd noticed those.

I helped Andrew adjust his helmet and harness. His skin felt cold and clammy. Whatever affected him was getting worse.

Spiro studied the etched plates on his helmet. "I've seen these before," he muttered. "In the deep..."

Ava's head snapped toward him. Another sound interrupted—not the grinding this time, but a low moan that seemed to emanate from the facility itself. The copper mesh on the walls vibrated.

"There's no more time." Ava grabbed a pack and her rifle. "We need to move. Now!"

"Which way will we go?" I asked, adjusting my hollow tube so it wouldn't tangle with the harness.

"I already said, down." She checked her rifle's action. "Always deeper into the facility."

I didn't like the way she said that, or how her hands shook as she loaded magazines into the pack. Someone this competent didn't show fear easily. What did the grinding sounds portend?

Then the moaning sound came again, and this time the lights did more than flicker—they pulsed in rhythm.

Andrew made a choking sound behind his faceplate.

"Stay close to me." Ava hurried toward the door. "Don't touch the walls. Don't look too long at any symbols you see. And no matter what you hear..." She paused, those blue eyes intense behind her faceplate. "Don't answer it."

With that encouraging advice, she opened the door and led us back into the facility's corridors. The relative safety of the shielded room vanished as we stepped out. Now there was only a rush to reach the deep to trick it for a time. How that would make any difference, or what we were trying to do after that, I didn't know yet. I didn't know what "it" was either.

I hurried after Ava, liking the shape of her ass as she ran. Then I chided myself, as it felt unfaithful to Livi. I shook my head. Livi was gone—

The wash of anger I felt at that helped me. I wasn't sure what dangers this place held. I sure didn't know enough about Dr. Ava Kraus.

I sighed. Livi was gone. I was underwater in Atlantis with an increasingly bizarre situation, and I trusted a Nazi's granddaughter to help us.

I definitely needed to keep my head in the game.

-41-

The corridors became stranger as we descended. The clean precision of the upper facility gave way to what seemed like organic curves, as if the walls had once flowed like wax. The symbols were different here too—more twisted and shifty. I kept my eyes forward, remembering Ava's warning about staring too long.

Our helmet lamps cast light and caused shadows. The facility's lighting still worked but grew increasingly unreliable, creating pools of darkness between stuttering overheads. The air felt thicker, almost oily against any exposed skin.

We passed a makeshift barricade—tables and equipment thrown together as if in desperate haste. Brass cartridge cases littered the floor, along with darker stains. Some of the cases were from MP40s—WWII Nazi weapons. But there were other signs too, the most interesting being the unmistakable marks of energy weapons I'd seen before on other worlds.

"Someone made a stand here," I said quietly.

"Two years ago." Ava didn't slow down. "It was a Krekelen expedition with Ophidian muscle. Like the others, they thought their weapons would be enough."

"You know about the Krekelens?" I asked.

"Oh, yes," Ava said. "You don't think my grandfather didn't understand that something else drove our country during the terrible World War? It took answers from Atlantis to understand some of that."

I'd never thought about that. How much of human history was stained by Krekelen interference? Had the bloodbaths of World Wars One and Two been partly on the reptilian shape-changers?

We reached a junction where the corridor split three ways. Spiro suddenly stopped, staring at markings above one passage.

"This way," he said. "The maintenance tunnels lead to…" He trailed off, blinking in confusion.

"How did you know that?" Ava asked sharply.

"I don't know," Spiro said. "The symbols, they just seemed…" He shook his head.

Andrew groaned behind us, swaying, but at least neither his nose nor his eyes were bleeding like before.

"He's right, though," Ava said. "The maintenance tunnels are our fastest route down. Assuming they're still intact."

I studied the passages. The one Spiro indicated sloped downward at a steeper angle. The symbols above it seemed to writhe when I looked at them too long.

Were Spiro and Andrew remembering more from their past? I still wondered if Andrew might have psionic power. Did the Pre-Great Catastrophe Atlanteans know about such things?

We started down the steeply sloping passage. The walls here were scarred with tool marks and energy weapon burns. Recent damage overlaid older wounds. The temperature was also rising noticeably.

Spiro trailed his hand along the wall, lost in thought.

"Don't do that," Ava said.

Spiro pulled his hand away, staring at her.

"It can track through that," she said. "We're trying to sneak through as it readies itself to break into my home. Think of it as a sniffing hound."

Spiro frowned.

"Just do it," I said.

Spiro nodded absently. "We maintained these corridors long ago. When the power cores needed..." He seemed to grope for words.

"Don't do that!" Ava snapped. "Don't try to remember— not here anyway and not yet."

We continued. The passage curved downward in a spiral. In time, more signs of battle appeared—blast marks and bullet holes. A broken helmet like ours lay in a corner, its faceplate cracked. The mesh had been torn away, as if by massive force.

"The Krekelens thought they could control it," Ava said, following my gaze. "They always think they can control it."

"Control what?" I asked.

Ava didn't answer. Instead, she pointed ahead where the passage opened into a larger chamber. "We need to be careful here. The floor isn't fully stable."

The chamber floor had partially collapsed, revealing older areas below. Ancient machinery lay exposed, still humming with power.

"The configurations are breaking down," Spiro muttered, then pressed his hands against his helmet as if shocked by his own words.

"There's a maintenance catwalk," Ava said, moving to one wall.

I followed her to where a narrow walkway clung to the wall, half-hidden by shadows. It looked barely wide enough for single file. Parts had corroded away entirely, leaving gaps we'd have to jump.

Andrew swayed; I grabbed his arm to steady him.

"I'll go first," Ava said. "Step exactly where I step. Don't look down for too long. And whatever you hear calling from below, don't answer."

She started along the catwalk. Andrew followed, then came Spiro, with me bringing up the rear. The metal creaked under our combined weight.

We reached the first gap. Ava crossed it with a confident

leap. The rest of us followed one after another. The second gap was wider. As Ava studied it, I heard voices drifting up from the open space—whispers in languages I didn't know, yet somehow understood.

"Come down... see the truth... remember who you were..."

"Don't listen," Ava said. "It lies. It always lies."

She backed up a few steps, then took a running jump across the gap. The metal groaned as she landed. One by one, we followed.

We were halfway across when Andrew stumbled; for a horrible moment, I thought he would fall. But Spiro grabbed and hauled him back. As Andrew sagged against the wall, blood streaming from his nose, I saw something move below.

I couldn't help it; I looked closer. A shape formed—vast, dark, reaching up. The whispers grew louder, more insistent as it did that.

"So close now... come see... remember..."

"Run!" Ava screamed.

We half-dragged Andrew as the catwalk shuddered. Metal groaned behind us as something pulled at it.

Ava reached the far side and helped pull us up. The last section of catwalk tore free just as I leaped, crashing down into the old chamber.

The whispers rose into screams of frustration, then faded.

We lay there panting, collecting our strength.

"It's getting stronger," Ava said quietly. "We have less time than I thought."

I watched her check her rifle with trembling hands. Despite all her experience down here, the dark thing frightened her as much as it did us. Maybe more, because she understood what it really was.

"How much farther are we going?" I asked.

"Too far," she said. "And that was just the first threshold. It gets worse from here, at least for a time."

I'd just about had my fill of these evasive answers.

As I helped Andrew to his feet, I wondered how many more thresholds we'd cross before we found what we were looking for.

Or before *it* found us.

-42-

The corridor ahead looked different. The walls had a wet sheen, though they were dry to the touch. Our helmet lamps cast shifting reflections.

"Something's not right," Andrew gasped. "It's... turning elsewhere. It knows we've left and wonders if—"

I was about to ask what he meant when every light died—both our helmet lamps and the facility's ancient lighting. The darkness felt alive, pressing against us.

"Don't move," Ava whispered. "Don't make a sound."

Didn't whispers count as sounds?

In the pitch black, I heard something slide across metal. Then I saw a faint blue glow emanating from the walls.

"It's projecting," Ava whispered. "Looking through memories. Don't let it find yours."

What the hell was she talking about now?

Then the glow intensified, becoming like a TV screen. I

saw Ophidian soldiers frozen in a tableau of horror, their weapons useless. Nazi troops firing at enemies they couldn't hit. Krekelens trying to shape-shift into forms that might survive.

A tendril of blue light extended from the wall and reached for Andrew. He screamed as it touched his helmet, the sound cutting off as if muted. The metal plates on his helmet began to corrode.

Ava rushed over and yanked him toward what looked like a maintenance alcove. "The shielding still works in these."

We squeezed in after her as the blue light probed more, lashing about blindly. I held Andrew up, feeling him shiver. Through gaps in the ancient shielding, I watched the tendril of light continue its search.

This grew as more tendrils reached out. Then they joined or coalesced into a shape—not solid, but suggesting immense mass. The mass moved like smoke, drifting through the corridor, as it seemed to sniff.

"The Krekelens thought they could fight it," Ava whispered. "Their shape-shifting, their weapons, nothing worked. It reaches inside, finds out what you really are before it devours."

"How did your grandfather survive it?" I whispered.

"He learned to hide and wait, just as we're doing now. The projections pass if you give them nothing to latch onto. In the end, though, it found my grandfather like it finds everyone daring to come down here."

The smoky, faintly blue-glowing mass drifted closer. My head began to pound as it did. Images flashed through my mind—Livi, Sky Island, the fiery staff burning Draconians. I gritted my teeth, trying to force the memories down.

The smoky mass paused. For a moment, I thought it had sensed us. Then it moved on, the blue light fading, leaving darkness again.

We waited several minutes before Ava dared to speak. "The facility's lights and our headlamps will return soon. Be ready to run. These projections are like antibodies. The deeper we go, the more we'll encounter, although not along a path we're going to use."

"Antibodies?" I asked. "Against what?"

"Us," she said simply. "Everything down here is a defense system. But defending against what? Or for what?" She shook her head. "Grandfather died trying to understand."

I didn't believe her about that. I would bet my bottom dollar she knew exactly what the thing defended and why.

The lights flickered back on. A moment later, she had us turn on our headlamps. Andrew's helmet was pitted where the faint blue light had touched it. The walls around us showed similar decay, except in our shielded alcove.

We moved quickly, watching for more blue reflections or tendrils of light. I understood now why previous expeditions had failed. How can you fight something that can turn your own memories into weapons?

The answer was obvious—you don't. You hide, run and survive. But we were heading deeper, toward whatever the thing was defending.

I had a feeling we'd find out soon enough whether that was a good idea or bad.

The corridor opened into what might have once been a research station. Old Nazi equipment mixed with Atlantean technology—workbenches, monitoring devices, recording equipment. Papers covered in German script were scattered across the floor, some marked with rust-colored stains.

"Grandfather's last outpost," Ava said quietly. "He wouldn't go deeper than this."

I studied the nearest workbench. Sketches showed an attempt to map the facility's lower levels. The later drawings grew increasingly erratic, with the neat German thoroughness giving way to frenzied scribbling.

"Here." Ava pulled open a drawer, removing an old journal. "This was his final entry."

I glanced at the open notebook. The writing was in English, which seemed weird: *The configurations align. Now I understand what sleeps below. God help us if it wakes. The Russians must never…*

"The Russians?" I asked, looking up. The rest after that had been illegible.

Ava shook her head. "His mind regressed at the end. He

remembered the terrible days of late 1944 and early 1945, especially when the Russians advanced across Poland."

Spiro had wandered to a wall covered in technical diagrams. Without touching the wall, his hand traced symbols that matched the plates on our helmets. "This was a monitoring station. We used them to... to watch for signs."

"Signs of what?" I asked.

Before he could answer, Andrew collapsed. Luckily, I was close and caught him before he hit the floor. His eyes had rolled back with trickles of blood seeping from one.

"The helmet won't protect him much longer," Ava said. "We have to decide now. Return to the surface, or..." She gestured at a massive door set into the far wall. Ancient symbols pulsed across its surface.

"What's down there?" I asked.

"The truth about the entity and why Atlantis really sank." Ava checked her rifle before staring at me. "The truth about what your friends really are."

The grinding sound returned, closer than ever. The room's lights flickered, and in the dimness, I saw blue reflections starting to form on the walls.

"Choose quickly," Ava said. "We're out of time."

I looked at the door, then at my companions. Spiro nodded grimly. Even Andrew, barely conscious, managed to whisper, "We go down."

The decision felt heavy, final, like stepping off a cliff in the dark. I still didn't know enough. How did Omilcar fit into all this? But if that blue glow attacked us again...

"How do we open the door?" I asked.

Ava moved to a control panel. "Like this." She pressed her palm against it. Ancient machinery groaned to life.

As the massive door began to swing open, I saw more symbols like the ones on our helmets. But these were different, more complex.

Beyond the threshold lay darkness.

"Let's do it," I said.

Ava took a deep breath and led the way.

"Go," I told Spiro. "Help Andrew."

The two ancient Atlanteans went next.

I decided to take a risk. I raced to the drawer where Ava had picked up a journal. There were more as I'd suspected. I grabbed the ones from the bottom and stuffed them in my pack.

This was a crazy adventure, and I was beginning to get a bad vibe from Dr. Ava Kraus. Why hadn't she gone down before? Or maybe she had. How did she know this held the answers to ancient Atlantis? Or did she read that from our minds? Or might it even be more sinister than that?

"Mr. Bayard," Spiro called.

"I'm coming," I said, hurrying to the massive door. As I passed it, the door began to swing shut. This was it, baby. We were committed.

-43-

My boots rang against the ancient metal flooring as we descended deeper into the facility.

We used the headlamps on our helmets, which washed over otherwise dark bulkheads. That made it eerie, as did the strange echoes around us. Maybe that had something to do with how deep we were, or it was an air pressure issue.

I kept the hollow tube ready, though my arms and body still ached from the megalodon battle. In truth, I'd been functioning, with frayed nerves, pushed on by the excitement of all this. I needed a break—as I was beat.

Ava had taken point, moving with a confidence that had started to bother me. In fact, her entire performance was beginning to feel... I'm not sure exactly. Three years alone in this place should have left some mark, some hesitation in her. Instead, she navigated the dark turns without pausing, her rifle held with practiced ease. She seldom checked landmarks unless one of us was watching her. She always seemed to know when we were, too. Nor did she show moments of uncertainty, ever.

I thought about that: over three years alone down here, with the grinding noises, the dead, and the debris from the old firefights. I'd have become a wreck. Would I even be able to look new people in the eye? Would I trust them with a dangerous mission like this, going deep with them when I knew that was super iffy?

Was Ava playing a game with us, using us for her own nefarious purposes? What might that purpose be?

One of my hands strayed on my pack where I'd stuffed the notebooks. Why had I grabbed them? It was distrust of Ava, wasn't it? That the journals might give me a clue about her and all this.

I might have nodded, but I had a feeling Ava would notice. What was I sensing about her? Man, but she had a great ass and kisser. After the past week stuck in a U-boat with these Atlantean scientists—

I had to quit thinking about her that way, or the others would think I was carrying a second gun in my pants.

What a mess. A Nazi babe led us and I distrusted the hell out of her. Yes, there it was—the truth at last.

I kept a careful distance behind Ava, watching the terrain. Captain Spiro followed me, with Andrew bringing up the rear.

It began to feel like a slog that I'd been on with a thousand switchbacks as the platoon worked up a steep mountain. That had been in Bhutan, in the Himalayan Mountains. Instead of switchbacks, we turned into new corridors, but they were all beginning to look the same in the damn darkness.

"We should rest," Spiro said after what felt like hours of descent. "If nothing else, the air's getting thinner."

I perked up, realizing the captain was right about that. My lungs had noticed it although my conscious mind hadn't. I was panting.

Ava studied us before she nodded.

We found an alcove that offered a bit of protection. It looked like an old maintenance bay with inactive machinery. Ancient tools hung on the walls, their purposes unclear to us.

I swear that Ava positioned herself where she could watch

all of us. She didn't laugh nervously or even with relief. Where was the psychological strain of long-term isolation? I'd seen what solitude did to men in combat zones. A few months could break the strongest minds. Three years alone in this place should have left deeper scars.

"I'll take first watch," I said. "The rest of you should try to sleep."

I needed some sleep, too, desperately, but I'd never get it thinking about the notebooks I carried. I was dying to start reading them. Besides, I think the coffee was still stimulating my system.

Ava hesitated, then nodded. She settled against a wall with the rifle across her lap. Her breathing settled into an unnaturally regular pattern almost immediately.

Okay, that wasn't strange at all. Did she trust the three blokes with her? Even if she did, that was a weird performance.

I watched as Andrew and Spiro settled down. Then I found a spot they couldn't see me right away.

I opened my pack and took out the first notebook. The writing was neat and exact, just what you'd expect from a Nazi scientist.

I began to page through it, looking for something interesting. It didn't take long to find. I focused and started reading:

Personal Journal of Dr. Werner Kraus Chief Scientific Officer, Project Übergang 15 May 1945

Today we have achieved what ancient man could only dream of in myth. The four U-boats of our expedition have crossed between worlds. I record this for posterity, though my hand trembles as I write. The enormity of what we witnessed... but I must be methodical. I must document everything precisely.

What began in 1938, during our first Antarctic expedition to Neuschwabenland, has culminated in this moment. I remember standing on the deck of the MS Schwabenland, watching our Dornier aircraft map Queen Maud Land. None of us expected to find what lay beneath that ice. The cave system we discovered in the western mountains held far more than the mineral deposits we sought for the Reich.

Those transfer rings—massive mechanical constructs buried beneath the ice. For six years, I studied their engineering, documenting the complex interplay of magnetic fields and gravitational lenses. The high command thought we were merely searching for a secret base location. Only those of us in the inner circle of Project Übergang understood the truth—that the Atlanteans had built a mechanical gateway between worlds.

I paused in my reading. How did they know it was Atlantean and a gateway? Maybe Dr. Werner Kraus had written the reasons earlier. This was crazy cool. Why did Antarctica seem to hold all the wild technology on Earth?

I shook my head and continued to read.

At 0347 hours today, our small flotilla reached the coordinates where we had retrofitted the chamber with diesel generators, diesel storage pods to top off our fuel tanks, and stabilizing equipment. U-2542 and U-2544, our Type XXI boats, took point on the hydraulic tracks, while our Type VIIs took up station behind them. Kapitän Heydrich ordered us to synchronize with the ancient mechanisms at precisely 103 meters—matching the focal point of the primary displacement ring.

The water temperature dropped precipitously as the massive flywheels began to spin. Several crew members reported the same disorientation we documented in our initial tests—that peculiar sensation of localized gravitational distortion. The hull creaked under impossible pressures. I feared we had miscalculated the structural tolerances.

Then it happened. The phenomenon began as a deep mechanical thrumming through the hull, not unlike the resonance tests we conducted at Kiel. The water beyond our viewing ports took on a peculiar distortion, like heat waves rippling through liquid glass. Kapitän Heydrich ordered full ahead, and we pierced what I can only describe as a temporarily stabilized discontinuity in space itself.

The transition lasted approximately 12 seconds. We experienced complete electrical failure, as our tests had predicted. In that darkness, many of us were certain we would die. The pressure on the hull was enormous. Later examination showed the steel had actually compressed by several millimeters.

When power restored, we found ourselves in what appeared to be an underwater cavern, illuminated by bands of phosphorescent organisms along the rock walls. The water here was different—denser, with unique mineral properties I must analyze further. Our compasses spun uselessly. The stars, when we later surfaced, were wrong.

But I get ahead of myself. We had barely oriented ourselves when the creature appeared. Far larger than any known marine species, it displayed both cephalopod and cetacean characteristics. Its size defied reason—easily twice the length of our Type XXI U-boat. It approached with terrible intelligence in its eyes. Only the quick thinking of Kapitän Heydrich, ordering an emergency wake cavitation, drove it away.

The creature's appearance validated the crude drawings we had found carved into the Antarctica chamber walls—the ones High Command dismissed as primitive art. The ancient ones had encountered these beings before, krakens as spoken about in Greek myths. What else from those carvings might prove true?

We have surfaced now, in darkness. The ocean stretches endlessly in all directions. There is no land in sight. The men try to maintain discipline, but I see the truth in their eyes—we can never return. The Durchgangstor collapsed behind us, just as the calculations suggested it would. The energy signature faded to nothing, leaving us truly alone.

I knew enough German to figure out that Durchgangstor meant Passage Gate. I thought of it as Ramsbotham Jump Gate, one I'd read about in Heinlein's 1955 novel, *Tunnel in the Sky*.

I keep reading.

We are committed now. The Führer's vision of establishing

205

a new Reich may be impossible here, but perhaps we have found something far more significant. These waters hold their secrets. The chamber carvings spoke of an advanced civilization. If even half of what they claimed is true…

Our four U-boats hold the future now—217 men, 12 women (all wives of senior officers), and 8 children. Plus our supplies, weapons, and most critically, the research materials from Project Übergang. We must find safe harbor soon. The Type VIIs are showing signs of stress from the transition.

I must rest now. Tomorrow we begin depth soundings and establish a search pattern. The men need a purpose. The pressure of the endless ocean weighs on all of us—both physical and psychological. Kapitän Heydrich has ordered regular maintenance checks on all pressure hulls. We cannot afford any failures out here.

When I close my eyes, I still see those gigantic flywheels beneath the Antarctic ice. What other wonders—or horrors— await us in these alien waters? We have crossed an ocean of stars to reach this place. May both God and science protect us in this new world.

—WK

After thirty minutes of reading, I heard water dripping somewhere in the darkness. The sound was regular, almost like a heartbeat. I caught myself counting the drops and forced myself to stop. These endless corridors would mess with your head if you let them.

What I was reading in this journal was spellbinding, some of the real but hidden history of the world. Some Nazis had escaped at the end of World War II—some of them to Atlantis. Who would ever believe me if I told them?

I kept reading. I couldn't help it. The doctor's account dragged my interest so I had to know what happened next.

-44-

Personal Journal of Dr. Werner Kraus Chief Scientific Officer, Project Übergang June 12, 1945

After twenty-eight days of methodical search patterns, we found salvation. What we discovered today exceeds our greatest hopes.

At 0715 hours, U-2542's sonar detected an unusual echo at 127 meters depth. Initial readings suggested structures. Given our previous disappointments with similar readings, Kapitän Heydrich was reluctant to risk another dive. However, our Type XXI's improved depth capabilities justified the attempt.

What we found was no mere ruins.

The underwater city (for there is no other word for it) rises from the seabed like a dream of lost antiquity. Vast structures of some glass-like material remain intact despite the crushing depths. Most extraordinary were the huge dome-shaped buildings, perfectly preserved. The engineering principles involved in their construction must be revolutionary—they show no signs of stress from the enormous pressure.

But it was what we found in one of the outlying structures that changes everything. It is a maintenance facility, perhaps, or some kind of manufacturing center. The equipment inside... I hardly know how to describe it. Machines that seemed to operate on principles we barely comprehended, yet with clear industrial purpose. Most incredibly, some still function after what must be thousands of years underwater.

Unterscharführer Weber, our mining engineer, believes he has already decoded the basic operations of several pieces of excavation equipment. The controls showed remarkable standardization—almost as if they were designed to be intuitive to users of any origin. We have begun cataloging everything systematically.

Our first successful salvage operation concluded at 1900 hours. The Type XXI's cargo doors proved adequate for retrieving smaller pieces of equipment. The real breakthrough came from discovering what appears to be ancient diving apparatus. After careful study, we were able to adapt it to work with our own breathing equipment. This allowed us to establish our first proper underwater work crew.

The diving suits are remarkable—far more flexible than our own gear, yet providing better pressure protection. With these, we can operate effectively even at this depth. Already, Weber's team has retrieved what appears to be a complete set of underwater cutting tools. The principles are similar to our own acetylene torches, but far more advanced.

Most significant is what we found in a sealed chamber— detailed technical schematics etched into metal plates. While the language is unknown to us, the technical drawings are clear enough. They appear to be maintenance diagrams for various pieces of underwater equipment. This will prove invaluable as we salvage more.

After lengthy discussion with the other expedition leaders, we have decided to establish our first base near this location. The site offers several critical advantages:

Proximity to salvageable technology

208

Natural concealment from surface observation

Depths accessible to our U-boats but challenging for more primitive vessels

Several underwater caverns suitable for concealed docking

Evidence of ancient power systems we may be able to restore

Tomorrow we will begin converting U-2544 into a semi-permanent base while the other boats continue salvage operations. The men's morale has improved dramatically. There is light in their eyes again—the look of men who see a future before them.

One troubling note: during our exploration, we found evidence of previous inhabitants, recent inhabitants. Hidden hatches had been forced open, equipment moved. Someone else has visited this facility, perhaps multiple times. We must accelerate our plans and establish proper defenses before we encounter them.

The Third Reich may have fallen, but here we had found something far greater—the technological legacy of an advanced civilization. We will learn its secrets, adapt its tools, and forge a new future in these waters. Our children will thank us for this discovery.

—WK

[Addendum: Technical notes on initial equipment recovery attached to following pages. Priority must be given to power generation systems and manufacturing tools. We have limited diesel fuel remaining and must establish independent infrastructure quickly.]

I heard Andrew shift restlessly in his sleep.

Realizing I'd been reading for quite some time and my eyes burned with fatigue, I put away the notebook, awed at what I'd discovered.

The fleeing Nazis had found the edges of ancient Atlantean technology. Furthermore, the scientist Dr. Werner Kraus approached the problems logically and forthrightly.

I wanted to read more, but I felt it prudent to hide what I'd discovered. For one thing, I wasn't sure how Ava would take my reading this.

Andrew sat up. His face was pale, and fresh blood trickled from his nose again. He wiped it away with the back of his hand, leaving a red smear that looked black in the dim lamplight.

Ava's eyes opened instantly at his movement—too quickly for someone who'd been sleeping. She sat up, looking around as if fully alert, almost like a lizard.

"I'm beat," I said. "Who stays up next?"

"I will," she said.

I nodded, laying down and falling almost instantly asleep. My eyes had been getting very heavy.

Soon, I dreamed about U-boats and terrible explosions, water pouring everywhere as I sought to escape a drowning death.

I awoke to escape a broken U-boat and fell back into troubled sleep almost right away. I hated this underwater facility. There were secrets and factions everywhere. What did Omilcar want with this place? How many people or beings worked on his side?

I woke up later, feeling even more tired than before. That was actually good. After a truly good night's sleep, I tend to wake up cranky at first. It's only as I get going that I realize my body has been refreshed.

We ate and drank from our rations and packed up, pressing deeper still. Instead of thinner air like earlier, the air grew noticeably heavier, almost humid. Condensation beaded on the walls, running down in rivulets that appeared to follow particular patterns.

Our footsteps echoed differently now, suggesting something that I didn't understand.

In time, another sealed door blocked our path, a massive structure clearly designed for security. While Spiro and Andrew struggled with the manual override mechanism, I watched Ava. She stood too still, like a predator waiting. There was no fidgeting, no nervous tics, nothing that struck me as human.

I frowned, thinking that seemed like an odd conclusion on my part. Was my subconscious trying to tell me something? Ava wasn't a predator—she had helped us and guided us down. I realized then that we didn't head toward any one particular thing. She'd spoken before about some kind of helmets and about reaching them. But how would these helmets help us in the end?

Before I could broach the topic, Ava spoke. "These old systems can be temperamental. If you could move aside, please?"

Spiro and Andrew looked back at her.

Ava waited, though she could have easily stepped beside them to handle it herself.

Instead, they moved aside.

Ava stepped up and pressed a specific sequence of controls. The huge door opened smoothly.

That wasn't suspicious at all. Why had she let them fumble with it if she'd known how to open it all along?

We passed through and continued our trek, doing little talking. Spiro and Andrew appeared to be lost in their own worlds, their memories surfacing more clearly than ever. Ava waited for something. I kept thinking about Dr. Werner Kraus's journal. I wanted to read more, but I knew I'd have to wait for the next rest period.

-45-

During our second rest period many hours later, I volunteered for first watch again. I noted that the machinery in this section looked more sophisticated, more alien.

Ava appeared to doze off against a wall, her rifle still at the ready.

Spiro and Andrew were exhausted, both of them soon snoring.

I picked my lookout spot and pulled out another notebook, thumbing through it before beginning to read again.

Personal Journal of Dr. Werner Kraus Chief Scientific Officer, Project Übergang August 3, 1945

After two months of careful salvage operations, we had our first encounter with the surface dwellers of this world. The incident merits careful documentation, as it will shape our future interactions with these people.

At 0430 hours, U-2542's watch crew spotted a sail on the horizon. Initial observation through periscope revealed a vessel unlike anything in Earth's maritime history—a massive galley propelled by both sail and oar power. Its construction was remarkable: twin-masted with an estimated length of 80 meters, wooden hull reinforced with some unknown metal at the waterline. The design showed sophisticated engineering principles despite its primitive materials.

Most striking were the oars—nearly 40 per side, each longer than a U-boat's beam. The synchronization of the rowers suggested a highly disciplined crew. By their size and positioning, these were clearly warriors, not slaves. Many bore elaborate armor that caught the dawn light.

After consulting Kapitän Heydrich and Standartenführer Wolff, we determined this was an opportunity we could not ignore. Our fuel reserves are critical, and these people clearly know how to survive on this endless ocean. We conducted a carefully planned contact.

U-2542 surfaced at 0545, maintaining 800 meters distance. The galley's reaction was interesting—they did not flee, but turned to face us and adopted what was clearly a defensive formation. Their discipline impressed even Standartenführer Wolff.

We launched our rubber boat with a carefully chosen contact team:

Myself (scientific observation)
Unteroffizier Meyer (our most "Nordic" looking sailor)
Dr. Hoffman (linguistics)
Two armed guards (concealed weapons)

As we approached, we observed their crew more closely. They are a race of giants—the smallest among them would stand eye-to-eye with our tallest men. Fair-haired and bearded, they could have stepped from Norse legend. Their leader, particularly, was a massive specimen with a forked beard and bearing that commanded instant respect.

Our attempts at communication proved frustrating. Dr.

Hoffman's expertise in Indo-European language roots was useless. Their speech has no correlation to any Earth language we know. However, they showed remarkable intelligence in establishing basic trade concepts through gesture.

The exchange that followed proved both profitable and informative:

We traded 10 kg of refined steel (ship repair plates)
Received in return:

Fresh fish and what appears to be cultivated seaweed
Two barrels of fresh water
A curious navigation device incorporating crystals
Samples of their metal hull reinforcement (pending analysis)

Most importantly, we learned they call themselves the "Sea Lords" (rough translation). They drew crude maps showing several surface settlements on massive floating platforms. This confirmed our sonar contacts from previous weeks. The encounter ended peacefully, but the strategic implications are significant.

While these Sea Lords are technically primitive compared to us, they are not savages. Their civilization has clearly mastered long-term survival on this ocean world. Their numbers must be substantial to crew such vessels. After extensive discussion with the leadership council, we have established the following policies regarding the Sea Lords:

Limited contact only—we cannot risk them discovering our base
Maintain massive technological advantage
Establish trade only through carefully controlled encounters
Never reveal our underwater salvage operations
Begin monitoring their major routes and settlements

Most critically: we must accelerate development of our defensive capabilities. While these Sea Lords seemed peaceful, their warrior culture is obvious. We cannot risk them eventually discovering our true numbers or capabilities.

Addendum: Analysis of their hull reinforcement proves fascinating. The metal is unlike anything in our experience— lighter than aluminum but with superior strength. More significantly, it shows signs of being salvaged from ancient Atlantean structures. The Sea Lords are scavengers of this world's past glories. This gives us a crucial advantage—we don't just salvage this technology, we can understand and reproduce it.

Tomorrow we begin mapping their trade routes. Knowledge of their movements will be crucial as we expand our operations. Still, I cannot help but admire their achievement. They have built a functioning civilization on these endless waters. But we will build something far greater.

—WK

[Technical notes on metal analysis and trade good specifications attached to following pages]

I looked up, thinking about what I had read. Dr. Werner Kraus was strategic. He indeed seemed like the right scientist for the job. I also recalled that both the Soviets and Americans after WWII had used captured German scientists in their space and missile programs. In some cases, those scientists had been instrumental in various successes, Dr. Werner Von Braun being a prime example of that.

This was getting interesting, and I wondered if there might be a passage concerning the Draconians.

I paged through the notebook, soon finding it.

Personal Journal of Dr. Werner Kraus Chief Scientific Officer, Project Übergang October 15, 1945

I must force myself to maintain scientific objectivity in recording today's events. The existence of non-human intelligences... even after all we've witnessed, this discovery challenges our most basic assumptions about this world.

At 0900 hours, U-2542's hydrophones detected unusual rhythmic sounds from the surface. Upon periscope observation, we witnessed something that would have seemed impossible two months ago: massive dirigibles patrolling in formation, each easily twice the size of our largest Zeppelins.

The truly extraordinary revelation came when we observed their crews through our Zeiss optics. The beings manning these airships were dinosaurian in nature, bipedal, roughly the size of small humans. Their physical characteristics suggest a completely separate evolutionary path from Earth life—yet they display obvious intelligence and technological sophistication.

Initial observation data:
4 dirigibles observed
Est. length: 180-200 meters each
Hydrogen lifted (based on cell structure)
Primitive but effective propulsion systems
Armed with projectile weapons (crossbow variants)
Sophisticated navigation systems (crystal-based, similar to Sea Lord devices)

At 1300 hours, the situation turned hostile. One of their patrol craft spotted U-2542 during a scheduled surfacing. Their response was immediate and coordinated. They dropped primitive but effective depth charges (black powder charges in pressure-triggered casings).

Damage report:
Minor hull breach on U-2542
Two crew injuries (non-critical)
Temporary loss of diving capability
Flooding in forward torpedo room

We conducted emergency repairs at depth while the other boats performed reconnaissance. This led to our most crucial discovery: the Draconians (designation based on their appearance) control several areas rich in underwater oil seepage. Their surface facilities, while primitive, are effectively placed for resource extraction.

This presents both a crisis and an opportunity. Our fuel situation remained critical—we had perhaps two months of diesel at current consumption rates. The Draconians' presence confirms exploitable oil deposits, but their control of the surface makes conventional drilling impractical.

After emergency council with all boat commanders and technical staff, we have formulated a new strategy:

Construct fully submersible drilling platforms using salvaged Atlantean technology

Locate oil deposits away from Draconian patrol routes

Establish hidden surface facilities for periodic fuel processing

Develop improved depth charge countermeasures

Maintain absolute secrecy regarding our base location

Design work has already begun. Unterscharführer Weber believed we could adapt Atlantean mining equipment for oil extraction. The challenge will be constructing facilities that can be completely hidden when necessary. That may prove impossible, but we will start there.

Most concerning is the obvious hostility between the Draconians and Sea Lords. We observed a battle between a galley and a dirigible yesterday. The Sea Lords showed remarkable courage but were ultimately forced to flee. This ongoing conflict could work to our advantage if properly exploited.

We have also noted something curious: the Draconians seemed to focus their activities around certain underwater ruins. This suggests they may have knowledge of ancient Atlantean technology. We must accelerate our salvage operations before they locate and claim the most valuable sites.

Implementation of our new strategy begins tomorrow. U-2542 and U-2544 will map potential drilling sites while our engineers begin platform construction. We must have at least one operational facility before winter.

A final note: Despite their primitive weapons, the Draconians' tactical coordination was impressive. We face an intelligent and organized species that may have controlled these waters for centuries. We must proceed with extreme caution.

The irony did not escape me—we fled here to escape one war, only to find ourselves in the middle of another. But this time, we have advantages our enemies cannot imagine.

217

Within six months, we should have fuel independence. Within a year, we should have weapons capable of challenging their air superiority. The Reich may have fallen, but here we will build something that will last a thousand years.

—WK

[Attached: Initial sketches for submersible drilling platforms, Draconian airship technical analysis, patrol route maps]

-46-

"The pressure's changing," Andrew said suddenly, waking from his fitful sleep. His voice sounded strained. "Can't you feel it?"

I could feel it: not just air pressure, but a sensation like static electricity that raised the hair on my arms. The walls seemed to thrum with subtle vibrations.

Ava's eyes snapped open at Andrew's words. For just a moment, something flickered across her face: recognition, anticipation, or worry?

I slipped the journal back into my pack before she noticed.

We gathered our belongings and stared downward again. Ava insisted we leave immediately, though she didn't elaborate.

Hours later, we passed sealed doors twice our height, marked with warning symbols. The corridor widened, the ceiling rising until our headlamps' light couldn't reach it. The

219

scale of everything had increased tremendously, as if we were entering some vast underwater or underground cathedral.

"Look," Spiro pointed to marks on the floor—deep scratches in metal that should have been nearly indestructible.

"That was from a previous expedition," Ava said smoothly. It sounded like she was reciting a prepared line, as if she'd been anticipating this moment.

I noted the signs of a fighting retreat—barricades had been erected and abandoned, while equipment had been dropped in haste. There were signs this had been a Nazi expedition—old equipment lockers stripped of anything useful, a broken gauge that still bore a swastika, artifacts of that nature.

"Over here," Spiro called. He'd found what looked like a research station—desks bolted to the floor and ancient monitoring equipment. If there had been papers, they had long since rotted away, but etched metal plates remained, covered in cramped German technical notes.

"They were studying something," Andrew declared, obviously intrigued. He ran his fingers over the etchings as if he could decipher the meanings that way.

I watched Ava. She gave no reaction to the signs of her people's failed expedition. There were no emotional responses at all from her.

We left the area and switched back and forth into new corridors, going down instead of climbing the Himalayan Mountains, unlike in Bhutan. The facility's hum grew louder as we descended. The corridors began branching more frequently, forming a complex maze. How did Ava know which route to take? She navigated without hesitation or frustration.

Three times, we took breaks, drinking and eating from our rations. I wouldn't have minded another cup of coffee.

After what seemed like miles of descent, we reached a vast chamber. Our headlamps revealed only hints of its true size. Ceiling lights had long ago ceased working down here. Massive shapes loomed in the darkness. I believe they were gargantuan machinery, although it was hard to tell. It reminded me of what we'd found on Chaunt Two many missions ago. Could there have been any connection between the Anunnaki of the Chaunt System and the Atlanteans?

We'd been trekking for endless miles. I was sure we left the surrounding sea and now trekked underground, descending far below the surface.

Spiro and Andrew were flagging, although Ava looked as chipper as ever. I felt beat again. What good would it do to drive us into utter exhaustion? It reminded me of a story about Genghis Khan. He hadn't wanted to promote a Mongolian "superman" to command of a troop because the "superman" would never know when his men needed a rest, as he never did. Maybe Ava was like that for us.

"We should stop here," I said. "We need some real rest before going further."

Spiro and Andrew nodded gratefully, although Ava worked to hide her annoyance.

Soon enough, we found a defensible position near a wall and set up a watch rotation. The facility's strange humming had grown louder, as I've said, making real rest difficult.

Like the other times, I took first watch again.

Ava lay down, her breathing immediately settling into that too-perfect rhythm.

Spiro and Andrew were genuinely exhausted like me. I waited until their breathing deepened into real sleep and I heard their first snores.

Despite my own exhaustion, I decided to keep reading to uncover more about the past.

I paged for quite some time, switching to the next notebook until I found this:

Personal Journal of Dr. Werner Kraus Chief Scientific Officer, Project Übergang December 23, 1946

I have delayed recording this entry for three days, struggling to find words adequate to describe what we have discovered. Even now, after 72 hours of preliminary investigation, I find my hand trembling with excitement as I write. This will be a lengthy entry—future generations must understand the magnitude of what we found.

The discovery occurred during our routine mapping expedition of the western abyssal trench. U-2542, conducting

221

deep sonar sweeps, detected an anomalous structure at 372 meters. Initial readings suggested another ruined city, but the scale... the scale was unprecedented.

When we illuminated it with our salvaged Atlantean flood lamps, even our most hardened U-boat commanders stood speechless. What we found was not merely a city, but an industrial complex of staggering proportions. The facility stretches for over three kilometers along the trench wall, much of it carved directly into the rock face. The engineering principles involved in its construction defy comprehension.

Initial Survey Data:
Main complex extends 3.2 km horizontally
Vertical extent: approximately 400 meters
Multiple pressure-sealed chambers
Intact power systems (still partially functioning)
Automated maintenance systems (some still operational)
Massive manufacturing spaces
Research laboratories
What appears to be a spacecraft construction facility

The latter point requires elaboration. The evidence is incontrovertible—the ancient Atlanteans possessed technology far beyond even our most fantastic predictions. The manufacturing equipment we've examined suggests capabilities that make our most advanced German engineering look primitive by comparison.

We have already recovered several smaller pieces of equipment. Our technical teams report extraordinary success in activating and understanding basic functions. Most remarkable is how intuitive the control systems are—almost as if they were designed to be comprehensible to less advanced civilizations.

The facility's layout reveals much about pre-flood Atlantean society. This was clearly a major industrial/research center, but it also contained living quarters, entertainment venues, and what appear to be educational facilities. The scale suggests a workforce of thousands. Yet more impressive is the integration of technology into every aspect of daily life.

Of particular interest is their water management technology. The entire complex operates underwater as easily *as it must have on the surface. This suggests they anticipated or planned for the flooding of their world. But why? The answer may lie in the deeper sections we haven't yet accessed.*

Our leadership council has been in continuous session for 48 hours, completely revising our long-term strategies. We are abandoning the surface facility construction program in favor of expanding this complex. All resources will be redirected to understanding and restoring these systems.

[Several pages of technical diagrams and notes follow]

Concerning Developments: Despite our enthusiasm, I must note several troubling observations:

Evidence suggests we are not the first to discover this facility. We've found signs of recent activity in several sections, though no direct contact yet.

Some passages show damage inconsistent with natural flooding or age. Something violent occurred here.

The deepest sections remain inaccessible. The sealed doors are not merely locked but appear to be deliberately contained. The warning symbols, while untranslated, are clearly urgent in nature.

Several of our more sensitive crew members report discomfort in certain chambers. Dr. Hoffman describes it as "psychic pressure" though I hesitate to use such unscientific terminology.

Most intriguing are the astronomical charts we found in one research section. They show not only this world's current configuration but also its pre-flood state. More importantly, they detail connections to other worlds—possibly explaining how we were able to travel here. The implications are staggering.

Unfortunately, strange occurrences continue to mount. Today we found a research log written in perfect German, though none of our scientists had been in that section. When we returned an hour later, the text had changed to ancient Atlantean symbols. More disturbing still, crystal arrays seem to respond differently to each person who approaches them. They pulse in patterns that match our brainwave studies, as if learning our thought processes.

Tomorrow we begin full documentation of the main manufacturing level. I have assigned our best engineers to study the power systems. The sooner we can restore main power, the sooner we can begin proper research operations.

A personal note: Looking at these wonders, I am struck by the parallels to our own situation. The Atlanteans clearly faced some catastrophe that flooded their world, yet they prepared for it. Their technology was designed to survive underwater, to be discovered and used by future generations. Were they leaving this for their descendants, or for others like us?

The Third Reich sought to build a thousand-year empire. Here we have found the remains of one that might have lasted ten thousand. We must learn from both their achievements and their ultimate fate.

—WK

[Addendum: Initial translation matrix for Atlantean technical symbols attached. Priority must be given to warning signs and operational manuals. Something in Dr. Hoffman's latest translations troubles me deeply, but verification is needed before recording those concerns.]

-47-

The German scientist's precise handwriting filled page after page, documenting his discoveries and growing unease. I kept one eye on Ava's sleeping form as I read her grandfather's journals.

Questions nagged at me: How could Ava survive down here alone for over three years? Why did she move like someone untouched by the toll of isolation? What was she guarding in this place?

Somewhere in the darkness ahead, metal groaned under pressure. I tightened my grip on the hollow tube, watching our supposed guide. If Dr. Ava Kraus wasn't what she claimed to be, then what was she? And why did I think she was something else?

I thought about Psi-Master Omilcar, about what he'd done to Livi and the experiment he'd conducted on the fetus of my son. I thought about Krekelen shape-changers and ancient secrets. The facility's hum seemed to grow louder as I did this, as if responding to my suspicions.

Despite all that, I felt on the verge of a revelation while reading these journals. Finding and reading them was critical, or so I believed.

I began to page once more, ready to read another section. It was only near end of the last notebook that I found this.

Personal Journal of Dr. Werner Kraus Chief Scientific Officer, Project Übergang January 17, 1947

I must record these events while they are still clear, though my physician advises against any mental strain. Seven men are dead. Twelve more are in various stages of psychological collapse. The facility's lower levels have been sealed, but the cost...

It began three days ago when we restored power to Section K-7. Initial tests were promising—the Atlantean matrices accepted our improvised connections, and energy readings exceeded predictions. Dr. Hoffman's latest translations suggested we had successfully matched the startup sequences.

The first warning signs appeared within hours. Three technicians reported severe headaches and distorted vision. We dismissed these as pressure-related symptoms despite being well within safe depth ranges. Weber noticed it first—how the affected men all worked near the secondary control arrays.

Timeline of events:

January 14:
0900: Power restoration begins
1300: First reported symptoms
1700: Technician Müller suffers severe nosebleed, removed to U-2544 sickbay
2100: Strange harmonics detected in power systems
2300: First dream incidents reported

January 15:
0200: Mass awakening event—entire crew reports identical nightmare

226

0500: Younger Müller (no relation to first) begins speaking in unknown language

0800: Crystal arrays showing unusual energy patterns

1100: First death—Weber's assistant found in restricted corridor, cause unknown

1400: Three more men reported missing

1600: Recovery team enters lower level, radio contact lost

1800: Hoffman reports translating new symbols "appearing" in previously blank panels

2000: Emergency shutdown attempted

January 16:

0000: Shutdown fails—systems appear to resist deactivation

0400: Mass hallucination event

0800: Second recovery team lost

1200: First appearance of the "shadows"

1500: Containment protocols initiated

1800: Hoffman successfully translates warning text

2100: Final casualty count determined

Dr. Hoffman's translation reveals the horrifying truth. The facility's deeper sections were not research labs as we assumed, but containment chambers. The Atlanteans were not merely studying something here—they were attempting to imprison it, whatever the thing was.

The warning text (partial translation):

"What dreams must remain sleeping"

"The deep mind must stay contained"

"When the crystals sing, seal the chambers"

What disturbs me most is how this alien entity (that appears to be the best explanation for all this) appears to test each individual differently. The affected crew members report increasingly complex interactions in their shared dreams. I believe the alien probes for weaknesses and catalogs our responses.

Last night, three affected men attempted to sabotage our containment systems in perfect coordination, though they were

227

in different sections of the facility. When questioned afterward, they had no memory of their actions. It appears that the entity is learning to use us.

[Additional text untranslatable—possibly degrades into warnings about "thought-forms" and "breaking of barriers"]

Critical observations:
Younger subjects more severely impacted
Some individuals show complete immunity
Copper shielding provides partial protection
Symptoms intensify with power levels
Some victims display unusual abilities before collapse

We have constructed emergency shielding using copper mesh salvaged from storage section A-3. Initial tests confirm it blocks the worst effects. All personnel now operate in shielded areas or with personal shielding.

Standartenführer Wolff wishes me to note we have observed strategic potential in these phenomena. I must formally record my strongest objection. This is not a weapon we can control. The entity or force we partially awakened shows clear signs of intelligence and purpose. The ancient Atlanteans sealed it away for a reason.

Containment Protocols Established:
Facility power levels strictly controlled
Lower levels completely sealed
Crystal arrays shielded when not in use
No direct interaction with primary systems
All personnel to use copper shielding
Mandatory psychological monitoring
No solo work in restricted areas
Children to be kept in shielded quarters

[Several pages of technical readings and medical observations follow]

Personal Analysis: We have discovered something that

challenges our fundamental understanding of reality. The Atlanteans possessed not only advanced technology, but also mastery of forces we barely comprehend. The distinction between their machines and these forces remains unclear.

Hoffman believes the facility served dual purposes— manufacturing and containment. The technology we hoped to salvage may be inextricably linked to whatever entity or power is imprisoned here. We cannot simply extract what we want and ignore the rest.

The question now is how to proceed. We cannot abandon this facility—it represents our only real chance at long-term survival in this world. Yet we dare not risk full activation. We must find a way to safely use the upper levels while ensuring the deeper containment remains intact.

Most troubling are Hoffman's latest translations. He speaks of references to "those who shape thoughts" and "masters of the deep mind." The implications... no, I cannot record speculation. We must deal in facts.

Tomorrow we begin installing permanent shielding around our active work areas. The dead will be buried at sea. God forgive us if we have awakened something that should have remained sleeping.

—WK

[Final note, handwritten in margin: Hoffman insists certain passages in the warning text are changing. Is that stress-induced hallucination? We must increase his copper shielding.]

This was alarming. It seemed the Nazis had awakened whatever we were now facing. Why hadn't Ava told us that?

I rubbed my forehead. This knowledge raised more questions than it answered. I was so tired. I needed time to process all this. Yet, how much time did we have left?

I rubbed my forehead again, wondering about the right thing to do.

I closed the notebook. My eyes were sore and tired. I hated this underground facility. I wondered: what had the Nazis done on Atlantis? They seemed to have awakened a horror, maybe the same horror that we'd witnessed as a smoky blue mass. It caused nosebleeds and headaches to Andrew, the most sensitive of us. The Nazis had clearly been terrified of whatever they'd found. So, what had they awakened?

I wanted to read more, but I didn't dare. Thus, I stowed the notebook and shook Captain Spiro awake. He opened his eyes and gave me a long, searching look.

"It's your shift, sir, if you don't mind."

Spiro nodded, but he carried an imperious and arrogant air I'd never seen before. His brown eyes seemed to burn with it.

Maybe because I was so damn tired, I hardly thought about it more than that. I lay down and drifted off to sleep.

I dreamed, and I heard myself moan in my sleep, waking

myself several times. After a moment of scanning my surroundings, I'd drift off again.

I felt claustrophobia, but not like being trapped in a sinking U-boat. This was bigger, more monstrous. Could it have been a memory? It wasn't mine. Then whose was it?

I sensed a monstrous entity. This was in the latest dream. Something had drawn it down from outer space—

Before I could learn more, someone was shaking me awake, shattering the dream.

I opened my eyes groggily.

"Come," Andrew said, speaking urgently. He straightened, looking down at me, sneering.

I had no idea why.

"You will," he said.

I frowned. Was Andrew reading my thoughts?

He smirked and turned away.

I got up and collected my gear, checking my pack to make sure no one had taken the notebooks. Then a premonition struck. Or maybe my dreams and possibly subconscious had finally reached an answer or answers. They'd seen the clues my conscious mind must have missed or failed to connect.

The headings for Dr. Werner Kraus's journals had ended in 1947. There were no 1948, 1950, 1960 or 1970 headings. In other words, there weren't any entries to prove that Ava had ever met her grandfather. I now doubted that Werner Kraus and his Nazis comrades had survived the horror they'd found in January 1947.

Perhaps there were other journals stashed away somewhere, but I doubted it. So if Ava had never met Werner Kraus, if there never had been a German Ava in the first place, who was the person standing over there with the shapely bod? Who led us down these chambers and had been in the facility for over three years? And given those questions, what did the real Ava stand sentry for?

I was starting to think I'd heard a lot of BS except for the good doctor's journals.

I cinched the backpack straps, picked up my hollow staff and wondered if I should activate it. I could use the protective glow to shield myself while I burned down the creature that

231

claimed to be Dr. Ava Kraus.

Who could mimic a human so perfectly that no one would detect it? A Krekelen shape-changer, without a doubt.

I thought back. Had Ava touched or brushed up against me at any point? No. The only time I remember her touching any of us was when she'd felt Andrew's pulse on his throat. He'd jerked as if touched by something hot. Krekelens were hot, much more so than any human. Andrew had also been too delirious to remember the touch or to rise then and protest. Perhaps the heat had even been comforting after a fashion.

If I were right about this, Ava the Krekelen would be exceedingly strong and difficult to kill because Krekelen aliens were strong and hard to kill.

Ava took point, heading out.

I watched her. This time, I didn't watch her contours with masculine appreciation for feminine beauty. Instead, I studied her mannerisms, applying my knowledge of Krekelen shape-changers.

Why would a Krekelen be down here in such a dangerous location? The answer appeared obvious. She was guarding something. What could she be guarding and how could she be doing it better than the smoky blue-glowing mass?

Did I know for a fact that Ava wasn't human? Without a doubt. It seemed obvious this morning, or whatever time of day or night it was in this underworld. We headed toward something distinctive, to helmets that imparted power.

"That is correct," Andrew said.

I turned to him, and he smirked with that superior attitude, only with more sass than ever before. I was getting heartily sick of it.

"But you're not going to do anything about it, Bayard," Andrew said. "As I am not the same person you defrauded on the oil platform."

The others stopped, looking at us.

I reached into my pack. Before anyone could react, I pulled out and slipped the psi-headband onto my head. Something happened with it. I didn't feel heightened awareness, but a blocking power. Had I flipped a switch with it, and if so, how had I done that? Maybe that I had was good enough for now.

I felt harder nausea than before so I wanted to puke. I also noticed that Mr. Smarty Pants, Andrew, no longer smirked at me.

Maybe my subconscious had done the flip switching. This block was better than gaining sight psionic ability as I had on Sky Island.

I grinned at Andrew.

He frowned—looking concerned—and said, "I concede, Bayard, you're dangerous after a fashion. But I have a most monumental task to complete. It would be best for you not to interfere with that."

"Have I interfered?" I asked.

"Perhaps not." Andrew turned to Spiro. "Do you understand yet?"

Captain Spiro nodded sharply.

Now Ava was staring at me, and then at the other two.

"Don't worry," Andrew told her.

"I'm not," she said. "I do wonder if you're going to be able to do what needs to be done."

"That would depend on several factors," Andrew said. "First, where are you really guiding us? Second, why are doing this? I believe it's time for us to have the confrontation."

Ava sighed and raised her rifle, aiming it at Andrew. "Like that, you can cease to exist if I so desire."

"Really?" Andrew asked, as if bored. "Well, how about…" He concentrated, staring at her.

Ava laughed, and for a moment, those brilliant blue eyes that I'd admired so much turned demonic red or Krekelen red.

This was news to me. One Krekelen, anyway, had finally learned how to disguise their normally give-away red eyes. Normally, or in the past, Krekelens disguised as humans had worn dark shades to hide their red eyes. This was a bad new development in their ability to mimic humans and walk among us unnoticed as aliens.

Andrew stepped back in astonishment, perhaps even dismay at his obvious failure to use his psionic power on her.

"You don't understand everything yet," Ava said. "We are immune to your powers. That was originally the reason for our… creation. You have regained some of your old abilities and doubtless knowledge, but these pale to what you should be able to achieve soon. We must reach the helmet chamber. There, you will augment your mental power with a psionic amplifier, a psi-helmet. Then, you will be able to achieve victory against your hereditary foe."

Andrew glanced at Spiro, and Spiro glanced back at him. Were they telepathically communicating between themselves? That would be where I'd place my bet.

"Yes," Spiro told Ava. "We agree with your assessment. How much danger is there to reaching the psionic amplifiers?"

I heard the grinding noises then, and Andrew swayed. He rubbed his forehead and cast about in fear, perhaps even in terror.

The noises seemed distant to me.

I turned to Ava. "Is the thing or process directed at us this time?"

She stared at me deadpan until her eyes widened with understanding.

"That's what I'm thinking," I said.

"What are you thinking?" Spiro said.

"Do you want to tell him or should I?" I asked Ava.

"Don't be coy, Mr. Bayard," Spiro said. "What can you possibly know that has a bearing on this?"

"I'm thinking Omilcar is in the facility," I said.

Ava hissed in an inhuman manner.

"None of that matters with that creature near," Andrew said. "Quick, Bayard, give me your headband."

"Why would I do that?" I asked.

"Quick, quick," Andrew said. "This is a matter of life and death. I believe your altered band will disguise my presence from the thing."

"Oh, yeah," I said. "That makes sense. What do you think, Ava? Is that a correct assessment?"

"Possibly," she said.

"There you go," I told Andrew. "Your supposition is correct. I'm giving you a gold star for that."

"Hurry," Andrew said. "Give the band to me. I'm sick of these nosebleeds and headaches."

"Well," I said, as if contemplating the idea. "How about

you screw off? How does that sound to you?"

Andrew stared at me, his terror warring with arrogant outrage. Then his eyes protruded as he screamed, "Don't you understand yet, you cretin? My life is vastly important, while you're a gnat in the scheme of things. Don't you understand that Atlantis can arise again, that we can finally fix the dread catastrophe?"

"You mean drain your world of water?" I asked. "How's that supposed to work? It would be a great trick if you could do it."

"Not that catastrophe, you fool," Andrew said. "Quick, quick, give me the headband before it's too late."

The grinding noises grew louder and closer. If the smoke monster had been after Omilcar, it seemed to have turned again toward us.

"There's no time for this bickering," Ava said. "We must run while we can and reach the helmets." She turned and sprinted, moving faster than any human could.

I didn't hesitate but sprinted after her, leaving Andrew and Spiro behind.

"I won't forget this, Bayard!" Andrew screamed.

"Run," Spiro said, dragging Andrew with him.

A moment later, they both started running in earnest after us.

Our helmet lamps' beams danced across the floor and walls ahead, amplifying the chaos. And all the while, the ominous grinding grew louder, closing in on us.

-49-

Ava—if that was indeed the Krekelen's name—skidded into yet another alcove after a long sprint. This one didn't have any antiquated tools but rather sophisticated mesh and dark metal etched with strange symbols that pulsed in green instead of blue.

I skidded near her, feeling the heat from her skin and smelling an acrid odor. Maybe that was from Krekelen sweat.

Shortly thereafter, Spiro helped Andrew stagger into the alcove. They both slid to the farthest corner and collapsed into it, panting, with Andrew sobbing quietly.

Ava—I'll continue to call her that for now—slid a panel before us, blocking the alcove from the corridor.

The grinding noises had come perilously close. I knew the thing, whatever it was, was hunting. For some reason, it didn't like this region of the facility, but it liked the deeper parts. I didn't understand why, and I wasn't going to ask any of these creeps for explanations.

The two Atlanteans seemed to be psi-masters, or whatever their kind were called on Atlantis. Both Spiro and Andrew, if that were their real names, certainly hadn't been scientists in the dim past. They had been mind-masters, telepaths. Were the ancient Atlanteans the originator of psionics?

I really didn't like this facility. It was too deep, possibly in the deep surface of the planet. It was away from everything and held an alien horror. I wanted to go home. All this craziness—I was finally homesick for Earth.

In this instance, what I wanted didn't matter squat. Instead, I endured like the others.

As the grinding became intimate—on the other side of the panel—I heard whimpering.

The green script on the dark metal writhed and pulsed. Then, the smoky blue entity we'd seen before drifted past. It didn't sniff, but it felt like it did.

By the dim green light of the glowing symbols, I saw Spiro clutch Andrew as if he was a father holding his child, with a hand clamped over Andrew's mouth, keeping him quiet. Andrew's eyes were wide and staring, and he squirmed, forcing Spiro to hold him tighter.

That's what I needed to see. Andrew lacked balls, toughness, manliness, call it what you like. When the going got tough, Andrew wilted. He'd done it on the oil platform and now here in the depths of this crazy facility. Perhaps it was time to choke him out for good.

Ava and I stared at each other, saying and doing nothing. Would the entity sense us? Would it devour us or break our minds?

I understood a little more what Dr. Werner Kraus had written. The most sensitive among them had been struck first. By sensitive, could Werner have meant telepathic—or perhaps exceptionally so? Did humans as a whole have latent telepathy or touches of it? That seemed more than possible. Maybe that's why some people had intuitive leaps and understood things that others didn't. Perhaps that's why they said sometimes that people who were really close, if separated by a great distance, knew the moment the other had died. There was some connection, something not directly related to what we call scientific about people.

I noticed that the grinding noise had moved past our alcove. What caused the grind? I didn't understand that, but I wondered suddenly if this entity was the reason for the Great Catastrophe of Atlantis.

Time passed and then Spiro exhaled as if exhausted. He removed his hand from Andrew's mouth and then pushed the other from him. Spiro didn't shove Andrew, just separated them.

Andrew's eyes no longer protruded, although his hands twitched. Another episode like that, and he might break entirely.

Finally, Ava removed the shielding before the alcove and stepped into the corridor, looking into the darkness with her lamplight. "It's clear. We can continue."

I glanced back and washed my headlamp over the two Atlanteans. They both looked exhausted with red circles around their eyes. Was I being too harsh on Andrew? The possibility existed.

"I'll give you a hand," I said.

"Don't touch me," Andrew said, shrinking from my outstretched hand.

Spiro didn't have the same haughty attitude, and I helped him up. He then turned around and helped Andrew. Then the two Atlanteans, weakened by what had just happened, began a slow shuffle down the corridor as Ava led us once more.

That was it for me, the proverbial last straw. What was the use of pretending when we were stuck down here with that thing? It seemed inevitable that we were all going to die soon.

"All right," I said, "let's drop all the pretenses. They're stupid at this point. You're a Krekelen, Ava." I slapped my pack. "I've been reading the diaries of Dr. Werner Krauss. I don't see any entries beyond 1947. So tell me, did any Nazis survive longer than that?"

"Yes," she said.

"Yeah?" I asked. "For how long?"

"I don't know."

"As slaves of the Sea Lords don't count," I said.

"This is a useless topic," she said.

"Fine," I said. "How do you like this one then? You're not Dr. Werner Kraus's granddaughter, are you?"

It took Ava a moment before she shook her head.

"So why not take your regular shape then?"

"This form seems to please you, as I've noticed you watching it."

"Yeah, like you Krekelens give a shit about that," I said. "Why are you here? Is it yet another way to screw the planet Earth and humanity?"

"On the contrary," Ava said, "you understand little of what we do. What you call screwing humanity is us trying to guide it into a better and more productive path than the murderous one they have chosen."

"Yeah, yeah, yeah," I said. "I've heard that kind of crap all my life, and I don't buy one iota of it. Humans need to be free, not controlled by some alien entity made in labs on the planet of Mu."

"Is that what you think happened?" she said.

"That's what I've been told."

"Omilcar told you this?" she asked.

"Yeah," I said.

"Omilcar, the so-called Great Sark of Mu?"

"That's the one."

"He's also known as a great liar, a great deceiver," Ava said. "Many amongst our council believe he should have been put down long ago." She shook her head.

Now I noticed that her movements were slightly alien. As good as this Krekelen was at mimicking, there were flaws in it. Maybe she wasn't as practiced as those on Earth were.

"I notice you're not denying my allegation," I said. "And you said a little bit ago that Krekelens were created."

"You did say that," Spiro said.

"None of it matters," Ava said.

"Then try this one," I said. "How long have you been down here? Has it really been three years?"

"The time I gave you is correct," Ava said.

"What about the megalodons?" I asked. "Were they yours?"

239

"Only partly, as I did not have full control of them."

"Where was Omilcar when he was doing his mental projecting while we faced the megalodons?" I asked.

"I would assume aboard U-2544," Ava said.

"You mean the Type XXI U-boat that came from Earth all those years ago?"

"Precisely," Ava said.

"Is U-2544 the last of the Nazi U-boats on Atlantis?" I asked.

"I believe it is, as it destroyed the second to last, the *Triton.*"

"These U-boats have been using the same parts all these years?" I asked.

"Of course not," Ava said. "They have each been refurbished time and again. But that is not the important point."

"Do Krekelens run U-2544 at present?" I asked.

"Yes," she said.

"Do those Krekelens belong to a different faction from yours?"

"Indeed so."

I nodded. "I get it. You think I'm going to die down here. That's why you can tell me all this, isn't it?"

"It is," Ava said.

"Are you going to try to kill me yourself when I'm asleep perhaps?"

"There is no need or desire on my part to do that," Ava said. "Despite your hostility toward me and my kind, it is good to have someone to talk to after such a long time alone. Krekelens are not like humans that wilt in isolation." Ava shrugged. "I'm performing a task, one we shall complete soon. Or rather, your two illustrious friends shall do so."

That was illuminating as the pieces were finally falling into place for me. "Psi-Masters can't affect Krekelen minds, can they?"

"You already know that," Ava said.

"Yeah, maybe I do," I said. "All right, let's keep going. We've come this far. So, what's the plan?"

"I'm going to stop Omilcar and those like him," Ava said. "These two will use the psionic amplifiers that will greatly augment their mental capacity. They will then be able to destroy Omilcar from afar."

I noticed that Spiro and Andrew were watching and listening to both of us closely.

"Why would these two do that for you?" I asked.

"The most basic drive would be to survive," Ava said. "Omilcar and his allies will surely kill them otherwise, as those of Mu and the mind-masters of Atlantis have always hated each other. Certainly, you gentlemen know this."

"I do, yes," Spiro said.

Andrew remained tightlipped.

"Interesting," I said. "So this enmity goes all the way back?"

"I think that is enough of a lesson for now, King of Sky Island," Ava said.

"How do you know that?" I asked.

"I have my ways," Ava said. "But… this once I'll give in to your curiosity. Those in the U-boat have contacted and tried to make a bargain with me. But I'm inflexible in this. I've been given my orders and I will accomplish them or die."

"Tell me about the smoke monster that's been hunting us," I said.

Ava shook her head. "I will not talk about that as it is not my secret to tell. Ask the two mind-masters. I don't know if they will deign to speak with you, but who knows? Greater miracles have occurred. Now come, the last lap is upon us. We must reach the psionic amplifiers soon, or we will never do so. I fear that Omilcar is down here, ready to challenge us with all his might."

Thus, we continued to trudge down the deeper corridors as some of the mysteries were starting to evaporate as I learned what was really at stake.

-50-

Why had the Krekelen taken the shape of Ava and put up those black-and-white photographs of figures in Nazi uniforms? Could the Krekelen have watched us through a viewing device as we came down on the Atlantean sled? That seemed like an elaborate setup. But Krekelens were thorough. I'd never met one so friendly. But perhaps it spoke the truth.

I had a thirst to know. Perhaps since Omilcar gave me the facts only to reveal they were false, my yearning to uncover the truth about the Harmony of Planets had grown stronger.

One thing was clear: Atlantean technology rivaled Anunnaki advancements in the Chaunt System. I wondered what the *Homo habilis* Philip would have said to all this.

Maybe, though, in the end, none of that mattered. What did matter was the reason I'd come to Atlantis. That was to kill Omilcar.

It was all about these helmets, the psionic amplifiers.

Omilcar desperately sought enhanced psionic power. That's why he'd destroyed my wife and my son-to-be—for more power, more control. We wanted the helmets and I'm sure Omilcar did as well—not only that, but it seemed that Omilcar and others from the U-boat were down here with us. They were probably racing for the helmet chamber just as we were.

"All right, you two," I said.

Andrew turned away from me, even as Spiro helped him down the corridor as we followed Ava.

"Captain," I said, "I've worked hand in glove with you on the *Triton*. I'm very sorry your crew died."

"They died because of you," Spiro said. "I could have gone back up and saved them, but you refused to help."

"Maybe you could have, sir. I don't know, but I doubt it. The point is that I've been aiding you, trying to work with you."

"That is as it should be," Spiro said. "All thralls of the great mind-masters of Atlantis should help and obey."

"That's how you're going to play it, huh?" I asked.

Spiro didn't respond to that.

I sighed. Both these little guys seemed vastly different from what they'd been like on the U-boat. Andrew had been difficult then, but not insufferably arrogant. Spiro had been okay then. Now, he held his head stiffly and spoke with a nasal quality, his manner imperious like a lord to a menial slave.

"Listen, Mr. Mind-Master," I said, "I have my headband. And so far, it's working fine to block you guys."

"So far," Spiro said.

I was about to level threats when I decided on a different approach. Honey usually worked better than vinegar.

"So, you guys are from before the Great Catastrophe—" It struck me then. I could learn what happened back then. "What caused the Great Catastrophe?"

No one answered.

"I'll tell you what," I said. "I'll make you a deal. You give me the data, and I'll help you against Omilcar. I'll also help you do whatever else you need."

"You will help us because you must," Spiro said.

"Not when I have this." I tapped the headband. "I also have

this." I held up the hollow tube. "I can incinerate you whenever I choose. That's mutual destruction. Oh, no, wait. It isn't mutual. I can take out your sorry asses as easy as can be."

So much for the honeyed approach.

"The Krekelen will shoot you if you do that," Spiro said.

Ava raised the barrel of her rifle, showing her willingness, no doubt.

"Look," I said. "Why not give me the answer. What's it hurt you? I've helped you to a degree. Wouldn't you—?"

I stopped. Telling him he owed me would be the wrong tack with these pukes.

"Look," I said. "I am the sovereign of Sky Isle, a realm on Mu. I have devices and machines I can trade with you later. Or I can be a puppet king for you on Mu."

The two exchanged glances, and I'm sure they were telepathically talking to each other.

Finally, Andrew shrugged.

"Are we almost to the chamber?" Spiro asked Ava.

"We have little time still," she said. "Can you detect Omilcar's presence?"

"I don't," Spiro said. "Do you?"

"No," Ava said. "But that doesn't mean he or some of the others doesn't have a way onto the station. I suspect they're trying to set up an ambush. Gaining the support of the killer you brought along could prove useful."

Spiro turned and looked down his nose at me. "I accept your offer, Bayard. You are now our puppet king on Mu."

I nodded because I didn't trust myself not to spout off something sarcastic.

"In the distant past," Spiro said, "when Atlantis was whole and we had started to send out colonies to the other planets, our engineers developed a mighty system to tap the molten core of the planet. They drove deep magnetic shafts to the core. But we did not understand at the time that there are things, creatures, entities in space that are so much different from us. The resonance of the molten core, amplified by the magnetic shafts, likely drew the creature from space. How many years it took for it to travel from wherever it resided until it finally came down onto our world and sought the core and the deeper parts…"

Spiro shook his head.

"The entity soon discovered it could feast off psi-master minds in particular, which it found a choice morsel. We didn't understand at first what we were fighting. Once we did, we tried many countermeasures. The creature struck back through those it controlled. Then a terrible, dreadful accident brought about the Great Catastrophe."

Spiro's features tightened.

"That is when we rushed to the stasis tubes. You see, we had anticipated something of the sort, which is why much has been preserved. As we fled, the great waters encircled the world. And we understood, by trying to battle the beast, the star beast, as we have called it—"

Spiro inhaled deeply.

"The star beast could go through just about anything, space, steel, dirt, almost anything. But for reasons we have not yet comprehended, it cannot pass through water, particularly salt water. Now an ocean covered our world, trapping the star beast as it thrashed about.

"Billions died in the Great Catastrophe, crushing Atlantean civilization. Yet, as I've said, many of us took to the stasis tubes. There, the star beast's hunger could not reach us. We had disappeared from its senses. We had hoped that after millennia, it would have starved to death and perished…

"From what I have sensed these past few hours, we came within inches of doing so. But intruders from your Earth in U-boats awoke it. They gave it sustenance because their poking about awoke many of ours which the star beast devoured.

"Still, the star beast is weak. With the helmets amplifying our mental powers, we might finally destroy it."

"What about Omilcar?" I asked.

"He thinks himself great," Spiro said. "But he needs his crutches to help him. I mean the staff with the crystal. It is Atlantean in nature. Surely, you must realize that. Those of Mu have thought to mimic our ancient and olden powers. Mind-Masters ruled Atlantean civilization because we were the greatest. None could compete against our mental dominance. Now, though there are but a few of us left, we will unite. We

245

will kill the star beast. Then we will awaken our world and use our great technological power. Once again, we will reach out, recreating the Harmony of Planets and ruling as is our natural right."

"Wow," I said. "That's an extraordinary tale. You've convinced me. I'm going to help you guys one hundred percent, because I think that is the way to go. With the technology I've seen and what you've done—"

"He is lying to you," Ava said.

"We know that," Andrew said. "We have been befogged in our thought ever since awakening from the stasis tubes. But we are not befogged anymore. Bayard, it's in your best interest to stand with us. We will give you more than any of the others will for your help."

"Sure thing," I said, "let's get to it."

"In that, you are correct," Andrew said. "We are almost to the chamber. Once we don the psionic amplifiers, the star beast will have to beware."

"Let's hope so," Ava said, "so that my long vigil in the depths of this watery grave of a world will be worth it."

-51-

I didn't like how quiet it had gotten. There weren't any grinding sounds, or even a sense of the star beast's presence. Had Omilcar found a way to divert the creature, to draw it elsewhere, perhaps?

I heard the soft hum of ancient machinery and the faint cycling of air. This reminded me of Bhutan, the sixth sense I'd developed to know when the shit was about to hit the fan. That prodded something else. It had been a nagging thought that had hovered just beyond my awareness. Now, it solidified, becoming a red line for me.

I needed to take care of this before I proceeded any further.

I hurried until I paced Ava. She glanced at me sideways.

When I didn't say anything, she whispered, "What is it?"

"I can't understand why you've been down here all this time. It isn't making sense to me, and that troubles me—a lot."

"What do you need to understand?" Ava seemed genuinely

surprised. "This is my duty. I perform it. That is actually more than you need to know."

I shook my head. "We're walking into it, lady. You said so earlier, remember? I'm beginning to wonder if you're deliberately taking us into an ambush to get us all killed."

"That is absurd. I most certainly am not."

"You see," I said. "That's just it. You're a Krekelen. That means I don't trust you as a matter of principle. That means I need a reason to do this because it makes no sense you being down here."

I stopped.

Ava stopped.

The two Atlanteans must have noticed, as they stopped behind us.

"If you don't believe me," Ava said. "What does it matter what I tell you?"

"You make a good point," I said. "Maybe if you gave me a reason that made sense, I could believe a Krekelen just this once."

Ava looked away. Was she thinking about it? What did Krekelens think about at a time like this? She turned back to regard me. "There are factions among us. Some hold to one belief and method, others to another."

"Okay," I said. "That's a start."

"My side believes the star beast is too inherently dangerous to attempt anything fancy with it other than containment. Far too many elements might backfire. I suspect you wonder about the grinding noises. We've put machinery in place that hinders the star beast. That sound is its resistance to it, I mean the beast's resistance. We cannot stop the star beast completely, mind you. I am down here monitoring the containment machinery, as someone has to. At the same time, I attempt to hinder those who would try to garner ancient Atlantean tech, and possibly release the star beast in the process. Once it escapes its prison, chaos could ensue."

"Does your side think the star beast will starve down here in time and die?"

"It does," Ava said.

"You're part of the conservative approach, the cautious

248

way," I said.

"That is one way to say it," Ava replied.

"And those on Omilcar's side?"

"They think they can destroy the star beast or use it like a weapon against others."

"So you're not leading Spiro and Andrew to the helmets so they can slay the star beast, but to defeat the others before they do something truly harmful."

Ava glanced at the two Atlanteans before regarding me again. "There is a possibility these two can slay the star beast with heightened powers."

I grinned at her. That was a load of crap if I ever heard it. She was using those two, but she didn't want to come right out and admit it. For a plan conceived so hastily, it wasn't bad.

Still, I did remember the journals. Werner had hinted at the entity using some of them. Could the star beast use any of us? That seemed more than possible. Had Ava been the sentinel here because she had even greater-than-normal Krekelen resistance to mind control?

Did I think she'd told me the whole truth finally?

No. I seriously doubted that. Ava was being tricky and double-dealing. That was normal Krekelen behavior. In this instance, though, I had a much different goal that had nothing to do with the star beast: that goal was to kill Omilcar. The star beast seemed bad, sure. Keeping it contained seemed wise. I could agree to that for the moment, so... in and out, baby. Kill Omilcar and get the hell out of this underwater, subterranean facility.

"I'm ready," I said.

Ava studied me.

"Let's do this," I added.

She glanced at the Atlanteans.

Spiro must have understood what her look meant and nodded. Andrew just waited.

Ava made a small sound that could have meant anything and continued to lead.

After rounding a corner, we approached a set of massive doors leading to what Ava called the staging chamber—the last major space before the helmet repository. The doors stood partially open, which was our first real warning. Everything else down here had been sealed tight as we approached. The other clue was the light shining from the chamber. It indicated the ceiling lamps worked.

"Hold up," I said. "I want to study this."

I eased to the partially open doors and peered within from the shadows. I didn't want anyone in there getting a bead on me.

The chamber was huge, easily big enough to house a small ship. Ancient machinery had been pushed to the walls, creating open spaces. Thick cables ran across the ceiling, vanishing into shadowed recesses. Elevated platforms and walkways provided multiple firing positions. The ancient equipment created plenty of cover. In the back, I spied hatches that must have led to the helmet chamber. They were shut, possibly sealed, or they had been hastily closed so we would think that.

Ava stepped beside me, also remaining in the shadows, and indicated equipment within the room. "If we could get behind there... we could start the engagement from a protected position."

I studied the possibility. Yeah, that was a good spot. Even if ambushers had tried to flank it... I would have seen them from here, then. That was an excellent location. Ava had a good tactical eye.

"They're waiting for us in here, aren't they?" I whispered.

"I believe so," Ava said.

"Are you ready to do this?"

She stared at me. It felt as if she wanted to tell me something. That passed, though, as she nodded and adjusted the grip on her rifle.

I wondered what she was holding back. After a moment, I shrugged. Pre-combat jitters were making it hard to think about other stuff.

"Let's do this on a count of three," I said softly.

"Agreed," she whispered.

"One... two... three."

Ava and I dashed within the chamber.

A second later, energy beams lanced out from multiple positions, their whine echoing off ancient walls. The air crackled where the beams passed, just behind us. We'd caught them napping, but the beams swept up fast to catch us.

Ava and I skidded behind ancient equipment. The smell of ozone burned my nostrils as the energy beams struck the now intervening machinery. This position offered excellent cover for the moment.

"They've stolen weapons from ancient armories," Ava said, as she positioned her rifle to shoot. "That could mean…"

"What?" I asked.

"Our adversaries are more dangerous than I'd envisioned."

That hadn't been what she was going to say.

I had no more time to ponder it as a man or Krekelen in human guise, and wearing tactical gear, rushed our position. Ava's rifle cracked three times, hitting him twice in the chest and once in the head. His gear had been useless, which meant her rifle, or ammo, was better than I'd thought. The man went down hard, his energy weapon clattering across the deck.

"Your attempt to foil us will be useless in the end," a man called out, although his voice was too precise to be human. "We will certainly secure the psionic amplifiers. Surrender now and save yourselves from death."

I rose from cover and activated my hollow tube. I'd tracked his voice back to a possible hiding position. Fire gushed as from a flamethrower against the hideaway. He screamed and fell into view, his human guise burning away as the Krekelen died. His true, ugly gray form was revealed in his final moments.

Ava picked off another attacker trying to work around our flank.

"We need to switch locations," I said, dropping back beside her. "This position is fast becoming too exposed. But before I tire myself from powering the hollow tube too much…"

I'd spotted the fallen energy weapon about twenty feet away.

"Cover me," I said.

Ava's fired again and again as I sprinted from cover. I snatched the weapon and dove behind an ancient console as energy beams cut through where I'd been.

The weapon felt alien but workable—trigger and power

cell, basic enough principles.

I'd slid the hollow tube onto my back and spied movement on a walkway above. I brought up the energy weapon and fired. The beam caught a man square in the chest, the force throwing him back over the railing so he screamed and thudded against the deck ten feet down.

"Three o'clock high," Ava called.

I swung the weapon around, beaming another man that changed into a Krekelen as he died. I fired an extra shot at his head, killing the alien for keeps.

The air filled with crisscrossing energy beams and bullets. The attackers had good positions but seemed like sloppy soldiers. That suggested to me most of them were Krekelens, not trained military personnel. Ava's shooting was a thing of beauty, though. She was a professional to the core. Every time they tried to maneuver, her rifle would crack and half the time another would fall or scream.

I kept mobile, shifting between places of cover, using the energy weapon for area denial. The combination seemed to be keeping them off balance. But something about their tactics bothered me. It seemed as if they were trying to pin us in this chamber rather than press the attack too hard.

That's when I realized I didn't know where Spiro and Andrew were? The Atlanteans had come in after us and where hiding somewhere in the back. Just as crucially, I hadn't spotted Omilcar yet.

"I think they're waiting," I called to Ava. "They must be setting up for something else."

"Then we must kill them immediately," Ava said.

Was that worry in her voice? Was there something she hadn't been telling me?

A new-old sound echoed through the chamber—not energy weapons or gunfire, but something closer to the grinding we'd heard before.

It struck me then that the star beast had left us alone for too long, given the choice morals of psionic meals it loved, gathered in one spot here. The grinding noises suggested the star beast was approaching, though it hadn't arrived yet.

Could that be Omilcar's plan to use the star beast against

252

us?

I had a feeling we would find out soon enough, and that it wouldn't be what I expected.

52

Of all the things, Omilcar the bastard emerged onto a high walkway, wearing his full regalia as the Great Sark of Mu. What was the murderous traitor up to?

His crystal-topped staff pulsed with power, but what caught my attention was the helmet he wore—dark metal and crystal, covered in the same symbols we'd seen throughout the facility. Had he already taken that from the helmet chamber?

Rage coursed through me at the sight of him. I aimed and fired, but the energy beam failed to reach him as the crystal atop the staff flared with power. The beam simply ceased about two feet from him.

I kept firing as hate seethed through me. Sure, Omilcar had created a force field. I would drain it—

"Duck!" Ava shouted.

An enemy beam grazed my shoulder, the fiery pain returning me to sanity. I rolled out of the line of fire and slithered across the deck, hurrying to a new position. I'd gotten predictable, so even these sloppy commandos had almost killed me. I had to control my rage and keep thinking. I ground my teeth with rage while trying to focus.

If you want to kill Omilcar, you have to think. I nodded, accepting that truth. As a professional killer, I would do what was necessary. Thus, I submerged my rage for the greater good.

"Enough of this!" Omilcar shouted. "Why not be reasonable, my friends? We have the superior hand. We can keep you pinned until the star beast arrives. I know you hear it coming. Join us, as we clearly know what we're doing."

I glanced at Ava.

She wasn't looking at Omilcar as I'd expected, but behind her.

I followed her gaze.

Spiro and Andrew stepped out from their hiding spot near the entrance. To my amazement, the two moved with confidence, perhaps even arrogance. What were they thinking?

"Get down!" I shouted.

The two Atlanteans ignored me. Could they stop beams with their own psionic force field? They both seemed more poised and self-assured than I'd ever seen them.

"You wear our heritage like a costume," Spiro shouted, his voice hard. "You understand nothing of its true purpose."

"Don't I?" Omilcar's helmet pulsed in time with the crystal on his staff. "Let me show you what a 'mere' psi-master of Mu can do with Atlantean power."

That sounded like an ancient grudge.

The battle that followed was chaotic. There were no energy beams, no physical attacks. But the air seemed to thicken and crack with invisible forces. Ancient machines sparked and shorted as waves of pure mental energy radiated from the three combatants.

Could that be harming the containment mechanisms?

I could feel the edges of their psionic contest even without possessing any of their abilities. I'd taken off the psi-headband so I could use the hollow staff. I'd kept the headband off while using the energy weapon to avoid the nausea it caused.

Spiro and Andrew stood shoulder to shoulder. It seemed that their combined wills created an invisible shield against Omilcar's assault. The psi-master's attacks came in waves, each one making the air ripple or flow from him to them, but failing to reach them.

"You're strong," Omilcar acknowledged after a moment. "But you're still fragments, broken things playing at remembered power. While I am whole and focused, the Great Sark of Mu!"

He aimed the crystal staff at them.

The attack must have hit like a hammer blow. Andrew staggered, blood trickling from his nose.

Luckily for him, Spiro stepped forward. He raised his arms and then aimed his fists at Omilcar. Was Spiro sending a psionic bolt at the Great Sark?

Omilcar used his free hand to grab a railing as if to steady himself. Something had shoved him.

"The helmet wasn't meant for you, you dog of an imposter!" Andrew wiped his nose and raised his arms, then aimed his fists at Omilcar. "You're corrupting its purpose, you freak!"

"Purpose?" Omilcar laughed, although it sounded strained. "You think small like all Atlanteans. You had power beyond imagining, yet you spent it cowering behind containment fields and force walls. You caged the star beast when you should have controlled it. I'm going to show you how to do that. Oh, I'm sorry. You'll be dead by then and won't see a thing."

The crystals in Omilcar's helmet seemed to align with the one on his staff as visible power surged between them. With both hands, Omilcar aimed the crystal-topped staff at Andrew.

The effect was immediate. Andrew crumpled like a puppet with cut strings. Whatever kind of blast that was must have killed him.

"No!" Spiro aimed his open palms at Omilcar. The rail before Omilcar bent, although the psi-master seemed unhurt.

"You see?" Omilcar said. "This is what the technology was meant for. Not hiding, not containing—but mastery, control!" He aimed the staff at Spiro.

I thought it was over, as that would be it, but Spiro held his ground as sweat poured from his face. "You dog from Mu, you'll never leave this place alive."

Omilcar laughed even as he half turned to address Ava. "Your faction has played it safe for too long, letting power beyond imagining go to waste. Join me. Help me claim this fantastic inheritance!"

Ava's rifle never wavered from Omilcar, although she hadn't fired. "We contain the star beast because we understand its volatility. We remember what happened when the Atlanteans tried to control it, the catastrophe that sank their world. Don't make their mistake."

"Bah," Omilcar said. "That was a momentary setback. This time we'll be ready. This time we'll have the helmets and the staff to bend the star beast to our will."

"You're insane," Ava said. "The containment systems are the only thing preventing another catastrophe. Without proper maintenance, which you're jeopardizing with his battle—"

Omilcar laughed again, although it seemed more strained than before. "You mean wasteful imprisonment. The star beast is power incarnate and raw possibility. With the psionic amplifiers, we can shape that possibility."

I aimed my energy weapon at Omilcar and pulled the trigger. Nothing happened. The psionic battle must have rendered our weapons useless. Was that permanent or temporary?

"This is your last chance," Omilcar shouted at Spiro. "Join me willingly, help me claim the rest of the helmets, and I'll let you live. Fight me, and..." He glanced at Andrew's body. "You can see the alternative."

I didn't know why the star beast hadn't shown up yet, though it seemed as if Ava and Omilcar did. We seemed to be at a stalemate.

Then a deep boom echoed through the facility, followed by the screech of tearing metal. The ancient machines that lined the walls in our chamber began to spark and smoke.

"No," Ava said, with real fear in her voice for the first time. "The primary containment grid is failing."

"Is the star beast coming?" I asked.

Ava stared at me with horror. "You don't understand. The

containment systems are more than just physical barriers. The ancient Atlanteans created energy fields that forced it to remain bestial and instinctive. That's why it appeared as smoke and simply consumed. But now... now its true nature could be emerging."

I had an idea what that meant.

"The star beast will possess and control others," Ava said. "That's why the Atlanteans feared it so much. That's why they sank their entire world to keep it contained."

Oh, shit. This was bad, ten times worse than what I'd imagined.

53

"We're out of time," Omilcar said, while still maintaining his mental assault on Spiro. "The star beast comes in earnest. It has perceived my deceptions that kept it from here. Now, Ava, decide, join me or—"

Another boom cut him off. The deck plates buckled as if something massive was moving beneath them. Cracks appeared in the walls.

I expected to see the familiar blue-tinged smoke monster seeping through the cracks. Smoke trickled through, but—

Spiro turned and gaped at something.

I expected the distraction would cost him from Omilcar. Instead, the Atlantean's features twisted as if in agony. He panted and blood seeped from his eyes. He shivered horribly and uttered croaks and groans. That only lasted for a moment, though it felt interminable.

Then Spiro smiled. It was a twisted thing. He looked

around as if seeing the place for the first time.

"Ah, it is so different like this," Spiro said, his voice higher-pitched than I'd ever heard it.

"Please, no," Ava whispered.

"Oh, yes, dear one," Spiro said, having heard somehow. "The long wait is nearly over."

Omilcar no longer attempted any psionic assault upon Spiro. He watched as if sickened.

"Friends, comrades and countrymen," Spiro shouted. "A new dawn has arrived on Atlantis. This is a glorious and magnificent moment. Ah, look, a Traveler. I perceived that you were different, Mr. Bayard. You will come in very handy, and quite soon, I assure you. I will leave my confinement much sooner than I'd anticipated."

Ava swung her rifle around and fired repeatedly. The bullets shattered Spiro's skull so it splintered. Then the former captain of the *Triton* slid down to the deck, dead.

Everyone stared at her.

That continued until one of the enemy soldiers screamed in a high-pitched voice. He shivered as if in dread and then pointed at Ava.

She shot him next, killing him, too. She fired at Omilcar after that, but the psi-master's power halted the bullets before him until they tinkled onto the grating, falling through it to the deck below.

Energy beams lashed at Ava. She moved with preternatural speed, ducking out of the way of them and out of sight.

That was all the cue I needed as I slithered to her fast.

"What's going on?" I panted.

"The star beast has discovered a new capability," Ava whispered. "It realizes it can use Travelers to escape. Didn't you hear it; didn't you see? It wants to possess psionic people like Spiro for their mental power, but it wants you so it can activate the teleportation system."

I thought about how Omilcar had used Livi's brain to escape from Sky Island via the obelisk. Could the star beast conceivably do something similar with me?

"I must kill you," Ava said. "I can't let the star beast possess you."

"The hell with that," I said, grabbing the barrel of her rifle as she tried to aim at me. She was a Krekelen, though, meaning she was much stronger than she looked.

In those few moments as we wrestled with her rifle—she trying to kill me, I fighting to survive—others screamed and laughed wildly. I was sure that meant the star beast was possessing them.

Then an energy beam struck her, and Ava twisted to the deck as she released the rifle.

Immediately, the firing ceased.

Ava was panting hard, staring at me from the deck. "Kill yourself, Bayard. Don't let the star beast possess you."

I jammed the psi-band that presently blocked mental attacks onto my head. Nausea struck, but I was confident it would shield me against the monster from space.

"That might make you invisible to the star beast," Ava whispered, "but its possessed servants will still be able to see you. They won't kill you, though. They need you alive to complete its escape from Atlantis."

"Bayard!" Omilcar shouted. "Can you hear me?"

His voice had become high-pitched. Did that mean the star beast possessed the Great Sark of Mu?

"Listen," Ava whispered. "I was chosen for this duty because I'm different from my brethren. My mind—even for a Krekelen—is uniquely resistant to possession. That's why I've guarded this place alone for over three years. But the others… I think the star beast might be able to possess normal Krekelens as well. Please, Bayard, don't let it escape from its prison."

"I don't intend to kill myself," I said.

Ava stared at me as the pain of the energy burn filled her. "Then kill the possessed and escape on the U-boat."

"Where is it?"

Ava gave me quick directions.

"If you're lying to me—"

"Give me my rifle," she said, interrupting. "I'll cover your escape."

"I'm not an idiot," I said. "You'll just shoot me in the back."

"I swear I won't," Ava said.

261

"I don't trust you."

"Then it's over. Can't you hear them sneaking up on us?"

I could, and a second later, nodded.

"You'll never defeat Omilcar if you don't trust me," Ava said. "I need the rifle."

"Damn you." I wanted to kill Omilcar more than stay alive. It was time to take a risk in order to achieve that.

I slid the rifle to her and crawled across the deck. I looked back. Ava moved up to her knees, stared at me with the rifle in her hands, and then laid it on a piece of machinery and began to fire at them.

I crawled faster, heading for a side exit. The last I saw of Ava, enemy soldiers fired energy beams into her, killing her. She reverted to her Krekelen form and melted into the primordial goo from which her kind originated.

I got up and dashed through the exit, racing for the U-boat Ava said was docked in a nearby chamber.

-54-

I ran down corridors, hearing the zombie horde chasing me. They didn't shout, but panted, their boots thudding upon the deck plates.

Had Omilcar joined them?

Then I felt the presence of the star beast. It moved around me in faint, almost imperceptible lines. I could feel the pressure bearing down. Could it see me then?

I didn't think so, as I saw the lines of nearly invisible power race ahead of me.

I supposed that meant there were more Krekelens and humans aboard the U-boat for it to possess. Would the star beast send the U-boat away or have the crew join in the capture?

The creature from the depths of space had given its plan away. It wanted the Traveler, me, in order to use the ancient teleporting system to go somewhere else. I suppose it could use

263

subterranean chambers and corridors to reach the sunken city and the obelisk there. That way, the star beast could bypass the oceanic barrier that trapped it on this world.

Omilcar, the fool, had set things in motion to free the cosmic horror.

I wanted to kill him. I could feel that pulse through my brain. Did that mean I wanted to chance the rest of humanity dying? No. As much as I loved Livi and my son-to-be, I couldn't let the rest of humanity perish because of my rage and hatred.

I'm not saying I grew in that moment. I didn't learn a damn lesson. I simply couldn't consign everyone else to hell for the sake of vengeance. I was single-minded and filled with hate toward the Great Sark of Mu, but I wasn't insane. I could—

Oh, hell, this was making me angry all over again. I ran like a coward. But what else could I do? The star beast was too vast, too horrible for me. An entire planet had faced the Great Catastrophe because of it. The space monster had downed a world. Possibly billions had died back then.

The legend of Atlantis was old, maybe already ancient when Solon of Athens heard about it. The Nazis had awakened the creature. The waking Atlanteans in their stasis tubes must have fed it just enough psionic energy to restore its power.

How long would it take this creature from outer space to die? Would the Sea Lords help it escape some day?

I turned corners and sprinted, but I couldn't put any distance between myself and the zombies chasing me.

I realized now that Spiro or Andrew must have sensed me on the Sea Lord galley through their latent psionic power. I had thought it some kind of tech thing. The Atlanteans must have used their psionic powers at other times during the *Triton's* journey without even knowing it.

Nazis, Krekelens, and the psi-masters of Mu—I was panting, my side aching. I couldn't keep this up much longer.

I looked back, and I saw them running, gaining on me. Omilcar was in the rear of them, his eyes bright with possession.

I was going to have to kill them. That would mean taking off the headband so I could use the hollow tube of Zeus. That

264

would risk the star beast possessing me. Should I kill myself to keep that from happening?

No. I was a man of the West and the Western tradition. I fought until I couldn't stand anymore. Maybe before capture I would pull the pin of a grenade. But I'd only do that if I could take the enemy with me. Otherwise, I fought to win even here at the entrance to hell.

I turned a corner and the corridor opened into a massive docking chamber. Through thick windows, I saw U-2544's dark hull. I spied a boarding tube pressed against thick rubber seals, while pipes and power conduits snaked between the U-boat and facility.

"Bayard!" Omilcar shouted in his high-pitched voice.

I skidded to a halt. I ripped the headband from my head and activated my hollow tube. I felt a twinge of heaviness strike me. It was vast and vile, space evil trying to control me.

Then the blue nimbus glowed around me. The assault on my mind weakened. I hoped that would give me enough to power this.

"You're getting off easy, Omilcar!" I shouted. "I was going to make it a hard death. You should have to face alien possession for ages."

Then I had no more time to tell the psi-master all the things I'd planned. Instead, I concentrated and willed fire to pour from the tube.

It did. Like a flamethrower on one of the Pacific Islands during WWII, fire poured from my ancient device. It licked out and fell upon the humans, Krekelens and psi-master of Mu that had given chase. They burned relentlessly.

I kept pouring fire on them.

It was horrifying as they kept coming, their clothes burning away and their flesh blackening and charring. I hosed fire, my hands shaking and my heart shriveling.

Omilcar burned and died, his reign of evil finally ended.

They all smoked until the last one fell and ceased moving.

I was afraid to stop, but I did. The blue nimbus around me ceased, and the star beast hit me like an avalanche.

I resisted the possession attempt as I passed the hatch and entered the boarding tube, hardheaded as ever. Pain wracked my body, and my vision blurred as my mind and eyes throbbed, but I pushed toward the U-boat, aware that its crew was the star beast's last chance for freedom.

I opened the U-boat hatch and entered with my hollow staff ready. The batteries powered the engines, which throbbed through the deck plates. Krekelens, or whatever humans remained aboard, were hiding from me.

I was bent over by the mental assault of the star beast, and thus I activated the hollow tube, creating the blue nimbus around me. That brought blessed relief.

Then I sealed the hatch behind me.

The first one died there. He was a Krekelen disguised as a naval officer, charging and swinging a wrench at my head. My staff flared, catching him mid-swing. His human shape burned away like paper in a flame, revealing the true Krekelen form beneath before it dissolved into charred flesh and goo.

I moved into the boat quickly and methodically, leaving nothing unchecked. These Type XXI U-boats were bigger than the *Triton*, but the layout was similar.

I rushed into the control room. Two of them were there, one throwing a cloak at me. He and the cloak burned. The other one rushed me with a hammer, but wasn't fast enough.

The smoke from their burning corpses and the stink made it harder to focus. I feared disabling the U-boat doing it like this. But I was out of options.

I could feel the star beast's panic. It hadn't worked as it thought it would. I could read that much from it.

Enemy shouts echoed through the U-boat.

I moved aft and incinerated another Krekelen. He turned into gray substance that quickly became jelly-like goo that dissolved.

I kept moving, burning another Krekelen, its death cry echoing off the metal bulkheads.

That was the last one.

Just to be sure, I did another sweep of the boat, stem to stern. I checked every compartment, every locker and possible hiding place. The officers' quarters held stores of energy weapons and Atlantean tech. But in a locked cabinet in the captain's cabin, I found something else—the transpar suit Omilcar had used to escape the burning dirigible.

I studied it, remembering my time on Garm, teaching the Neanderthals how to use these. This was the same kind of design.

Omilcar had used the suit to soar away from certain death. Maybe it could carry me where I needed to go.

I was wasting time, and I sensed that the star beast was causing me to linger and hesitate. With leaden step, while hearing its vain promises in my mind, I headed back for the control room. It was time to cast off for good.

The U-boat's engines struggled as I guided it through the endless ocean. I'd burned out several systems while eliminating the Krekelens, and more equipment had failed during my hasty escape. But the boat had held together long enough to reach the sunken city where I'd entered Atlantis.

I'd found charts in the captain's cabin marking the location.

My hands were steady on the periscope as I scanned the waters ahead. Would the star beast be able to make one last attempt? I hadn't killed it—not even close—just kept it from escaping its watery prison.

There—massive structures of some glass-like material rising from the seabed. The sunken city looked different from this angle, more alien.

Movement caught my eye as a vast shape detached itself from the structures below, rising with terrible purpose. It was the kraken. Damn, but it was bigger than I remembered. Its body was easily twice the length of the U-boat. Those intelligent eyes fixed on the craft as massive tentacles began to spread.

Could the star beast be controlling it?

I sealed my pack and checked the transpar suit's controls one last time. I remembered well how to use this.

The kraken closed in, its tentacles reaching for the U-boat. I set the engines to full ahead and locked the helm. I would let the beast chase the empty U-boat. I had other plans.

I sealed the suit, powered it up, and moved into a different compartment. There, I blew the emergency hatch. Cold water rushed in as I triggered the suit's systems. Energy coursed through the material as I surged against the stream and out of the U-boat into the open water.

The kraken's tentacles coiled around the U-boat as I shot past. Its ancient eyes tracked me, but the beast remained committed to its original target. I heard the hull beginning to crack as I sped higher.

The transpar suit carried me up through the darker water into the sunlit layers near the surface. Then I banked around and dove, pushing the suit's systems. The pressure mounted as I plunged toward the sunken city.

I could see the obelisk rising from a seaweed-covered courtyard. It looked just like the one on Sky Island, but darker. Green-black growths covered its base, but the pyramidion still gleamed red.

My lungs were already burning as I landed beside it. The suit could keep the pressure at bay, but it couldn't generate air. I had a minute at most.

Send me to Sky Island on Mu, I thought at the pyramidion.

The crystal began to pulse with familiar energy. But it

seemed to hesitate, as if questioning something. That could be the star beast somehow.

I'm a Traveler. You know that. Send me to Sky Island on Mu at once. That is a command.

If the star beast had one more trick left—

But no, light began to build within the crystal. Behind me, I sensed more than saw the kraken releasing the broken U-boat, turning its attention toward this new disturbance.

The pyramidion's light grew stronger as it beamed me. I felt the familiar sensation of stretching. Then I shot upward, heading, I hoped, back to Sky Island on Mu.

I had escaped, kept the star beast imprisoned, and slain Omilcar. I didn't know about the future—

That was my last thought as the interstellar journey began.

-56-

After my journey through deep space, thunder echoed as I materialized atop the ziggurat of Sky Island. The flashes of lightning that accompanied interstellar teleportation faded, leaving me alone in the gathering dusk. The transpar suit pressed against my skin, my pack and hollow staff a burden like the memories I carried.

I stood there, letting the wind wash over me, so very glad to be done with the alien star beast. Like all interstellar journeys, upon landing, I felt fully restored in strength and energy.

At last, I looked around and saw the large moon illuminating the floating island, providing more light than Earth's moon at its fullest.

It felt strange being back—like waking from a bad dream to find your world out of alignment. I was out of sorts, a ghost, it seemed. Once, Sky Island had been a place of happiness and joy. I had been the king of Mu who was going to fix everything. What a sick, sad joke that turned out to be.

I sighed and gazed upon the grim laboratory buildings. They loomed against the darkening sky. Perhaps ghosts lived in them.

A Draco Pterodactyl screeched.

I noticed then that many of the pterodactyls rested on the tops of the block buildings. Two of them seemed to be feeding on something, a grim sight that felt oddly fitting.

The pterodactyls meant the riders were still here. I wondered what Forkbeard had been doing during my absence.

When I'd left, I hadn't been sure I would ever come back to the scene of such wretched crimes. But after killing Omilcar and escaping the star beast, I hadn't known where to go. I'd decided to return to my friends, to those who had grieved with me, who had gotten drunk with me in order that I wouldn't weep alone.

I drew a deep breath. Everything seemed different on Sky Island except for one terrible thing. Livi's death felt raw again. We had planned such a magnificent future together. The Great Sark of Mu had painted such promise back then.

I shook my head, pushing such thoughts aside. That was finished. The psi-master was dead, his schemes buried in the depths of another world. He hadn't unleashed more horror on the universe. I'd stopped two monsters on Atlantis.

"Lord Bayard?"

I turned to find a young rider staring up at me from a lower step, wide-eyed. He must have been near the ziggurat on watch duty and raced up here after I'd arrived, after the thunder and lightning ceased.

Without waiting for any response, the young rider turned and leaped down the great steps of the ziggurat to pick up a mallet and ring the gong that hung nearby.

Its deep tone echoed across Sky Island. Soon I heard shouts and saw big warriors rushing from the block buildings to the ziggurat. They came armed as befitted the tough fighters.

I descended the ziggurat with the transpar-suit helmet in the crook of my arm. I wanted them to know who I was. I carried the hollow staff in my other hand, the sign of my monarchy.

Towering Forkbeard arrived first at the foot of the ziggurat.

The giant warrior stopped as if in shock at the sight of me, his beard whipping in the wind. He lowered his double-bladed axe. For a moment, he seemed unsure whether to kneel or embrace me. Then his face split into a massive grin and he clasped my arm warrior-style.

"My lord," Forkbeard said in his powerful voice. "We feared... You've been gone for weeks. We had no word and began to wonder..."

"It is done," I said. Forkbeard surely knew what I meant. "Psi-Master Omilcar will never trouble us again."

I figured there was no need to talk about the star beast, not yet, anyway.

Hard satisfaction crossed Forkbeard's biker features. Then worry replaced it. "Much has happened in your absence, lord. Ophidians have—"

A distant horn interrupted him. It wasn't the deep notes of the pterodactyl riders' gong, but a sharper, alien sound. It seemed to drift up from far below, possibly from the ruins of the Dark Citadel.

Were people camping down there? No, Forkbeard had said Ophidians. Yes, Ophidian and Draconian tribes lived in the rugged lands surrounding the Dark Citadel. Perhaps Omilcar had allowed the Ophidians to infiltrate the Dark Citadel before he'd left.

"I thought the lightning and thunder would have delayed them," Forkbeard said. "But no, they are right on schedule."

What could that mean?

More of the pterodactyl riders had gathered around us. They now parted and followed Forkbeard and me as we moved to the edge of Sky Island. We stopped at the ubiquitous guardrail that ringed the island, peering down at the dark, misty land below.

Something rose from the ruins—a shape surrounded by crackling energy. As it climbed higher—it was some kind of sky raft—I could make out Ophidian warriors on its surface, manning what looked like primitive catapults.

"We believe they found the raft in the lower chambers," Forkbeard informed me. "As you can see, it is a flying machine, possibly of ancient design. They tested it nightly

273

now, threatening to climb up here in the dark. They never dare do this during daylight, although I wish they would."

The great raft reached about halfway up to Sky Island. Rocks and spears launched from its surface, propelled by the catapults. The missiles all fell well short of us, raining back to the mists below.

Riders made as if to summon their pterodactyls, some of them putting the whistles to their lips. The great beasts watched from the tops of the block buildings. Forkbeard waved the riders back.

"That's a useless idea," he told them. "The Ophidians can't reach us yet and we'd be fools to fly in the dark even with the bright moon this night." He turned to me. "Each evening, they climbed higher and learned more. Soon..." He shook his head. "We should speak privately, lord. There is much to discuss."

I watched the Ophidian raft begin its descent, soon disappearing into the mists that had formed near the ruins. My grip tightened around the hollow staff. I'd come home hoping to find peace, needing it, in fact. Instead, I'd returned to a siege in slow motion by snake people. Perhaps Omilcar had helped the Ophidians slip into the Dark Citadel before he'd left. That might explain the missing computers.

Maybe this was fitting, though. The king of Sky Island couldn't just hide in his grief. My people, as few as they were, needed me—not just as a ruler, but as the premier warrior.

I snorted to myself. Isn't killing my specialty? The last chambers of the underwater Atlantean facility and the U-boat had proven that. I silently cursed the star beast for forcing me to kill in such a wanton fashion.

I turned to Forkbeard with a question forming in my mind. Why did some of Mu's toughest warriors cower on Sky Island because of a few Ophidians? That seemed wrong. I needed to uncover this mystery.

"Tell me everything," I said.

"Perhaps if we go inside, lord," Forkbeard said.

"Yes. That sounds like a good idea. Let's go inside."

Forkbeard led me into his planning chamber. Maps and sketches covered one wall, depicting the Dark Citadel and its surrounding territories.

"It began three weeks after you left," Forkbeard said, settling his massive frame into a chair. "We discovered the Ophidians were down there. They're likely the ones who removed the computers. Then our scouts started reporting activity in the lower chambers."

"What about the platform?" I asked.

Forkbeard nodded. "They assembled it in secret piece by piece. We didn't understand what they were building at first. We raided during the day, but they were waiting and used the catapults and spear throwers. Given the size and shape of the ruins, we would need to land to dig them out. I didn't want to use the riders like that. Perhaps that was a mistake, but I can't be certain."

I waited, listening.

Forkbeard heaved a sigh. "Then one night, that thing rose from the ruins." He gestured at a detailed sketch. "With each test flight, they add more: better weapons, reinforced armor, and other upgrades. The power nodes—they're using old technology we don't understand, although I think you might, lord."

"How high can the raft go?" I asked.

"The highest we've seen is two-thirds of the way to Sky Island. They're quite methodical. The Viper King—their leader—is a massive Ophidian wielding an enormous cleaver. He doesn't hesitate to use it as he lops off heads if he gets angry enough. Even so, the Viper King is cautious. He makes sure each modification works before adding more."

Forkbeard's face darkened. "We tried stopping them one night. I lost six good men trying to sabotage their equipment. The snake people were waiting, damn their eyes."

I rose and examined the latest sketches. The platform—now a massive raft—had grown significantly, bristling with weapons and reinforced armor. "How many warriors can it carry?"

"A hundred, maybe more," Forkbeard said. "And they're learning fast, able to maneuver it better each night. It will probably be three or maybe four nights before they try for the island. When they come, it'll be with everything they have, maybe double the number of what it carries now. They will outnumber us significantly, and we won't be able to use our mounts. Frankly, Sire, I've been thinking about abandoning Sky Isle. Unless you have an idea, I don't know that we can hold here."

I nodded slowly, thinking about the hollow tube's capabilities and about what the transpar suit could do.

Two hundred Ophidians with armor and catapults hurling rocks and spears at the riders on foot... it would be the wrong fight at the wrong time. Normally, the pterodactyl riders would raid from above, hurling javelins and swooping low to strike with claws. The riders couldn't do that if the Ophidians hid in caves, crevasses or the ruins of the Dark Citadel. The riders couldn't do that at night, but would be forced to face the enemy on foot. The Viper King, or Omilcar before he left, had thought this through.

There wasn't time to bring more warriors to Sky Island. The closest would be at the city of Tsargol. I wasn't sure I wanted them on the island anyway.

I looked at Forkbeard. "Get some rest. Tomorrow we'll observe their preparations in detail. I want to see exactly what we're dealing with before we commit ourselves."

Forkbeard stood.

I did, too, clapping him on a burly shoulder. "You've done well holding your ground when you probably wanted to retreat. The Viper King is doing this the smart way. Now that I'm back, I'm not going to let him get away with it."

Forkbeard nodded, heading for the door. He paused and turned to me. "It's good to have you back, my lord. The men have missed their king."

I gave him a nod of thanks.

After he left, I stayed in the chamber, studying the sketches. The Ophidians had built something formidable while I was gone. But they didn't know what I'd brought back with me.

Tomorrow, I would uncover what I needed to know.

Would I stay on Sky Island after this? Part of me said to go, leave forever. Would I leave to return to Earth? Frankly, I didn't know. If the Ophidians were Omilcar's scheme, I wanted to destroy it no matter what.

Maybe I needed to call a place home, and build something from it. Maybe I could eradicate the Ophidians and Draconians, or find a way to send them to a planet they would like. Wasn't it wiser to let each race claim its own planet rather than waging endless wars across them all?

I rubbed my jaw. Was I truly fit to be king? First things first, I decided. Tomorrow night, I would closely examine the Ophidians and their raft to prepare for the battle ahead.

-58-

The next night, an hour after sunset, the alien horn sounded from the Dark Citadel. I stood at Sky Island's edge, watching power nodes flicker to life in the darkness. The transpar suit clung warmly to my skin as the massive platform began to rise.

According to Forkbeard, the Ophidians had doubled their usual complement—at least eighty warriors manned the catapults, with another forty standing by for reinforcements. Metal armor gleamed dully in the glow of their power systems. I spied targeting arrays on—

I activated the zoom function on my transpar helmet visor, focusing on the details. To my surprise, the Ophidians had uncovered a few larger energy weapons. Those looked more sophisticated than anything I'd seen in the sketches last night.

The Ophidians had likely discovered weapon lockers near the same underground chambers where they'd pilfered the raft.

Forkbeard stood beside me, his posture rigid with tension.

"They're coming higher than usual, lord."

He was right. The platform rose steadily, pushing past its previous limit from last night.

Forkbeard pointed out the Viper King. The huge Ophidian stood at the forward edge, his scaled hide reflecting the crackling energy that surrounded them. He studied our defenses with what appeared to be cold reptilian intelligence.

Where had Omilcar found that old boy? I was more certain than ever that this had been part of the Great Sark's ultimate plans. Omilcar had spent too much time in the Dark Citadel when the Ispazars had run it. He had worked with Ispazars, Ophidians, Krekelens and humans, and betrayed them all at one time or another. Maybe it was fitting the star beast had possessed him at the end. It let Omilcar know what it felt like just before he burned.

The Viper King waved his cleaver and chopped the air with it.

Catapult arms swung, sending the first volley of rocks dangerously close to the underside of Sky Island. I was beginning to think the catapults were a ploy. The real danger was from the heavy energy weapons, three of them.

I had been observing through the visor's zoom function for some time. Those heavy weapons were linked with thick cables to the power nodes that fueled the anti-gravity pods of the raft. Twelve special Ophidians in long red robes serviced those weapons. Perhaps they belonged to a priestly caste or an ancient order of weapon-smiths. I didn't know. But I knew they were the key to this assault, or practice assault this night.

I cast a sidelong glance at the big warrior beside me. "They're mapping the island," I told him.

Forkbeard grunted. "And no doubt testing our responses, or lack of them. They undoubtedly know we can't counterattack effectively at night."

Why didn't the Viper King fly the platform up to us and expel his warriors onto the island proper? Maybe they flew every night in order to lull the riders. When the attack came, it might come as a surprise.

The platform began a slow, deliberate circuit around our position. It appeared that they'd added stabilizers to compensate for wind, letting them hold steadier firing positions.

The Viper King directed each maneuver with precise swings of his huge cleaver.

"I'd say they're almost ready for the main event," Forkbeard growled. "Another day or two of testing will be it."

I nodded. It was smart of them to come at night when our pterodactyls were useless.

The alien horn sounded. The platform began its descent, eventually disappearing into the dark mists below.

"If you don't have a plan, Sire," Forkbeard said. "I believe we should leave by tomorrow."

I watched the last power node vanish into the mists.

Forkbeard waited.

At last, I looked up at him. "I don't believe that will be necessary, my friend."

"You can defeat them?"

"From what I've seen tonight, yes, I believe I can."

I would have to take into account those heavy energy weapons. Still, I didn't think they were ready for my big trick. They might have hoped to surprise us. Tomorrow night, I intended to surprise them.

-59-

The next night, the Ophidian platform rose once more, power nodes crackling with ominous blue-white arcs that split the darkness. Silhouettes of warriors lined the edges, their scaled armor reflecting flickers of manufactured lightning. This time, they had packed the platform with twice as many fighters. Perhaps they believed they were finally ready to conquer Sky Island.

I glanced at Forkbeard, his beard braided tight for battle.

"Good luck, lord," he said.

I triggered the transpar suit's power and launched myself from the edge of the island. The cool night wind whipped past my suit as gravity pulled me downward. Behind me, I heard Forkbeard's sharp intake of breath as I plummeted into darkness.

Then the suit responded to my thoughts. My fall turned into flight, slicing through the air like a diving falcon. Starlight glinted off the suit. I banked hard left, adrenaline surging and my heart pounding. This was glorious.

Below, the Ophidians swarmed across their massive war raft. They didn't spot me until I was nearly on them. I skimmed low, close enough to hear many of them hiss with fright or rage.

The Viper King shouted and brandished his cleaver.

The red-robed Ophidians manhandled their energy weapons, no doubt desperate to lock onto a target that moved too quickly for them.

I activated the hollow staff and felt it vibrate to life. I aimed, and ferocious, molten plasma beamed into the nearest cluster of starboard power nodes. Even with the helmet, I smelled the ozone and scorched metal.

Ophidians screamed as their machinery dissolved into molten slag.

The platform lurched sideways, sending several Ophidians stumbling, a few over the edge to plunge into the darkness. Those aboard tried to regroup, hissing commands. I could see their Viper King in the center, fangs bared in fury as he attempted to coordinate a defense.

I didn't plan to give them time for one.

I flew to the opposite side, pouring plasma into energy weapon mounts. Sparks erupted, lighting up the platform.

There came a whine of overloading nodes. I darted under the raft and let the staff's power wash over it. The ancient metal groaned, buckling under the onslaught. One by one, power cells exploded with deafening force.

The proud flying raft that had threatened Sky Island mere minutes ago now quivered, mortally wounded.

Under the harsh orange glow of flaming wreckage, Ophidian warriors leaped from the doomed platform, some grabbing tattered blankets to make chutes, I suppose, others plunging with terrified shrieks. I caught one glimpse of the Viper King, scales glinting in the hellish light, arms raised in a final snarl of defiance as the platform's deck gave way beneath him. Then he fell with the rest.

I soared back up to Sky Island, exhaling a deep breath I hadn't realized I'd been holding. Behind me, the Ophidian raft

282

crashed into the ancient ruins, an eruption of flame and twisted metal. The explosion lit the night, scattering debris everywhere.

A roar of celebration went up from the watching pterodactyl riders gathered on Sky Island. Their voices rang out in triumph.

Forkbeard met me as I landed. His grin was as broad and fierce as a triumphant bear. "By the ancient gods, lord, that was—"

"Just the beginning," I said, powering down the suit and wrenching off the helmet. The cool night air felt refreshing against my damp skin. "Tomorrow, we begin eliminating them—all of them. The Dark Citadel, the surrounding ruins, everything. We'll show the Ophidians that Sky Island is no longer merely defending itself."

Forkbeard studied me, the torchlight dancing in his eyes. Then he nodded. "The men will follow you anywhere after this. The king has truly returned."

I turned to gaze out over my domain—those ancient buildings lit by crackling torchlight, the watching pterodactyls, and my loyal warriors, a hardy handful who had once raided at will. For a moment, my thoughts returned to Livi, a bittersweet ache tightening in my chest. I would miss her dearly. I couldn't say how often I would travel to other worlds now, or if I'd ever see the Terran companions who had battled the Krekelens on Earth. Would I make it to Vega? I let the questions swirl in my mind like drifting embers.

Below us, I heard an Ophidian horn once again. Its mournful note carried up to the island like a challenge... or perhaps a final cry of defeat.

I might return to Earth someday. I might seek out old friends or lost allies. For tonight, though, my course was clear. I would secure my little kingdom—my Sky Island—and let fate unravel the rest in its own time.

I straightened my shoulders as I surveyed my warriors. Atlantis was safe for now. Mu had gotten rid of a devil of a psi-master. I had claimed my vengeance to quell my grief. Now, I could begin anew and face whatever the future held.

The End